November 2

The Day of the Dead in Sicily

November 2

The Day of the Dead in Sicily

By Ettore Grillo

Strategic Book Publishing and Rights Co.

Strategic Book Publishing and Rights Co., LLC
USA | Singapore
www.sbpra.net

For information about special discounts for bulk purchases, please contact Strategic Book Publishing and Rights Co., LLC. Special Sales, at bookorder@sbpra.net.

ISBN: 978-1-951530-66-2

To my wife, Hyunok Kim Grillo

CONTENTS

Chapter One Introduction 11

Chapter Two The Epitaph on Giuseppe Chiarello's Tombstone .33

Chapter Three A Story Extracted from the Diary of
Pasqualino Butera 51

   My family 51

   Life in the Army 57

   The First Engagement 64

   The Second Engagement 77

   The Marriage 83

   The End of the Story 95

Chapter Four The Limiti Family Tomb 103

Chapter Five Visiting More Tombs 121

   Katia's Tomb 121

   Eraldo's Tomb 123

   Gerlando Sferrazzanetti's Tomb 124

   Antonio Colinari's Tomb 125

   Gioacchino's Tomb 127

   Romualdo Fischietti's Tomb 128

   My Parents' Family Tomb 129

   Napoleone Colajanni's Tomb 130

Giulio Sperlazzari's Tomb 131

My Great-Grandfather's Tomb 133

Giacomino's Tomb 136

Chapter Six Meeting My Cousin Luigi 139

Chapter Seven The Wheel of Fortune 155

The Reggiani Family 155

Lucia the Businesswoman 164

Lucia and Farmer Peppe's Wife 178

The Two Families go to Mass 185

Lucia Begins a New Life 193

Lucia Wants to Move to Enna 206

The New Joint Venture 212

New Life in Enna 215

Antonio Emigrates 222

Antonio Gets Rich 229

Antonio Returns to Calascibetta 232

Chapter Eight Walking in the Cemetery at Night 239

Chapter One

Introduction

Enna is a small city on a plateau in the center of Sicily. Its founding dates back to time immemorial. It is called the navel of Sicily. It is part of the Erei Mountain chain and is located at an altitude of about one thousand meters above sea level. Like all Greek cities, Enna was a city-state with its own government and its own mint. It minted a coin called an *ennaion*.

Enna shared the same language and religion as Greece. The primary goddesses worshiped were Demeter and her daughter, Kore. Nobody knows exactly where the temples of Demeter and Kore stood, but it is certain that the main temple of Demeter in Sicily was in Enna. Being the goddess of the crops, Demeter was invoked to have a good harvest. It is said that during time of famine, even the Senate of Rome used to send a delegation to Enna to propitiate Demeter.

The people of Enna buried the dead by digging small rooms in the rock, usually facing south. In the room, painted terracotta vases were placed next to the corpse. Tombs have been excavated that included well-preserved skeletons and red- and black-figure vases. Sometimes in the mouth of the skeleton was found a coin. The Greeks believed that to get to Hades (the kingdom of the dead), souls had to pay a fee of one coin to Charon, who ferried the dead across the Acheron, a river that divided the world of the living from that of the dead.

Enna has always been a city devoted to religion. When Cicero, the great Roman orator, came to Enna to collect evidence against the governor of Sicily, Verres, who had snatched away gold and statues from the Sicilian temples, he was so surprised by the religiosity in Enna that he had the feeling that its inhabitants were *omnes sacerdotes* (all priests).

When the Arabs conquered Sicily, they changed the Latin name Henna into *Catrum* (castle) *Hennae* (the genitive of Henna), which in the Arabic parlance became Castro Ianni, and then Castrogiovanni in the Italian language. This final appellation lasted until December 6, 1926, when Castrogiovanni was elevated to the capital of the province and was given back the ancient name of Enna. It essentially just dropped the *H*, which is always silent in the Italian language anyway.

A short distance from Enna stands the town of Calascibetta. As the crow flies, the distance between the two places is about two kilometers, but the winding road that connects them is about seven kilometers long. They both are located on the summits of two small mountains. While Enna has an average height of a thousand meters, Calascibetta is a bit lower, about nine hundred meters above sea level.

They have almost the same climate, cool in the summertime and cold in the winter. Fog, which is caused by low clouds, often envelops them. A valley dotted with olive groves and almond trees lies between the two mountains. It is green for most of the year and golden yellow during summer due to the lack of rainfall and the scorching sun.

However, the geography of the two places is quite different. While Enna stands on a plateau with sheer cliffs, Calascibetta rests on the slope of Mount Xibet.

They both have been inhabited since ancient times, as evidenced by archaeological findings, but it is believed that the real foundation of Calascibetta took place during the Arab period. As Enna was an impregnable stronghold, the Arabs settled a military camp on Mount Xibet, waiting for the right moment to launch an attack on Enna, which was occupied by the Byzantines. The siege lasted for a long time. While the Arabs remained camped on Mount Xibet, they boosted the tiny town situated there, developing the commerce and agriculture. Furthermore, they built mosques and palaces.

A dense, self-sown forest of locust trees, cypresses, and other local plants surrounds Enna. It is so green and thick that it bewitches whoever looks at it. An uncle of mine told me that when Mussolini came to Enna on a state visit, he was enchanted by the beauty of the mountain. When he arrived at the hillside, he was so impressed by the woody slopes that he ordered his driver to pull the car up to the roadside, and Mussolini kept walking on foot because he wanted to admire the beauty of the incomparable view of Enna seen from the valley below and breathe its fresh air.

Seen from Calascibetta, Enna appears inaccessible. The steep rocks conceal some paths through which you can walk up to the top of the mountain. It is said that the Arabs were able to break the siege thanks to the help of a traitor banished from Enna, who in the nighttime showed them one of those concealed, dangerous, narrow paths through the rocky slopes.

A further growth of Calascibetta took place during the Norman period. As the Arabs had done two centuries earlier, the Normans also camped on Mount Xibet during their thirty-year siege on Enna, which was an Arab fortress this time.

The Normans built churches, monuments, a castle, and the city walls in Calascibetta.

The Aragonese came to Calascibetta after the Normans. King Peter II of Aragon, who became the king of Sicily, built the Royal Palatine Chapel in 1340 on the ruins of an old Arab fort. He loved Calascibetta and died in the town in 1342.

In spite of everything, Calascibetta remains a small town compared to Enna. Its population is about five thousand, while Enna's is thirty thousand. These days, there are both elementary and middle schools in Calascibetta, but a few decades ago there was only the primary school. Middle school, government offices, hospital, big supermarkets, high schools, university, and most of the businesses were in Enna.

Nowadays, from the Belvedere of Enna, it is possible to see a long line of cars and buses on the winding road that links the two places during rush hour. The citizens of Calascibetta go to Enna to work, for school, shopping, and so on. The students that want to go to school in Enna only have to take a comfortable bus from Calascibetta's main square, Piazza Umberto (Umberto Square), and within about fifteen minutes they can reach their school or university in Enna, but it was not so easy one century ago.

Many of Calascibetta's citizens have jobs in Enna. Often, they keep their residence in Calascibetta and come and go during the day from and to their working place. Sometimes, they move to Enna and live there. Obviously, to get a decent job, qualifications are required. With a degree or a high school diploma, you can aspire to get a good position.

A long time ago—I am talking of a time before World War II—the road link between Calascibetta and Enna was not easy at all. Most people moved from one place to the other on a donkey or a mule; you could count the people in Calascibetta who owned a car on the fingers of one hand. Only a few well-to-do families could afford to send their children to study in Enna. The bus service didn't exist. Therefore, boys in Calascibetta who wanted to attend middle school and then high school or technical school had no choice but to rent a room from a host family in Enna and live there. It was quite uncommon for girls to go to school outside their town. Most girls interrupted their schooling after elementary school.

The family of one Calascibetta's most eminent citizens, Giuseppe D'Angelo, rented a room in Enna to allow him to study there. Later, he achieved a degree in philosophy and was elected president of the Sicilian Region. He was a good politician who loved both his hometown of Calascibetta, and Enna.

It is said that some students, not having enough money to rent a room in Enna, covered the distance between the two municipalities by walking. It must have been a challenge, because Enna is at least a one-hour walk from Calascibetta. Furthermore, in the winter, weather conditions are prohibitive.

Although Enna and Calascibetta are in Sicily, an island with a temperate climate, the weather is quite inclement during the winter. It is windy and, above all, foggy. The citizens of Enna have nicknamed the fog *la paesana* (the fellow citizen), for it often envelops the city like a cloak. Seen from below, the fog looks like a wide hat on the head of the plateau. Once, snow used to fall on Enna and Calascibetta, but these days, due to global warming, snow has become rarer and rarer.

The plateau on which Enna stands is not completely flat. There are three areas that are a bit elevated and gently slope down to the center of the city. Seen from above, the area looks like a triangle. On one tip is an old castle called *il Castello di Lombardia* (the Castle of Lombardy), which is still accessible, even though a few towers have fallen into ruin. On the other tip is the Franciscan Monastery of Capuchin of Montesalvo, and on the third tip is the cemetery, which lies on a hillock. In the center of the triangle is the Piazza San Francesco (Saint Francis Square) and Belvedere Marconi, the viewpoint of Enna. People stroll in these places in the evenings during the summertime, for the weather is mild and the view from Belvedere Marconi is unique. They can admire the illuminated towns as well as Mount Etna, which occasionally releases fiery flashes from its central crater.

The Castle of Lombardy stands in the highest part of the city. It was a military castle. According to some authors, it took its name from the Lombard soldiers who stayed in the fortress during the Norman period. The best-preserved tower is called Pisana Tower. It was built by Frederick II of Swabia and was so named because it was manned by a garrison of soldiers from Pisa.

The Castle of Lombardy was considered impregnable. Later, it was converted first into a prison and then into an open-air theater, called the theater closest to the stars, due to its altitude. In fact, it was situated at an elevation of one thousand meters above sea level. These days, neither the prison nor the theater exists, but tourists come and visit the castle and climb the steps to the top of the Pisana Tower. From up there, they can admire valleys, mountain ranges, villages, towns, Lake Pergusa, Mount Etna, and the Tower of Frederick on the other side of the city.

The Monastery of Montesalvo lies near the center of Sicily. An obelisk symbolizing the geographical center of the island stands just a few meters away from the monastery.

According to some, in ancient times, the pagan feasts of Ceres, Kore, and Dionysus were celebrated in this place. Then, around the year 1300, a Catholic church was built there to replace the pagan festivals with those in honor of The Most Holy Mary of Visitation. The monastery is adjacent to the church. Once it teemed with Franciscan monks, but nowadays its many cells are almost all empty, except two or three where monks still live.

The cemetery is large enough to look like a town. It has broad avenues and tall tombs. Many tombs are similar to small houses. They have a room inside with walled niches and an altar where Mass was once celebrated on November 2.

I dare say that the cemeteries in Sicily are unique. I have visited some burial places while traveling around the world, but they were completely different than the Sicilian cemeteries, for every population on earth has its own way of treating the dead, depending on its culture and traditions.

In Italy, before the Napoleonic edict, the dead were buried in the churches. Later, this custom fell into disuse.

In the Capuchin Catacombs of Palermo, the friars used to embalm the dead. It is still possible to visit the underground cemetery of the monastery where the embalmed corpses are displayed. Through this practice, the Franciscan friars wanted to draw attention to the frailty and transiency of human life.

The Franciscan friars of Rome did something similar in the Capuchin Church on Via Veneto. In the crypt of this church the bones of about four thousand Capuchin friars are displayed. With the bones, the friars made chandeliers, chairs, tables, decorations on the walls, and other objects in the Baroque style. Also in this case, the Capuchin friars aimed at making people meditate on the impermanence of life.

In Korea, I couldn't see any family vaults. They set the dead into the ground and then made a womb-shaped mound. They called it the womb of Mother Earth, the final abode of the body, but cremation was also practiced in Korea.

In some tribes that I visited in Tanzania, the dead were buried in front of the house where they had lived, but before being placed into an underground niche on the side of the pit that had been dug, the dead person was put on a chair in front of his house for a few hours. This way, the relatives and friends could offer condolences to the family.

In America, I couldn't spot any chapel in Arlington National Cemetery in Virginia, near Washington, DC. I just saw a vast expanse of graves. Even the president of the United States had been buried in a grave. What impressed me for its simplicity was the grave of Robert Francis Kennedy. It was located at the foot of a grassy hill. On it was just a cross on one side and a small tombstone with the name Robert Francis Kennedy and the dates of his birth and death on the other. At that time, I meditated for some minutes in front of the graves of John and Robert Kennedy. They were my idols when I was a teenage boy.

When I was about to leave Arlington, a guard approached me, saluted me, and then shook my hand. I was shocked! Did the souls of the Kennedy brothers order the guard to treat me as a special guest?

The Catholic Church devotes November 2 to the commemoration of the dead. In days past, Enna's cemetery swarmed with people, and Masses were celebrated both outdoors and inside the tombs, which had an altar in the room. Before the Second Vatican Council, a priest came and celebrated Mass in my grandmother's tomb every year. There were about thirty persons that attended Mass in front of her tomb and took Communion on that day. Later, after the Second Vatican Council changed the rite of Mass, it became inconvenient to say Mass in the tombs, which had the altar against the wall. With the new Catholic rite, the priest had to stand behind the altar and face the audience. There was not enough room to set another altar in the tomb. Therefore, no more Masses were celebrated in Enna's cemetery tombs. These days on November 2, one Mass is said outdoors in the main avenue of the cemetery.

On the Day of the Dead, I stay in the cemetery more than usual. I like visiting the tombs adorned with flowers and lit candles. Often, I stumble onto a photo of someone I knew when they were alive. I am surprised to see how many acquaintances of mine join the ranks of the dead year after year. Death chases all of us. It plays tag with humans. Even if we run fast, we cannot avoid being touched by it sooner or later.

My maternal grandmother, Paolina, used to keep a few chairs in her family tomb, for herself and her family, relatives, and friends that came to visit the tomb or had the chance to pass by it.

I remember that when I was sitting inside the tomb with her, my attention was caught by a beautiful picture framed with fine black wood in front of the altar on the right side. The black-and-white photo had been enlarged, but the graceful features of a handsome young man with a line in his wavy black hair and a sweet smile on his lips were unaltered.

The photographer had done good work. The face portrayed in the photo seemed to be surrounded by white clouds. The young man looked like an angel. The portrait stood on a triangle-shaped wooden pedestal. My grandfather had made this for his son, who had died in his prime and whom he had loved much. On November 2, my grandmother used to put a vase with yellow chrysanthemums and red cockscombs in front of the portrait of her son.

In the tomb were six white, marble-walled niches, three on each side, one above the other. The lower niches were about two meters above the floor. A name with the date of birth and death had been carved on the tombstone of three niches. In the other three niches, the marble had no carving because they were empty. Sooner or later, a body would be set inside each of them.

The altar was covered with a white crocheted cloth. In the foreground of the altar were the pictures of my grandfather and his two sons that had died before their time. Behind them were the pictures of my great-grandparents and my grandfather's brother. Their bodies had been put under the tomb, not in the niches. In fact, in the back of the tomb was a tombstone that covered a small door to access the underground part. In other words, only the closest family members of the founder of the tomb rested in the niches. All the other relatives, supposing they were allowed to be buried there, were placed in the underground room.

Sitting in the tomb, my grandmother used to say the rosary and pray for the souls in purgatory and her beloved husband, Ciccino, who had passed away, still young, at the age of sixty-eight. Sometimes she talked about this and that with some friends of hers or relatives that occasionally entered the tomb.

Often, I stayed in the tomb with her. I sat on one side and she on the other near the enlarged portrait of her dear son. One day, she told me that one drop of blood had leaked from the niche where her husband had been buried. On that occasion, she dipped her finger into the drop of blood and licked it. That is how much she loved her Ciccino!

At that time, I didn't think about my death. Obviously, by sitting inside the tomb next to my grandmother, I had an idea of what death meant, but I believed that the issue of death concerned only others, not me. I couldn't imagine that someday I would die like everyone else. I was just a child! But from the age of about twenty onward, the theme of death has conditioned me. Of course, I have lived my life. I have had my love stories and my job, but whenever I thought about my death, I was seized by anxiety and panic attacks. I feared being annihilated. Perhaps I feared death so much because I didn't have enough religious faith, which claims that there is another life after death, or at least we are not completely annihilated. For me, there was no afterlife. *We disappear into thin air, like sparks*, I thought at that time.

After my grandmother died, the framed, enlarged photo of her son disappeared too. I never saw it in the tomb again. Apparently, those who inherited the tomb considered the portrait too cumbersome and intrusive!

Usually on November 2, after entering the cemetery, I go through a kind of ritual. First of all, I visit my grandmother's tomb. Since I don't have the key to enter it, I cannot put flowers in the flower holders, nor I can light a candle. I confine myself to peeping through the glass door to see whether the tomb is well-kept or not. I also stand in front of the tomb for a few minutes to say a prayer for those who are buried there. Then, I move to another tomb.

After climbing down the stairs between the two main avenues in the cemetery, I visit my parents' tomb and those of my friends. Then, I stroll through the cemetery, starting from the lower part of the hillock and ending in the upper part.

Ever since I was a child, I have visited the cemetery in my hometown of Enna on November 2, the day of the Festival of the Dead. In this cemetery, most of the burial sites are tombs; there are not many graves, except for a very small area that the municipality has allotted to the burying of very poor people.

The Day of the Dead in Sicily is one of the most awaited events, but the traditional celebration has changed over the years. Once, children believed that the night before November 2, the dead brought presents for them and left them in the nooks of the rooms. In the early morning, they searched for the toy surprises and finally found them. How happy they were!

This happened during my childhood. Nowadays, this tradition has almost disappeared, having been supplanted by Santa Claus and the stocking of Epiphany, an ugly old woman that also brings children gifts. But during my childhood, neither Father Christmas nor the Epiphany existed in Sicily, so the only chance to receive gifts was on November 2.

Obviously, parents hid the gifts in the house, pretending that they had been brought there by the dead, and prompted us children to look for them and find them. However, we really believed that the gifts came from the dead. The symbolic meaning was clear. By receiving the presents, children were taught to respect and love the souls of their dead relatives.

On November 2, we used to eat special cakes called *ossa de murti* (bones of the dead). They were whitish, looked like bones, and were very hard to eat. Only youngsters with strong teeth could chew them; nonetheless, they were delicious.

The custom of visiting the cemetery, not only on November 2, but also during the whole year, was widespread in Enna. I knew a man who worked at my uncle's firm who every Sunday went to the cemetery to clean up his parents' tomb, change the flowers in the holders, and light a candle. The typical flowers to offer to the dead were chrysanthemums and cockscombs.

I also knew a student who in the afternoons did his homework in the cemetery. He used to bring his school bag and sit on a step in front of the entrance to a big tomb that had an overhang. He studied there for hours, even in the winter when it rained or when the cemetery was covered with a blanket of fog. Apparently, the silence and peace of the place fostered his successful life. He became the president of an important university in northern Italy. I still remember his features. He wore a mustache even when he was a boy. He was a bit plump and looked effeminate, but he was not like that at all. He married one of the most beautiful women in Enna and they had a child together.

As for me, I preferred to stay away from the cemetery. In my opinion, the living should stay with the living and the dead with the dead. Going to the cemetery often was like fleeing from society, from life, so I used to go there just once a year.

As time went by, something changed in the cemetery. The black-and-white photos were replaced with color photographs, and the small wax candles were replaced with modern electric grave lights. Now, the vases in front of the altars are full of exotic flowers. I couldn't spot even one of the beautiful cockscombs that once stood out inside the family tombs. Apparently, the old Sicily was disappearing!

My Christian name is Mario; my family name is Chiaramonte. I am light-skinned and about one meter and seventy centimeters tall. The color of my eyes is between green and light brown. I was born in Enna at a time when the old Sicily was still alive. It was the sunny island where some women knew the secret to rid children of their intestinal worms and of the evil eye through arcane practices. It was the old Sicily where goats walked in the streets, and the shepherd milked them in front of the houses and sold milk to the housewives. What a fresh product it was! Apartments didn't exist, and people warmed up their houses by using braziers. Fruit and legumes had a natural taste. Hens brooded their eggs, ate wheat, bran, and leftovers, and were free to scratch around. It was the old Sicily where fields were plowed by oxen, the wheat was reaped by farmers' hands, mules and horses trampled the spikes in the threshing floor, the wind separated the chaff from the grains of wheat, television had not been invented yet, and people gathered in the houses to chat about this and that. It was the old Sicily where people breathed unpolluted air, the water of the sea, lakes, and rivers was clean, and the terms like plastic, pollution, climate change, global warming, and hole in the ozone didn't exist in dictionaries.

I come from a family of traders. I liked my father's job, but my parents had different ideas about me. My mother wanted me to become a priest. On the other hand, my father considered me not cut out for business at all. He spurred me to study for a degree and then do a job different than his. Both of them were right. Every time I started a business, it was a disaster. I didn't have the cunning or the good luck, which are both needed in business.

I studied hard and earned a law degree. I then did an apprenticeship at a law firm in Catania and later at my uncle's law firm. After two years of training, I started my own, but I was irresolute about my life and my job. Sometimes I dealt with civil causes, other times with criminal matters. Once I moved my firm from Enna to Catania and then again from Catania back to Enna. I practiced as a lawyer in my hometown until the age of sixty-three, and then I quit my job. After I retired, I started traveling around the world.

When I turned eighty, my visits to the cemetery became more frequent. Perhaps I unconsciously wanted to get acquainted with the place that would host my body for the years to come. Walking along the tombs, I meditated on the end of my life. I looked inside my body to see whether it contained a kind of immortal energy or not, but I couldn't see or feel anything. Maybe I really would disappear into thin air at my death! Nevertheless, I didn't give up my meditation, and I continued to look inside myself.

Living until the age of eighty was a good accomplishment for me. From then on, every year I spent on earth would be a gift from heaven. Some of my friends had passed away in the prime of their lives. One died when he was just fourteen. I didn't have much time left, so I had to finish my quest now. After death I could do nothing.

What did I want to realize? First, whether or not there is life after death; second, whether or not the soul exists. Assuming that the soul exists, is it something good or bad? In the course of my life, I had many arguments with others. Some of my enemies rested in this cemetery. I wanted to visit their tombs, talk with them heart to heart, soul to soul, and understand why they acted so badly toward me.

Strolling in the cemetery, I tried to recollect my past. How many chances had I missed? When I was just a boy, I used to play as a center-forward on a football team in my hometown. At that time, I often arrived alone in front of the goal after having dribbled the ball past the defenders and the goalkeeper. The goal in front of me was clear, but instead of taking a shot on goal, I kicked the ball across the goal mouth. How was that possible? Was my foot crooked? I think it was because of my mind, not my foot. Unconsciously, I didn't want to be a winner. At the time, it would have been enough to gently push the ball over the goal line to win the game, but I didn't.

When I grew into an adult, the same thing happened to me in relating to others. I inexplicably threw away the chances that life offered me in the same way as I did when I missed the goal. Above all, it happened when it came to love. I was about to conquer the heart of a woman, but at the last moment, when her heart was about to open to me, I unconsciously demolished what I had built.

With the wisdom of hindsight, I guess that there could have been a cause behind my failures. Maybe God wanted me to follow a spiritual path away from mere human achievements and successes. Who knows! Is it possible that God has a plan for each of us?

In the past, to try to discover whether a soul harbored inside my body, I opened my heart to many kinds of spiritual experiences. Even though I was Catholic and had no intention of giving up my religion, I decided it wouldn't be a sin if I also did my research outside of Catholicism. So, not only did I attend Protestant churches, but I also approached Buddhism, Islamism, Hinduism, and other religions.

The Protestant churches I visited mostly based their worship on praising God and Jesus by singing. Unlike Catholic churches, there were neither images nor statues of saints. It was a good experience for me to attend those places of worship. Both the Catholics and the Protestants worshipped the same God, only the mode of doing it was different.

In India, I visited a few ashrams: Osho Ashram in Pune, Sai Baba Ashram in Puttaparthi, Amma Ashram in Kerala, and Ramana Maharshi Ashram in Tiruvannamalai. They were places rich in spirituality. Of note, the dynamic meditation I did at Osho Ashram helped me to get rid of the childhood conditioning I had acquired from my family and society.

The ashram where I stayed a bit longer was that of Ramana Maharshi. In it was a bookstore that contained books about him. I bought a little book by him entitled *Who am I?* Apparently, both Ramana Maharshi and I had experienced the fear of death. When he was a boy, he had the feeling that he was about to die. After that experience, he left ordinary life and devoted himself to meditation and to watching himself. He wanted to find out his real nature, whether he was his body or something else more subtle. Finally, after a long time spent meditating, he got enlightenment. According to Ramana Maharshi, the most effective meditation consisted in looking inside oneself and asking, "Who am I?"

Ramana Maharshi used to meditate in a cave. He always stayed in the cave. A sadhu who was devoted to him begged for food for him and took care of all his needs. After Ramana Maharshi's fame spread, many people came to the ashram and asked him questions. He replied to all of them and seemed to have the power of reading others' minds.

When I arrived at Ramana's ashram, he had been dead for a long time. In the early morning, I used to go to the cave where he meditated, and I tried to put his teachings into practice. I closed my eyes, looked inside myself, and asked, *Who am I?* In spite of my endeavors, I never learned anything about myself. It was as if I was empty inside. I could only feel my body and nothing else. Maybe I was a being without a soul!

A few years went by before I attended a Zen Buddhist meditation center in the woods of a Korean mountain. The drinking water flowed from the ground naturally. There were about ten buildings in the area. All of them were made of wood in the traditional Korean style. My roommate was the only one who spoke English fluently. With him, I met the Zen master. We bowed in front of him, and then he started talking while my roommate translated his words into English.

The Zen master told me how I should meditate, and for this purpose he gave me a *Koan* (key words to meditate on). My *Koan* was "What is this?" As I had done at Ramana Maharshi Ashram, while I stayed at the Zen Buddhist meditation center, I looked inside myself for almost one month and asked myself the *Koan* continuously from morning to evening. I just focused on the question and strove not to think about anything else.

This kind of meditation was a bit different from the Ramana Maharshi's *Who am I?* Actually, according to Zen doctrine, the truth cannot be expressed in words, so we cannot say in words what we are. We may be flesh, energy, or illusion, who knows! So, I watched inside myself to understand what kind of substance I, the watcher, was made of. At that time, I didn't discover anything about my real identity, but the meditation was useful. By doing it, I purified my mind and understood how useless and even dangerous a mind is that wanders in the clouds. Being here and now is a good start for any spiritual search.

I also attended yoga centers in my hometown, in New York, and in the Bahamas. In New York, besides doing yoga, I also studied Sanskrit, which was believed to be the oldest language in the world. While in the Bahamas, I also practiced Bhakti Yoga, the yoga of devotion.

Besides doing the spiritual practices I mentioned above, I read a lot of books about religions and enlightened masters: books on Sufism, Gurdjieff's fourth way, Osho, Saint Augustine, and so on. I also read the Bible, the Koran, the

Bhagavad Gita, and other holy scriptures. Furthermore, whenever I sensed that something supernatural or mysterious had occurred somewhere in the world, I ran there.

The opportunity to meet the Sufis came during my stay in Rabat, the capital of Morocco. As soon as I arrived in that city, I tried to get information on how to find the Sufis. My host family told me that it would be impossible for a non-Muslim to enter a mosque, but perhaps the Sufis would make an exception for me.

I went to a *zawiya*, a Sufi lodge. I entered there and exchanged a few words with a man sitting in the hall. He was reading a book in Arabic.

"Good afternoon, sir. Sorry for disturbing you. I am doing research on life after death. I heard that the Sufis are mystic. Being mystics, you Sufis may know the truth. Could you tell me what you think about this topic?" I asked.

He stopped reading, lifted his eyes to me, and shook my hand. "Nice to meet you. From your accent, I guess you are Italian, yes?"

"Yes, I am Italian. Actually, I am from Sicily, which is not far from Morocco. The Arabs stayed in Sicily for about two and a half centuries. We have the sane blood in our veins."

"Please, sit down. I am a professor at the University of Rabat. You are lucky to have met me. I have described the Sufi way on a CD."

He stood up, took a CD from a drawer and handed it to me.

"Before coming to this *zawiya* again, you must watch this CD. Then you will be allowed in. However, I will answer your question right now," said the tall, olive-skinned Sufi.

"To know the truth about the afterlife," he continued, "you must purify your heart first, and then you can get the answer you are looking for, even in this life! If you invoke the name of God, you will cleanse your heart little by little. The core of Sufism is '*La ilaha illa Allah,*' there is nothing to worship other than Allah. You hold too many gods inside your heart: money, success, fame, and so on. You have to drop all these gods from your heart and worship only Allah; that is God."

I went to the *zawiya* every Saturday for almost two months. Everybody was warmhearted to me. They prayed to God mostly by chanting. The *zawiya* vibrated with their devotional songs. I didn't know how to sing in Arabic; otherwise, I would have joined them. At the end of the prayer, we sat on the floor and consumed the Arab traditional food called couscous. We ate that delicious dish with our hands.

Finally, the day of my departure from Rabat came, and I left Morocco with my heart turned to my Sufi friends. I miss all of them.

To deepen my quest, I joined an esoteric group. This experience was useful to me and broadened the horizons of my mind. However, I have to say that my writing has been the best way to know myself, others, and the meaning of life. I don't want to say that religions, my esoteric experience, and reading books have taught me nothing. Not at all! I just want to stress that what I have achieved through my writing I couldn't get from other sources. In my opinion, writing is more powerful than psychoanalysis.

My writing is like seeing my mind reflected in a mirror. By and by, as I was creating a book, not only did I discover something new inside myself, but I also understood human behavior a little better. It was as if my pen scratched and then stirred up the deepest layer of my mind. My writing helped me understand how to overcome my shortcomings, difficulties, and fears. I could see things as they really were because my detached view of reality was more objective and serene while I was writing. Through my writing, I realized that, most likely, the quality of my relationships with others depended on my make-up and the law of attraction. I attracted good or bad people, good or bad situations, that suited my good or bad mood, the weakness or strength of my character.

Unfortunately, despite my efforts, I had discovered nothing about the afterlife. I didn't even know anything about the existence of the soul. Do we really have a soul inside us? Supposing it exists, what happens to the soul when one dies? Does it migrate into another body? Does it remain trapped inside the dead body? Does it move to another planet, to another star? Are paradise, purgatory, and hell just illusions or real places where souls live? If these places exist, where are they located? In different parts of the universe? Where is the hell where souls burn? Is it in the underground of the earth?

In my opinion, research on the afterlife is the most important study one can do. Maybe the leaders of the world don't think they will die. Their minds are engrossed in mundane affairs all day long. Why, instead of fighting for trivial things, don't they budget some money to research the human soul and the hereafter?

My wife once said to me, "You worry about death too much. Why don't you write a love story? Readers are fascinated by romances."

I pondered on my wife's words. She could be right. Maybe I was too involved in my quest on life after death. So, I followed her advice and tried to write something about affairs of the heart, but I found it very difficult to make up the plot. I am not able to invent a story. I can only write about myself, my life, or the events that really happened that I saw with my own eyes or I heard with my own ears.

The theme of life after death has not been the only concern of my life. I also wanted to learn something about human nature. Is it good? Is it bad? Do good and evil exist? I hadn't achieved great results. Notably, I couldn't understand human behavior.

In my opinion, some people I came across in my life were mean to me. Is my judgment of their inner being right? Maybe they misbehaved only with me but they were good with others. How can I ever come to know the deepest layers of a human being, their mind, soul, and good or bad nature?

Everybody thinks he is right while others are wrong. As for me, I thought I was an honest and sincere man, and I couldn't understand why there were insincere people on earth. Whenever I came across someone that acted falsely with me, I was literally petrified. *How is it possible that there are people so unfair?* I thought. Sometimes I had a feeling that I had a soul and doubted that a person that had betrayed me had one. *How can a soul be so treacherous?* I asked myself.

There was a friend of mine who swore that he considered me as his brother. I believed in his words, but later I found out that what he had said didn't match his feelings. I couldn't understand why he showed himself different from what he was inside.

I once knew a woman that said to her boyfriend, "I love you." But those were just fake words. She wanted to marry him for his money. There was no love at all. For me, a sincere and even credulous person since childhood, it was inconceivable to act as a hypocrite. I was not able to cheat anybody.

Due to my job as a lawyer, I have met people so greedy that they even gave up their family ties for the love of money. I knew a woman who, while her sister was dying, made her sign a will that allotted her all the inheritance at the expense of her siblings. Then, an interminable lawsuit ensued. Both the plaintiffs and the defendant died when the case was still ongoing. They had spent a lot of money and wasted their energies to get nothing!

In Enna, most men of my age spend their time in the clubs for the old people, where they can play cards, watch television, chat about their experiences of life, their school time, their first loves, and similar things. Thus, the days pass!

There are also some workaholics in Enna that keep working until late in life. A cousin of mine still manages his firm at the age of eighty-six. One great attorney even pleads criminal cases at ninety years of age!

As for me, I spend my old age reading books, traveling, visiting places of worship whenever possible, writing, and walking in Enna's cemetery once in a while to meditate, question myself, and add some more data to my quest for information on the afterlife and human behavior. Who spends a better life? The elders in the social clubs, the workaholics, or me? I don't know. Few living beings on earth are allowed to attain the ultimate truth. In my life, I have just tried to be honest and consistent with myself and my writing. I have never written in one way and then acted in another. This has been enough for me to be satisfied with what I have done.

Chapter Two

The Epitaph on Giuseppe Chiarello's Tombstone

Not all the tombs in Enna's cemetery are rooms with walled niches and an altar. Some tombs have Spartan features; instead of a room, they have a small glass window in the facade and a tombstone. On the ledge between the glass window and the tombstone, the relatives put candles, flowers, and the pictures of their departed loved ones. Often, enameled photos are fixed on the facade. This kind of burial site is quite small, usually less than two meters high.

Sometimes, as if he wanted to make up for the tomb's Spartan structure, the one who built it thought to engrave an epitaph on the tombstone to embellish his burial site. Of course, there were also epitaphs in the tombs of the rich. However, they were not common in Enna. I dare say they were occasional. As I was curious about those kinds of inscriptions, I sometimes walked through the tombs and found some good ones with deep meanings. Most of them were passages from the Gospels, while others were prayers to God. Some epitaphs expressed the poetic vein of the tomb's owner.

One day, while I was walking on a narrow path near the entrance to the cemetery, turning my eyes to the right, I spotted a little tomb about one meter and eighty centimeters tall. The facade was gray, with two small light posts on each side and an iron-framed glass window. Inside the light posts were two lit candles. Peeping through the glass window, I saw no pictures on the ledge. The facade was bare. No enameled photos had been embedded in it. It was unusual. Maybe the tomb was too old and dated back to a time when photography had not yet been invented, or perhaps it was so bare for some other reason. However, it didn't look derelict. An epitaph had been carved in the tombstone behind the glass window:

> Here rests Giuseppe Chiarello,
>
> a fragile earthenware vase amid iron vases.
>
> Can you figure out my life on Earth, o passerby?
>
> My bones lie here, while my soul soars high.
>
> I can see you standing in front of my little tomb, o passerby.
>
> I enjoy talking to your heart, o my dear friend.
>
> Now, take it from me.
>
> My meekness prevailed over the bullies, at last.
>
> The rich and the powerful could not buy immortality,
>
> while I, with my humble heart, won eternity!

Giuseppe Chiarello's epitaph touched my heart. I read and reread it. To my eyes, it was a charming poem. The metaphor seemed to convey an idea about what his life had been like. He compared himself to a fragile earthenware jug among iron jugs. How could he ever succeed and compete with iron jars—that is, with people stronger, more aggressive, and more cunning than him? Was he the loser? It seems that he won at last.

I left Giuseppe Chiarello's tomb and kept walking on the cemetery's main street. Not far from there, a tall, majestic family tomb full of carvings and floral themes stood out. The room was decorated with stuccoes in the baroque style. Portraits of the Duke of Capodarso and his wife, Baroness Bianca, stood out on the altar. The tomb looked lifeless and neglected—no flowers, no candles. The plaster had peeled off in some places, and mold had appeared between the floor and the walls.

If there had been a contest to award a prize to the most beautiful tomb in Enna's cemetery and I had been a member of the jury, I would have voted for Giuseppe Chiarello's little tomb, because of its originality and artistic spirit. The gorgeous noble-family chapel of the Duke of Capodarso was cold, while Giuseppe Chiarello's heart was still throbbing in his tiny tomb, thanks to the epitaph.

I felt that he must have been a poet. It was just my feeling, nothing more. I had never heard of him in the literary circles in my hometown, but who knows! It is possible that a good poet falls into oblivion.

Even saints can be forgotten by their fellow citizens. This happened in Enna, the birthplace of Saint Elijah of Enna, also called Saint Elijah the Younger, to distinguish him from the prophet Elijah. He was born in Enna around 823 when the city was a Byzantine fortress. His baptismal name was Giovanni. When the Arabs occupied Sicily, they took Giovanni prisoner and sold him as a slave in Africa. After Giovanni was set free, he started preaching the Gospel and arrived in Palestine, where he became a monk and received the new name of Elijah. He was a great traveler and a wise man. He traveled to Egypt, Persia, Rome, Greece, the Sinai Peninsula, and so on to spread the Gospel. He founded a monastery in Seminara, Calabria, an Italian region near Sicily, where his body now rests. The fame of Saint Elijah's wisdom and holiness spread throughout the world, so much so that the emperor of the Eastern Roman Empire, Leo the Philosopher, invited him to stay in his court. Saint Elijah set off for Byzantium, but he died on the journey.

This saint is worshipped both by the Catholics and by the Orthodox Christians, for the Eastern Schism had not begun at the time of Saint Elijah the Younger, when there was only one universal church of Jesus Christ. The feast in honor of Saint Elijah of Enna is celebrated every year on August 17.

Strangely, this great saint is unknown in his hometown. No one in Enna had ever heard of Saint Elijah the Younger until a historian wrote a book about him. I too learned about him after attending a lecture on the Middle Ages at Ennaion Library in Enna.

The same thing could have happened to Giuseppe Chiarello. He could have been a good poet or writer whom his fellow citizens had ignored. I decided to dig into his life, and the following afternoon, I went to the public library to find some clues about him.

The city library in Enna is renowned for its meticulousness in preserving things related to the history of the city. The clerk, with bristly hair, a short-bristled beard, and thick glasses, had a bored look while sitting behind the counter at the entrance. His job consisted of writing on a slip of paper the number of the shelf where a book could be found whenever somebody requested it, but there were not many book seekers in Enna's library. Nowadays, it is much easier and faster to do research on the Internet to find what you are looking for.

The clerk was well-known in Enna for organizing meetings with poets. Even though he didn't have enough schooling, by attending his tedious job at the library, which allowed him plenty of time to read books, he became a scholar. He had read hundreds of books about how to get enlightenment. His name was Peppe Salamone. He once gave me the useful tip to visit some ashrams in India.

He had founded a literary association called "The Friends of Poetry." I sometimes attended their meetings, which were held in the elegant fourteenth- century hall of the library. To my surprise, there were more poets in Enna than I had expected. Some of them, in my opinion, had psychological problems and looked a bit strange. This is not so odd. Misfits are often good poets. In Italy, there was a great and maladjusted poet named Giacomo Leopardi who wrote superb poems. He is still alive in my heart. He lived a solitary existence and was quite unsociable, but generations of students have studied his sublime poetry at school.

Since Peppe Salamone had dealt with poets for a long time, I figured he had to know something about Giuseppe Chiarello, supposing he had written poems.

"Good morning, Peppe!"

"Good Morning, Mario. Did you enjoy the last meeting with the poet from Aidone who presented his new book of poems at the library? What about his haikus? Did you like them?"

"Those haikus were a surprise to me. I didn't even know that this word existed in the dictionary before I came and attended the meeting at the library. Thank you for inviting me."

"It was my pleasure, Mario. You are a scholar and a friend of mine."

"I have made research on this kind of poetry. I have found that haikus are a literary form of expression born in Japan. Is it like that?"

"Yes, it is as you say. Some Japanese poets were able to convey an idea or feeling within just three lines made of seventeen syllables."

"The haikus by the poet of Aidone were nice. I liked them. I wouldn't be able to make a poem with seventeen syllables."

"In fifteen days we'll have another meeting. This time, a poet from Enna will present her poems. She is a professed feminist and the first and last woman, as far as I know, to get a job as a bricklayer. Women don't do this kind of work in Enna, so don't miss her lecture!"

"I'll do my best to take part in this event."

"How can I help you today? Do you need a book or a magazine? Or anything else?"

"I am looking for a book written by a poet or a writer—I don't know exactly—by the name Giuseppe Chiarello. Have you ever heard about him?"

"Yes, I have. In the afternoons, he used to come to the library, take a seat at a table, and write something. From a distance, I could see that he wrote in prose. I don't know what his writing was about. He died a few years ago. He had also written some poems, but he couldn't make a book with them. Every now and then he joined our meetings at the literary association. On one occasion, he brought an old cousin of his with him. She recited his poems plainly, with no inflection. I had the feeling that nobody liked his poetry, for it was too sad, and also a bit confused, in my opinion."

"The epitaph I read on his tomb was beautiful," I said.

"Beauty is in the eye of the beholder! So we may have different opinions about Giuseppe Chiarello as a poet. He was an amateur poet, in my opinion, but don't take my judgment on him as gospel truth. Deep down, I am not a professional literary critic."

"Do you know anything about him?"

"Yes, I heard that he was a victim of his wife; even his daughters didn't respect him. Once, I asked him to hold a lecture about poetry, but he refused. He was too shy to be the center of attention. I heard that he had also written something in prose and strove to publish his manuscript through Primo. Do you know him? He is the main bookseller in Enna. If you ask him, he will have more information about Giuseppe Chiarello than I."

"Thank you, Peppe. I'll ask the bookseller. He is also a friend of mine."

"Don't miss attending the next meeting with the feminist poet."

"Don't worry. I will come, Peppe."

"If you come across an unknown poet or writer, tell them about our association, The Friends of Poetry. They can present their works here at the library. I like discovering new talent."

"Of course, Peppe. I'll tell them to contact you. Bye for now, Peppe."

"Bye, Mario."

Primo's bookstore was in the upper part of town, near the Castle of Lombardy. It had a mythological name, Demeter's Bookstore. Booklovers and booksellers are destined to meet, so Primo had been a friend of mine for a long time. I had been one of his first customers. He was short but held his head high like a cockerel. Rightly, his bookshop was the best in Enna. At work, he dressed in a jacket and a tie, while he wore casual clothes outside of his job. Due to his dark complexion, he always wore light-colored jackets.

Once, his bookshop was very busy. Later, with the coming of the Internet, sales slumped. These days, 50 percent of books are purchased through the web, maybe more; I don't know the statistics exactly. I seldom purchased books from him, for I preferred to buy them, as well as other items, through the Internet.

When I entered his shop, I saw a few customers lounging about the shelves. Apparently, in spite of the Internet, there are still people that enjoy touching the paper of the books, opening them with their hands, and flipping over the pages before they decide to make the purchase. For a few readers, even the quality of the paper is a motivating factor to buy a book.

Primo had arranged a few shelves in a corner of his bookstore where only books by authors from Enna were displayed. If Giuseppe Chiarello had gotten his manuscript published, his book should be there.

On seeing me, Primo stood up, came towards me, and then hugged me.

"How are you doing, Mario?" he asked, smiling with happiness as if he had found a lost, valuable object.

"I'm doing well!"

"I haven't seen you for a long time. I know you are a great traveler who spends at least half of the year abroad, but when you are in Enna, you can come here and say hello to an old friend of yours."

"When I am in Enna, I mostly stay at home. I read, write, and meditate for about an hour a day. Now and then, I go to the cemetery, but I haven't forgotten you. You are still my friend. Do you know I turned eighty last month?"

"Congratulations! You look much younger. I heard that you even buy your shoes through the web. Is it true? You should help the economy of your hometown, instead of purchasing everything on the Internet."

I felt a bit ashamed. He had told the truth about my Internet mania. However, I didn't want to disappoint him that day.

"Yes, what you said is partly true, but today I am here to buy a book from you. I want to purchase *La Storia di Enna* (*The History of Enna*) by Paolo Vetri. Do you have it?"

"Of course I have it. Paolo Vetri is one of the most important historians in Enna. I have his book in two editions, one is in paperback and the other in hardback."

In no time, Primo took the two editions from a shelf. How he could memorize the location of all the books in his shop was a mystery to me. He was really a good seller who loved his job.

"Which one do you like?" he asked.

"Which one do you advise me to buy?"

"I recommend the edition in hardback because of its fine paper. Moreover, it contains illustrations of both Enna and the former Castrogiovanni."

"I'll purchase the edition in hardback, Primo."

While he was wrapping the book, I introduced my question about the man from the epitaph.

"Have you ever heard about a man named Giuseppe Chiarello?" I asked.

Primo lifted his wondering eyes and stopped wrapping the book as if a powerful spell had turned him into a piece of wood. Then, his blood started to flow again through his veins, and he slowly turned to me.

"Yes, I knew him personally. I think I was the only friend he had. He had been a warrant officer in the army. After he retired, he came and lived in Enna until he died. How did you hear about him?" Primo asked with a trembling voice.

"While I was walking in the cemetery, I stumbled across his tomb. There was an epitaph engraved in the tombstone. I liked it and thought he must have been a poet or a writer."

"I can only say he was a very good man. The meekest and sincerest person I had ever met in my life. If it had depended on me, I would have made him a saint."

"Was he from Enna?"

"Yes, he was, but he traveled every day from Enna to Caltanissetta until he quit his job in the army."

"How old was he?"

"He was about twenty years older than me. Therefore, he must have been seventy-six years old when he died."

"He died quite young, didn't he?"

"You must know that he suffered many hardships. In the evening, he used to come to my shop and leaf through the pages of a book. He was a scholar on the history and culture of the Sicilian people. He enjoyed books by Napoleone Colajanni, a great writer and honest politician from Castrogiovanni. In my opinion, Enna was made the capital of the province out of respect for him. Nowadays, honest politicians are a rare commodity. Don't you think so?"

"Yes, I agree with you, Primo. I don't like politicians, but let's not talk about them, otherwise we'll eat our hearts out. Rather, tell me something more about Giuseppe Chiarello."

"Like you, he detested politicians, but he didn't dislike social themes. He had a prejudice against northern Italians. According to him, Sicily was superior to northern Italy in its culture and traditions. He had read all the books by our local authors, from Nino Savarese to Alfredo Rutella, a good poet. Even though Giuseppe had blue eyes and was light-skinned, he felt he had Arab origins. 'Every Sicilian has at least one drop of Arab blood in his veins,' he said to me one day."

"I heard from Peppe Salamone, a friend of mine who works at the city library, that Giuseppe Chiarello used to go there in the afternoons and write."

"Yes, I know. Every day after he left the public library, he came to my bookstore with his manuscript in hand. He asked me to keep it in a safe place until he finished writing it. He didn't want to take it to his home, and rightly so. His wife and two daughters were three harpies. They would have been capable of throwing away his work just to displease him. Therefore, I kept the manuscript in the counter drawer. He stayed in my shop until closing time, and then I walked him to his home. What a dear friend he was!" said Primo, his eyes moist with tears.

"Sometimes he told me about his campaign in Russia during the Second World War. He covered thousands of kilometers on foot in Russia, with temperatures of twenty degrees below zero. Many troops died then, but his strong body went through the ordeal."

"What about his family? I didn't spot a photo in his tomb."

"He was married and had two daughters. People knew he was henpecked. *Vox populi vox Dei!* It means that what people say is the truth. Sometimes, he looked depressed. The three witches he kept at home—that is, his wife and daughters—vexed him too much. He was a good man. If you are too good, others take advantage of you. It is easy to fall into the trap of the sly. We live in a world populated by ravenous wolves! There is no room for meekness. People of success are smart, cunning, and aggressive hypocrites and cheaters. Don't you think so, Mario?"

"No, I don't, Primo. In my opinion, the world belongs to the good ones, on the condition that they are alert. Alertness is the secret to success, not cunning."

"I hope you are right, Mario."

"Tell me something more about Giuseppe Chiarello, please."

"Okay. When he wanted to write something, he went to the library, sat at a table, and wrote by hand."

"Did he publish his manuscript?"

"No, he didn't. He couldn't find a publisher."

"Why didn't he publish his work by himself?"

"It was impossible. His wife managed his money. When he was nothing but skin and bones and unable to walk and get out of his house, I visited him at his home almost every day after I closed my shop. I was very cautious, because the three bitches could listen at the door. I couldn't talk with him freely. One evening, when the three wild beasts were eating their meal and I was staying at his bedside, Giuseppe asked me to find a publisher for his manuscript."

"Why were those three women, his wife and daughters, so terrible? Maybe you have a prejudice against them. I can't believe what you say about them. You depict them too badly, in my opinion."

"They were appalling. His wife used to wait for me to come behind the door to the street, as if she had nothing better to do. She opened the door before I even rang the bell. At first, I greeted her. She never replied to my greeting. She just fixed her viper eyes on me and pointed her finger towards her husband's bedroom. Not a single word came out of her mouth.

"Her younger daughter was as fat as a cow. When she came across me, she made vulgar gestures at me. For instance, she lowered her hand to her cunt, glared at me, and snarled with a defying look. Her sister's nature was maybe not so bad. She always had her hair in curlers. Her face resembled that of her father, except for her hair, which was pitch-black. However, living with her sister and mother, she complied with them. Sometimes, she behaved worse than them. One evening, she even dared to give me a kick when I opened the door to leave that goddamn house full of negativity and filth."

"Your words upset me, Primo."

"Yes, what I have just said to you is really horrifying, but that is not all of it. I have never seen so dirty a house. Once, I asked to go to the bathroom, and the girl in the curlers pointed it out to me. I opened the door. On the right was a pile of dirty, evil-smelling clothes beside a basin. I headed for the toilet, but seeing it encrusted with shit, I gave up peeing. I was about to vomit. The sheets in my friend's bed smelled ripe. I asked Giuseppe if they had been changed. 'Don't ask me anything, please. I don't know anything about housework,' he answered. Peeping at one of the rooms, I saw it full of plastic bags that contained something. Made curious, I asked Giuseppe about it:

"What do those plastic bags contain?"

"My wife keeps clothes, socks, towels, shirts, and similar things in them," he answered.

"Don't you have a closet?"

"Yes, we have it, but it is more convenient for her to keep clothes outside the closet."

"Can she easily find the clothes she puts in the plastic bags?"

"I don't think so," he replied, "for she continuously complains about not being able to find anything."

"There was also not enough light in the house. Only a feeble gleam filtered from the kitchen door. For the rest, the rooms were illuminated by the city lights. When I left Giuseppe's bedroom, I had to be careful to avoid stumbling into all kinds of objects like brooms and buckets. If it had not been for my friendship with Giuseppe, I would have never put my foot in that sinister house. For me, those three women were mad as March hares."

"Don't judge anybody, Primo. You cannot know the ultimate truth. After many years of studying and pondering human behavior, I have concluded that the lack of love makes people become mad. There was no love in that house. Nobody loved Giuseppe, and Giuseppe loved nobody. For that reason, his wife and daughters behaved strangely. When a woman loves her husband, she can't do such awful things. But you cannot condemn the three women and acquit Giuseppe. He was responsible for his hard luck, just like his wife and daughters. If he had loved them, it would have been impossible for them to act so badly. His lack of love toward them made them become wicked. Now, let's change the topic, Primo, please. I feel disgusted."

"Don't you want to know the end of the story?" he asked.

"Yes, tell me what happened. Did you help your friend find a publishing house?"

"Of course I did. I told him, 'Don't worry, Giuseppe. I'll find a good publisher in Palermo. Once in a while I go to that city to get books from my suppliers.'"

"Have you ever read his work?" I asked.

"No, I haven't. Once, I took his manuscript in hand to get an idea what it was about, but I couldn't read it, for his writing was so tiny that I needed a magnifying glass to pass an eye over the manuscript. I didn't have enough patience.

"I contacted a publishing house in Palermo. When I happened to go to that city, I went and met the chief executive officer and showed him the manuscript. He leafed through a few pages and immediately gave it back to me. 'Our publishing house has a long and glorious tradition. Usually, we don't publish works by unknown writers. However, type the manuscript and then let's meet again,' he said.

"I tried to find a typist, but I couldn't. Nobody wanted to do the job. Finally, I found a typist who accepted typing Giuseppe's work, but she asked for too much money, in my opinion. So, in the evening, as usual, I went to Giuseppe's house. The three ogresses controlled my movements. When I felt they were not listening at the door, I whispered in my friend's ear, 'Giuseppe, I found a typist, but she wants to get paid a lot. According to me she asks for too much money to do the job.' 'I can afford it,' he replied. 'My wife keeps the key to the safe. Ask her. She will give you the money for the typist.' Knowing the character of the venomous snake, his wife, I didn't ask her anything. Six months later, my friend Giuseppe died without having the joy of getting his manuscript published."

"I am sorry for him. He was really an unlucky man," I said.

"I am eaten up with remorse now. I should have paid the typist. I was a miser on that occasion. We humans tend to spend money to achieve the most trivial and futile things, but not to help our neighbor. We are inhuman beings, not humans!"

At that moment, a tear ran down Primo's face and fell onto the counter.

"Don't have scruples, Primo. You did your best to help your friend."

"I also contacted some local publishers," Primo continued in a choked voice, "to please my friend, Giuseppe, but with no avail. Finally, I gave up my endeavors."

"Did you inform your friend about your efforts to get his manuscript published?"

"Yes, I did. As I told you before, I visited him every evening after I closed my shop. He was becoming thinner and thinner. He seemed not to care much about the publishing of his work anymore. He had more serious problems to tackle."

"Where is the manuscript now?"

"I keep it at home. It is precious to me."

"Can I purchase it?"

"How do you dare ask such a thing of me? No, the answer is no. I can't sell it. It is a keepsake, but you can come here and read it anytime. I'll bring it here. I'll keep it in the drawer of my counter just for you."

"Do you know why his writing was so tiny?"

"Yes, I do. He said that by writing in that way, he could control his thoughts well and express them easily. For me, that was absurd. In my opinion, if you have inspiration, you can put it in black and white regardless of the tool you are using to convey your ideas. You may have a pen, a pencil, a laptop, a typewriter, or you can write in bold, italic, in small or big letters. It doesn't matter. Only inspiration is the basis of good writing."

"I don't think so, Primo. There are authors who can't get inspiration if they are sitting in front of a laptop. Once, I knew a writer who used to record his voice on a recorder, and then he transcribed it on paper. Other authors may need pen and paper. As for me, I get inspiration only if I write in English, though my first language is Italian. I don't know why. Maybe I was born into an English-speaking country in a past life, who knows!"

"Are you joking, Mario? There are no past lives. We live only once."

"Can I borrow the manuscript sometime and read it at home comfortably?"

"No, you can't."

"Do I have to stand in your shop with the manuscript in hand?"

"Of course not! You can have a seat in that corner of the bookstore. I'll get you a chair, a small desk, and a magnifying glass, so you can come here and read it peacefully anytime."

"Okay, thank you, Primo. I'll come here starting tomorrow."

The following day I entered the bookstore. Primo was waiting for me. He took the manuscript from the drawer and handed it to me.

"Handle it with care!" he stressed.

"Don't worry. It is in good hands."

He had arranged everything for my reading. I put the manuscript on the small desk Primo had provided for me, sat on the chair, and started reading it with the magnifying glass. It took about one hour to read a single page. Even though the writing was clear, the letters were too small. One page was equivalent to ten pages of normal writing. I kept going to Primo's bookshop for the whole month of November and read the manuscript one page a day. It was nothing but Giuseppe Chiarello's diary, which ended six months before his death because he was not able to walk outside his home and write at the public library anymore. The names of the characters were different from the real ones, including his own name, which he had changed into Pasqualino Butera. I think he wanted to preserve his anonymity.

It was a sad diary from the first to the last. Perhaps the sadness of the manuscript had been the main reason that nobody wanted to read it. It is said that words, both spoken and written, create vibrations. Obviously, Chiarello's manuscript emanated sad vibrations towards those who held it in their hands. The tiny writing might also have been a contributory factor to deter readers.

Not many people are inclined to read or listen to sad stories, but life is not a bed of roses! These days, violence and immoral behavior rage across the world. There are children that kill their parents and mothers that kill their children. Drugs upset people's minds. Thousands of emigrants die trying to cross the Mediterranean Sea to land in a country other than the one where they were born. Poverty afflicts a great part of the world population, above all in Africa, India, and Latin America. Wars lead to devastation and death. Shouldn't we talk about these topics? Most people like reading stories of success or joyful, carefree books, supposing they even read books these days. Who would ever care about Giuseppe Chiarello's gloomy life? However, since I found his diary interesting and educative, I selected the most relevant passages and made a short story out of them.

I didn't write much about his campaign to Russia, for the diary was incomplete about that part of his life. He probably couldn't write anything while he was actually at war. In my opinion, when he returned to Italy after the war, he repressed the memories of the hardships he had suffered while in Russia.

Of course the diary was written in Italian, but I wrote the short story of Giuseppe Chiarello's life, as well as this entire book, in English for more than one reason. First of all, these days, English has become the language that many people throughout the world can speak and read easily. I like to address the world when I write something. I am a man beyond race and nationality. For me, only individuals exist, not nations. If it depended on me, I would turn the world into only one country, with only one world government and only one currency. Second, I like the English language; I find it very precise. Moreover, it has much more lemmas than other languages. This allows me to express myself in a more complete way.

Paradoxically, this short story based on Giuseppe Chiarello's life will be read by few readers in his hometown, for few people in Enna are able to read a book in English. Maybe in the future things will change for the better, I hope.

Through this, my little book, Giuseppe Chiarello's life will be remembered in many countries in the world, but it will be ignored in his hometown, as was Saint Elijah the Younger.

Now, let's have a look at his life story. It may not be considered interesting by some, but it is definitely unique. His diary has been helpful to me, for thanks to it, I now better understand human misery and can approach my neighbor, whoever they are, with a more serene and open mind.

Chapter Three

A Story Extracted from the Diary of Pasqualino Butera

My family

I am Pasqualino Butera. I was born in Enna three years before it was raised to the rank of provincial capital and changed its name from Castrogiovanni into Enna. My mother, Assunta, had been married twice to two brothers. After her first husband, the elder brother, died, the younger one married her. My mother said that the two brothers were different in both complexion and character. The first husband was haughty, dark, and wore a thick mustache; the other was shy, blond, and with blue eyes. As for my mother, she was dark in complexion, rather short in stature, had an aquiline nose, and piercing black eyes that inspired fear. She always wore black clothes that made her look like a bird of prey. She was the harshest and strictest person I ever met in my life. I never dared to look her in the eyes.

From her first husband, my mother gave birth to my sister, Giovannina. My brother Filippo and I were sons of her second husband. Filippo was two years younger than me. As my mother's first husband had been left a widower and had had three daughters, Filomena, Luciana, Mariannina, and a son, Serafino, from his first wife, my sister Giovannina had three sisters and one brother, while Filippo and I had cousinhood ties with my sisters' siblings.

Giovannina was dark-skinned like her parents, while Filippo and I resembled our father. None of us inherited my mother's rough features and her aquiline nose. I hardly recall my father, for he died when I was four years old. My mother used to keep two silver-framed pictures of her two husbands on the chest of drawers in her bedroom. Two small electric candles were always on in front of each of them. In the pictures, the two husbands didn't look like brothers at all. They didn't share any features. I don't know much about them, their characters and their lives, for my mother seldom talked about them.

Due to my mother harshness, my brother Filippo came up so repressed and conditioned by her that he seldom opened his mouth to speak. He was a bit open with me, but whenever he was with others, he tightened his lips as if they were two shutters. At the age of fourteen, he started his apprenticeship as a blacksmith. The job suited him, for he didn't need to talk while he forged iron or beat it on the anvil to shape it.

Filippo was unluckier than I. At night, while sleeping, he used to wet the bed. This continued until the age of eighteen. Every time he wet the bed, my mother beat him violently. Finally, she resorted to a specialist, who diagnosed that Filippo was born with a cleft in his spine. Due to this malformation, he wet himself at night. When he turned eighteen, the ailment disappeared. It was not his fault if he wet the bed. The situation was caused by his disease. I couldn't understand why my mother acted so badly toward him.

Being the daughter of my mother's first husband, my sister was two years older than me. When she was twenty-five years old, she received a proposal of marriage from a man fifteen years older. My mother opposed the marriage with all her might, because the suitor was well known for being a pederast, but in the end, my sister's unceasing tears softened my mother's hard heart, and she got the permission to marry the one she loved. She didn't have children with him. To my eyes, he looked like a homosexual. Who knows, maybe my mother had been right to oppose the marriage.

During my childhood, I don't recall having had friends, except for my cousin Serafino. My meekness prompted my schoolmates to make fun of me, so I preferred to remain aloof from others. Sometimes, my cousin made a fool of me too. To him, I was credulous and a bit retarded.

One afternoon, my cousin came home and asked me to play football. My mother was out. She had gone out to buy some flour at the mill. Play is an irresistible decoy for a child. I couldn't resist joining Serafino, so I left home, unbeknownst to my mother.

We played in the square in front of the Church of San Cataldo, which that afternoon the children had turned into a playground. Serafino explained the rules of football to me. It was not difficult for me to understand that the most important thing was to kick a goal. It was the first time I had played with other children. Before that day, I used to stay at home. Although I was not tall, I had an athletic body, so I easily scored five goals. I was filled with elation. But happiness is like a little bird. It flies away when you approach it!

While I was playing in the square, my mother passed by. She looked at me and headed home. She said nothing to me. I thought I was allowed to continue my football game. I scored two more goals and then I went home.

When I rang the doorbell, my sister came and opened the door. She motioned me with her hands not to enter because there was trouble brewing at home, but I didn't understand her, so I crossed the threshold like a lamb that enters a butcher's shop. My sister closed the door behind me. I was making my way toward my room when my mother, who was lurking, leaped on me as a tiger on a fawn. She hit me hard all over my body and then pinned me down with her bony hands and fingernails as sharp as those of a feline. She screamed as if she were possessed and bit my arm and shoulder repeatedly.

I felt like I was going to die. My siblings looked at the appalling scene with their eyes full of terror and their hands on their heads. They couldn't do anything to rescue me.

"Next time you leave home without asking for my permission, I'll kill you." Knowing my mother's fiery temper, I thought it actually would be possible for her to kill me.

At night, my sister came to my room and woke me up. She held a bottle of alcohol in one hand and a cotton ball in the other.

"I'll disinfect your wounds."

"Thank you, Giovannina, you are a good sister," I said to her, sobbing.

"Don't cry, otherwise you will awake Mom! In this case, she will beat you *and* me."

I can't forget what Giovannina did for me that night. Yes, love exists on earth. It is more powerful than evil.

From then on, I didn't play football again. Fearing my mother too much, I never went out to play with those my own age. Playing was forbidden to me. I just stayed at home, doing my homework or just sitting on the chair and waiting for the passage of time.

I couldn't endure my mother's strict discipline. My life was sheer hell, but there was nothing to do to change my plight. We children had been taught to obey our parents, otherwise we would have been excommunicated.

The only freedom I had during my childhood was to have a nap after lunch. It lasted for two hours, sometimes even longer. I enjoyed sleeping. During my afternoon naps, I sometimes spoke during sleep. Other times, I had wonderful dreams. I often dreamed of being an eaglet flying over the valley from Enna to Calascibetta. I spread my wings and let myself be rocked by the wind until I alighted on the pinnacle of the Church of Carmel in Calascibetta. From up there, I watched the children playing in Piazza Umberto and the passersby walking in Via Giudea. I was just a bird. I was not allowed to play with the children of humans.

Afterward, I left the pinnacle of the Church of Carmel and flew to the bell tower of the Royal Palatine Chapel, the highest point in Calascibetta. From there, I admired the valleys where the crops swayed in the wind and watched the peasants hoeing the vineyards. I lifted the eyes to the sky, but I couldn't spot other eagles. Of course, there were other birds in the sky—pigeons, crows, sparrows, swallows, and so on—but they couldn't play with an eaglet. They belonged to another breed and were scared of me, a rapacious bird. After a couple of hours, I flew back home and perched on my bed just before my awaking.

Until the age of fourteen, my only diversion was going to school in the morning. My classmate was my cousin Serafino. He was four years older than me. Being a dunce at school, he had failed four times. He made little progress at school until I caught up with him. Every morning, he picked me up from home, and together we went to school, which had been set in a former convent of Franciscan Sisters not far from my home. We stayed in the class for four or five hours, and then I had to run home within ten minutes, not more; otherwise, my mother would have beaten me.

During my school life, two situations baffled me. There was the English teacher who used to come into the class with the daily newspaper in hand and then address the students. "Boys, be quiet and don't disturb me. I want to read my newspaper. Meanwhile, you can review a lesson or do whatever you like, but do not disturb me. Understood?"

He perused the newspaper for the entire hour, and then he left the class. "See you tomorrow, boys," he used to say to us with a faint smile and waving his hand after the class was over.

During my first year of middle school, I had an excellent physical education teacher, but the following year things changed. The new physical education teacher was not much different from the English teacher I mentioned above. He also used to read the newspaper in the classroom. The only difference between the two was that the physical education teacher didn't greet us, because when we entered the gymnasium, he was already seated at the desk with the newspaper spread out on it. He didn't even have enough time to lift his head towards us!

How was it possible that nobody complained about those pseudo teachers? What did the headmaster do? I could have informed my mother, but she was an unpredictable woman. She could have said that I had invented the story. She could have considered my complaint as a lack of respect for my teachers and then beaten me.

Life is not all sunshine and roses! It is also made of teachers that don't do their duty and of mothers too harsh with their children. We cannot change life nor build a better world, because there are myriads of characters, myriads of minds, and myriads of hearts on earth. People tread on their own track that never meets another's. Everyone fends for himself. I don't deny that selfless people devoted to the good of others may exist, but they are quite rare. However, good or evil, all people we come across in our life are useful to our growth, including those who hurt us, because thanks to them we understand life better and strengthen ourselves to better face the inevitable misadventures we encounter in life.

When I turned fourteen, I stopped going to school and trained as an apprentice with a tailor. As happened when I went to school, after leaving the tailor's workshop, I ran home.

Staying at home, I was terribly bored. We didn't have a radio. Television had not been invented yet. Sometimes I reread my books of geography and daydreamed about being in this or that country and living another kind of life.

Time doesn't pass equally for everybody. A businessman is always busy and complains about not having enough time. A convict is forced to spend the entire day in his cell doing nothing and having a lot of time at his disposal. Of course, time never passes for the latter. Waiting for the passage of time, a convict is more tired than a busy businessman at the end of the day.

Like a convict, I waited for the passage of time. I looked forward to being eighteen. Then, I would enter the army. I would become a man. My mother would have no power over me anymore.

Life in the Army

When I received the draft card, I felt released, even though it was wartime and the army could send me to the front line. It was mandatory to serve in the army. My mother had no choice but to let me leave home.

Military discipline can't be worse than my mother's harshness, I thought. But it was a false idea to believe that by changing environments I would also change my bad mood. A new environment, new air, a new sky can't bring serenity of mind. You must have serenity inside yourself, for it cannot come to you from outside. My inner frame would remain the same even though my environmental context changed. The time I had spent in solitude during my childhood and adolescence had made me too shy, introverted and unable to socialize. My condition would remain unaltered not only in Enna, but also in the army and any other place on earth where I chose to live. Moreover, the hard life I had spent with my mother had made me suspicious of human beings and had hardened my heart.

I was posted to an infantry regiment based in Pordenone, a city in the northeast of Italy. When I arrived at the barracks, the other conscripted soldiers seemed like strange beings from distant lands. Quite often they spoke to each other in a dialect I could not understand. While the Sicilian dialect is understandable by all Italians, the dialect of the people from northern Italy cannot be understood by everyone.

Even though I was suspicious and fearful of the other soldiers, I strove to open my heart to them, but whenever I opened my mouth to say or ask something, my heavy Sicilian accent prompted the Italians from northern Italy to mock me. In fact, our regiment was made mostly of northern Italians.

Some of my companions-in-arms did not call me by my real name but by the epithet of *Terrone*. I had never heard such a word before. It was an insulting and racist term those from northern Italy used to offend the southern Italians. Actually, for them, Sicily was not part of Italy. They considered themselves a superior race, while we Sicilians were rude and illiterate peasants.

"I overheard that to come to Sicily we need a passport. Is it true?" a soldier asked me one day while giggling.

On that occasion, I didn't reply to him. I just looked him in the eye and kept reading a book I had in hand.

"You don't look like a Sicilian. Your eyes are blue, and you have chestnut hair. Surely, you must descend from the Vikings who conquered Sicily long ago. You can be proud of your Viking ancestors. They came from northern Europe. Therefore, they were a superior race. Why don't you change your horrible Sicilian accent?" a soldier who looked a bit friendly told me one day.

This time I answered him. "My Sicilian accent is better than yours. When you speak, I can't catch the meaning of what you say. Your parlance is full of anacolutha. Instead, try and speak Italian correctly."

My companion-in-arms didn't reply to me. He just burst into laughter and went away. Maybe he didn't know what an anacoluthon means.

Another day, a soldier nicknamed me Mafia. I, the meekest and humblest person in the world, unable to kill even a fly, was mistaken for a gangster! I tried not to react to the insults I received. Most of the time I pretended I had not heard or understood what my companions-in-arms said to me.

A few soldiers from southern Italy changed their accent to be accepted by northerners. After a few days, they started speaking like them. With the new accent, they had fewer socialization problems.

Racism is widespread all over the world. It belongs to the animal nature of human beings. Humans defend their countries and preserve their races as well as animals—lions, dogs, wolves, and so on—defend their territories. Both humans and animals prevent strangers from mixing with them.

I once heard that an immigrant to France went to the registrar of births in the French city where he lived and changed the Italian family name of his newborn child into a French name to get him accepted by his schoolmates when he was of age to go to school. I also heard that in the United States, a very famous actor changed his Polish name into an English one to advance his career.

Another episode of racial discrimination against the Sicilians was told to me by a schoolmate. He was from Enna, but he had lived for some time in Biella, a small city in the north of Italy, with his family and had gone to school there. He told me that whenever a classmate of his gave a party, they invited all the other classmates except him. They left him out. He didn't attend any of the school parties that year, for he was not of the same race as his classmates. He was a Sicilian!

One of my companions-in-arms was from Apulia, a region in southern Italy. According to him, the southern Italians were despised only by the northern ones, while the Sicilians were despised by everybody, even by the southern Italians.

These are facts I witnessed or heard of, but I suppose there are many other episodes of racism every day in the world.

After some time, immigrants usually integrate into their new city, region, or country. Some of them forget their origins and even deny the land where they were born and raised. This happened to my Aunt Serafina, who migrated to

Turin when she was over forty and stayed there for about ten years. Whenever she came to Enna for summer holidays, she spoke with the accent typical of the citizens of Turin. In the past, I talked with her in the Sicilian dialect, but now she seemed to have forgotten her first language. When I asked her to tell me something about the monuments in the city of Turin, she pretended not to understand my Sicilian dialect, and she always replied to me in Italian with a northern accent.

One evening while I was out of the barracks and strolling in the street, I approached a couple of girls, hoping they would agree to exchange a few words with me, but when I opened my mouth and started to introduce myself, one of then cut me short.

"Go back to Palermo!" she shouted.

It was a tremendous wound for me.

Despite everything, I never spoke like the northerners while I stayed in northern Italy. Changing my accent would have been like betraying Sicily, the homeland of Empedocles, Archimedes, Nobel prizewinner for literature Luigi Pirandello, Nobel prizewinner for literature Salvatore Quasimodo, Vincenzo Bellini, and many other great men. How can people from northern Italy say that we Sicilians are illiterate! The Italian language was born in Sicily at the time of the Sicilian Poetic School, whose main exponent was Jacopo da Lentini.

I ignored my companions-in-arms, and they ignored me. What disturbed me most was being called a mafioso. Obviously, they tarred everybody with the same brush.

Because of the Mafia, we Sicilians are seen with suspicion everywhere, not only in northern Italy, and are the object of racism throughout the world like colored people, maybe even more. Many Sicilian workers in the coal mines of Belgium were discriminated against. They couldn't go to the cafeterias or to the restaurants like others. Usually, at the entrance to leisure places, a board was placed with these words written on it: "Entrance forbidden to dogs and Italians."

How can a Sicilian ever be a racist! I think it is impossible for us to discriminate against people according to the place where they were born or the religion they practice. If somebody asked me what I dislike most, I would answer him with no hesitation, "I dislike racism."

While I was in the army, I came to know that the Italian government had enacted a bill to discriminate against races, especially Jewish people. This kind of law simply disgusted me.

My first days in the army were quite demanding, not only because of racism, but also for the harshness of military life. At dawn, the sound of a trumpet woke me up. I had to get up immediately, and then, within twenty minutes, I had to poop, wash myself, shave, undo my bed, arrange the blankets and the sheets so that they took the shape of a cube, get dressed, and finally go to the soldiers' gathering. I was used to doing things slowly. The new lifestyle upset me.

I was tremendously insecure about myself and my relationships with others. I had a lot of confusion in my mind. I thought that sooner or later I would be declared unfit for service. I felt that such an eventuality would have been humiliating for me, so I decided that I had to solve my mental and temperamental problems at any cost. I just needed to find the right foothold to continue my climb to the serenity of my mind.

One day a week I stood sentinel at night, so I had enough time to think about how to solve my problems. During the four hours I was on sentry duty, while pacing in the area I had to watch, I looked up at the sky and tried to find a way to discover the causes of my insecurity.

I had certainties about nothing. I believed that the barracks, the other soldiers, and my life itself were nothing more than an illusion projected by my mind. Things didn't exist in reality. I was unable to even distinguish sleep from wakefulness. I thought and rethought on how I could find certainty about myself, the world around me, and the way I should relate to others. Then, I looked inside myself and saw my mind as if it were a messy room where chaos reigned. The bed, closet, chairs, desk, and all the objects were stacked on top of each other indistinctly. Of course, I couldn't understand the world with such a confused mind. I had to find a way to put my mind in order and at ease.

One night when I was pacing up and down a bastion of the barracks, the moon radiated its silver light beams over the fields, and I found a starting point to bring clarity inside me. *If I am able to think, it means that I am alive and exist. I am not nothingness. I just need to keep calm, put away my anxiety, and let life be my teacher. By living life, I will solve my problems naturally, for life will tell me how to do it. There is no better teacher than life itself,* I thought.

Little by little, I began to adapt to military life. After we completed the training period, which lasted nearly a month and a half, there wasn't much to do in the barracks except wait for the passage of time. Sooner or later we would be sent to one of the war fronts. Occasionally, we went to the shooting range to train with rifles and hand grenades.

The training officer realized that I was hopeless at handling arms. Consequently, he assigned me to the support area. I assisted the official in charge of military supplies of food and barracks equipment.

Soon after the war broke out with Russia, my infantry division was sent by troop train to Ukraine. The plan of the Italian government was to penetrate deep into Russian territory in support of our German allies, but we couldn't go beyond Ukraine by train, because the tracks in Russia had a different width than the rest of Europe. On the other hand, we couldn't continue our advance into Russian territory by truck, because even though it was September, during the night the water in the radiators of the trucks froze and made them unusable. Antifreeze had not been put in the radiators because nobody expected that the temperature would drop below zero. Therefore, we had no choice but to continue our advance on foot.

Every day we covered about fifty kilometers. At first, the local population welcomed us as their liberators from the Soviet regime, but as we entered Russian territory, people became increasingly hostile. At first, we achieved some success against the Russian armed forces, but then we realized that we were unable to cope with them. After the Russians caught an entire army of German soldiers in the battle of Stalingrad, we beat a hasty retreat.

The Russian winter was merciless. Our equipment was unsuitable for the terrible weather. We walked on the frozen ground with hobnailed boots that were unsuitable for snow. Our feet almost froze. Tens of thousands of my fellow soldiers died. Unlike the German and Russian soldiers, we didn't have enough white snowsuits to camouflage ourselves on the icy steppe and were easy targets for the Russian riflemen.

Even when I served in the army, I didn't give up my nap after lunch. Whenever I had the chance, I dozed for a while after a meal. One afternoon during the Russian campaign while I was taking a nap, my battalion moved and left me sleeping in a nook of a shed. When I woke up, I found myself alone in the snowy steppe. I would have frozen to death if a Russian farmer had not taken me to my battalion with his tractor. You can find a generous heart everywhere, even in your enemy in wartime. Except for that time I was carried on the Russian peasant's tractor, I walked Russia on foot during the retreat. I can't count exactly how many kilometers I did on foot, maybe two thousand or even more.

I was not much worried about my life, because being born in Enna, I was used to cold. Moreover, the German army covered our retreat. The Germans were better equipped and better armed than we Italians. The only thing that terrorized me was the hissing sound of the Katyusha rocket launcher called Stalin's organ. It fired rockets every two hours. Even after the war was over, I thought I heard those goddamn Katyusha rockets while I was sleeping.

After the war, I remained in the army and became a warrant officer. I stayed in Milan for a year, but I had Sicily in my mind and in my heart. I didn't feel like staying far away from my home island. I requested to be transferred to Sicily, and one year later my dream came true.

The First Engagement

I was posted to the recruiting center in Caltanissetta, a city near Enna. I lodged at my mother's house and went to my workplace every day by bus. It took about half an hour to go from Enna to Caltanissetta.

Staying with my mother, I had to obey certain rules, especially punctuality at dinnertime, six o'clock in the evening. After dinner, I was allowed to walk on Via Roma, but it was forbidden to get home later than 9:30. My mother said that if I was late, she would be worried about me and pass a sleepless night. So, for her sake, I returned home on time.

It is said that every Sicilian has at least one relative in America. It may be true. As for my family, we had relatives on my father's side in Brooklyn and Queens, New York, and on my mother's side in Newark, New Jersey.

Sometimes, the Sicilians who emigrated to America long ago, as well as their descendants, came to visit Sicily, the land of their origins. At the time, only the rich could afford to purchase air tickets. Most people crossed the Atlantic on ocean liners.

Since the Internet had not been invented yet, correspondence between relatives who lived in America and those in Sicily happened through second-class mail. Calls on the telephone were inconvenient and expensive. Not many families, including mine, had a telephone at home.

Every month, my mother received a letter from her sister, Concettina, who lived in Newark. Aunt Concettina used to insert a one-dollar banknote in her letter as a gift for me. I was the only child who still lived with my mother. My sister and brother were married and lived on their own. I was happy to receive those dollars from my aunt. It was unusual for me to be an object of love.

One day, inside Aunt Concettina's letter, besides the one-dollar banknote, there was a good piece of news. The daughter of her husband's brother, of Sicilian origins, planned to visit the land of her forefathers. Aunt Concettina asked my mother to host her niece for about one month. She had an aunt in Villarosa, a town near Enna, but she wanted to spend her holidays in Enna because she was interested in the history and legends of our hometown and wanted to visit the mythological places. As she was a relative of my uncle, there were no blood ties between her and us.

"What do you think? Can we host her?" my mother asked me. It was unthinkable for my mother to ask my opinion about what to do when I was a boy, but now she was becoming old, and the harshness of her heart had subsided a little bit.

"I think we can do it, Mum. Giovannina and Filippo's rooms are empty now. The American girl can stay in Giovannina's room. By the way, how old is she?"

"Aunt Concettina wrote in her last letter that she had turned twenty last April. Therefore, she is ten years younger than you. If I accept to have her as a guest, you'd better be very respectful to her. Otherwise, I'll scratch your face as I did when you went to play football unbeknownst to me. You remember that?"

"How can I forget, Mum? You left me with a scar on my arm. Don't worry. I'll be polite to her. What is her name?"

"Rita, said my sister."

"How can we communicate with her? The Americans speak English. I don't know even a single word of their language."

"My sister said that Rita is able to speak in the very old Sicilian dialect, so we can understand her, I think."

"Very good! Will she arrive in Italy by airline?"

"No, she will cross the Atlantic Ocean on the *Andrea Doria* liner and will land in Genoa. Then she will take a train to Enna. When she arrives at the Genoa railway station, she will send me a telegram, so we will know her arrival time beforehand and can pick up her at the train station in Enna."

"We'd better arrange a taxi, Mum. However, I am not available in the morning because I have to work in Caltanissetta. If she arrives in the morning, you will have to pick her up at the station alone. How will you recognize her? Do you have any photo of her?"

"No, I don't, but my sister said that Rita is very tall. It is unusual for a Sicilian woman to be so tall."

"Maybe we'll have to arrange a special bed for her."

"Let's meet her first, and then we will decide what to do."

Two months later, the postman delivered a telegram to my mother. It was written in the Sicilian dialect: *"Rita arriva dumani sira e cincu e mmenza a stazioni ferruviaria di Enna"* (Rita will arrive tomorrow evening at five thirty at the railway station of Enna).

"Very good!" I said to my mother when she showed me the telegram. "We can go together."

The Enna train station was in the valley between Enna and Calascibetta, at an altitude of 693 meters above sea level. It served both Enna and Calascibetta. It was a small train station with only four tracks. At that time, the line was not electrified, and the trains climbed up slowly through the sloping fields. There were no fences between the tracks and the countryside, so the train whistled continuously to warn the peasants of its transit.

It was May. The fields were still green, and a light breeze made the crops sway. The train made its way through the olive thickets, and the sound of its whistle was audibly closer and closer. Before long, the train would arrive at Enna's railway station.

Besides my mother and me, there were about twenty persons who waited for the arrival of their families, relatives, or friends. Finally, the train arrived. The passengers opened the doors from the inside and began to get off the train. A girl ran to hug her boyfriend in military uniform. A coffee seller in a white jacket with a tray full of cups in his hand shouted, "Coffee, coffee, cappuccino," and walked fast on the platform along the train cars. A porter took a big bag and other smaller bags from one of the train's windows. Overall, there was a lot of hustle and bustle in the station.

At long last, a tall and lean beautiful girl in a colorful dress got off the train. As soon as I saw her, I had the feeling that lightening had pierced my heart. I was shocked by her beauty. She looked like one of the actresses I had seen in American movies, and she was even more beautiful. *She must be Rita*, I thought.

"Put my bags in the cart and follow me!" the long-legged girl with an authoritarian voice said to a porter who obeyed her swiftly though he didn't understand her words in English.

My mother and I waved at her, and she also waved at us, smiling. She kept smiling all the way, and then she bent her knees and hugged my mother, who was at least thirty centimeters shorter than her.

"*Sugnu Rita* (I am Rita)," she said, turning to me.

"*Sugnu Pasqualinu e chista ye me matri* (I am Pasqualino and this is my mother)," I said.

"*U tassì ni sta aspittannu dda ffori. Amuninni fora!* (The taxi driver is waiting for us outside. Let's go out)," my mother said.

"Okay, let's go!" Rita said in her language.

The porter loaded the bags in the cab, and Rita gave him a dollar tip. He took the banknote and made a low bow.

I had never seen a woman so tall in my life. She was twenty centimeters taller than me, but I liked her. I liked everything about her: her curly short hair, her black eyes, her long legs, her sinuous body. She was the woman of my dreams.

When we arrived home, I took her two suitcases to the room where my sister had lived, but the bed was too small for Rita. To make her sleep comfortably I moved another bed to her room, joined one crosswise to the other, and then tied the spring bed bases with a rope to keep them steady.

Rita had planned to stay with us for a month or so, and then she would move to Villarosa to spend one more week with her aunt, her father's sister.

At dinner, my mother served *spaghetti alla norma*, which was spaghetti with tomato sauce, basil, fried eggplant, and salty ricotta. Rita found it delicious. She gave us the gifts she had brought from America. There was a tie for me and a black lace shawl and a multicolored fan for my mother.

"What would you like to see in Enna?" I asked her.

"I want to see everything. I don't know anything about your city."

"Would you like to visit the churches first?"

"Yes, I would. Is it possible to see the temples of Demeter and Kore?"

"Those temples don't exist anymore. In Enna, the cult of Mary replaced that of Demeter. I can take you to Lake Pergusa. It is not far from downtown Enna. According to myth, Ades, the god of the underworld, came out of one of the caves scattered in the woods that surrounded Lake Pergusa, with his chariot pulled by four black steeds. At the same time, Kore was plucking flowers with her mother, Demeter, and some nymphs by the lakeside to weave them into garlands.

"To allure her, Ades disguised himself as a splendid narcissus. Kore was enchanted by the color and scent of that beautiful flower and walked away from her mother and the nymphs to pick it, but suddenly the narcissus turned into Ades, who grabbed Kore, put her on his chariot, and abducted her. Then, Ades lashed his steeds, which, as fast as the wind, immediately headed for his underground kingdom.

"Demeter was desperate. She looked for her daughter everywhere, but to no avail. Then she turned to Zeus, who knew where Kore was kept, but he seemed not to be inclined to displease his brother Ades, who had a wife at long last. After Kore became Ades's wife, she was given a new name, Persephone.

"Demeter was the goddess of agriculture and fertility. As an act of revenge against Zeus, she made the vegetation on earth wither. Things were getting complicated even for Zeus, the king of gods! But Ades persisted in his refusal to give Persephone back to her mother. However, he couldn't help complying with Zeus's wishes, who wanted to break the deadlock between Ades and Demeter.

"Zeus suggested a solution acceptable to both parties. Persephone would stay for six months with her husband in the underground and for six months with her mother, Demeter, on the earth's surface. So it happened!

"The myth symbolizes the alternating of the seasons on earth. In autumn and winter, when Persephone is in the underground, vegetation is lifeless, while in spring and summer, when Persephone stays with her mother, plants and trees flourish."

Rita listened and gaped at me. She was bewitched by my account.

"I want to see Lake Pergusa and the cave from where Ades came out. Could you take me there?"

"Yes, of course. We can go to the lake by bus, and then we can walk to the cave," I answered.

I hoped to be left alone with Rita, but my desire clashed with my mother's preconceived ideas. She was an old-fashioned Sicilian woman. Her sister, Concettina, had put her niece in her care. Therefore, my mother felt responsible for Rita's moral conduct. What would happen if Rita and I were left alone? I could kiss her or even do something more! According to the Sicilian mentality of the time, a man shouldn't lay a finger on a woman before marriage. For my mother, it was unthinkable that I go out with Rita alone, but how could I express my feelings to the girl I loved with my mother clinging to us all the time?

The following day, my mother, Rita, and I went to the lake. We walked amid the woods, looking for the mythic cavern from where Ades had come out, but I couldn't spot it. There were a few caves in the area, but I was not sure which one had been used by Ades. I didn't want to give wrong information to Rita. However, she didn't care much about the cave, for she was enchanted by the green of the trees and the blue of the lake water.

"Even though America has wonderful landscapes, I find Lake Pergusa unique. I can feel the presence of Demeter, Kore, and the nymphs and envision them plucking flowers and making garlands. This is a magic place indeed," said Rita.

Meanwhile, my mother was getting tired of treading on uneven ground, and we had to put an end to our walking through the forest by the lake.

At the end of the day, lying in my bed and closing my eyes, I had the feeling that mythic Lake Pergusa, which had made Ades fall in love with Persephone, had also triggered a spark of love between Rita and me. It was just my feeling. I could be wrong. I just waited for the right moment to open my heart to her.

"I'd like to see the sea. Is it far from Enna, Aunt Assunta?" Rita asked my mother one morning.

"I don't know. I have never seen the sea. I have always lived in this mountain in the center of Sicily. When Pasqualino returns from Caltanissetta this afternoon, we'll ask him about the sea. He should know where it is," my mother answered.

At dinnertime, Rita resumed her question about the sea. "Could you take me to the beach, Pasqualino?"

"Yes, I can. We have many beaches in Sicily. The nearest ones to Enna are in Catania, Gela, and Cefalù. The busses to Catania are more frequent, so we'd better go there. We can set off in the early morning and come back in the evening. Yes, we can definitely go to the beach, but we have to ask my mother for permission," I said, looking at my mother shyly.

"Can I go to the beach with Pasqualino, Aunt Assunta?" asked Rita.

"You and Pasqualino alone?" asked my mother, opening her eyes wide.

"Is it possible?" insisted Rita.

"Not at all! My sister entrusted you to me. You must stay with me while you are in Enna."

"In that case, we can go to the beach together—that is, you, Pasqualino, and myself. What do you think about that?"

My mother was a curious woman. She didn't want to miss the only chance she had in her life to see the sea.

"We can go to the beach on Sunday, on the condition that Rita always stays next to me," said my mother, turning to me.

"Do you know what people do at the beach, Aunt Assunta?"

"Tell me. I have no idea about that."

"People swim," Rita replied. "One goes to the beach just to swim. When I am in America, I go swimming in the ocean. We are taught swimming at school. By the way, do you know how to swim, Pasqualino?"

"No, I don't. But we can go to a sandy beach this Sunday. The water is shallow there. There is no danger for those who can't swim."

"I'll teach you how to swim."

"Is it not dangerous?"

"Not at all! It is easy. You will learn it soon."

On Sunday morning, we set off early for Catania. My mother had prepared a picnic bag with fruit, sandwiches, a bottle of orange soda, and three glasses. After one hour and a half, we arrived at a beach in Catania called La Playa. We entered a lido and hired a cabin to change our clothes, an umbrella, and three sun beds. My mother kept wearing her black dress, while Rita and I exchanged our clothes for swimming suits.

The sun was scorching that day, and the sand burnt under our feet. We remained under the umbrella for a while. Meanwhile, Rita smeared a special protective lotion that she had brought from America on her skin.

"Pasqualino and I are going to swim," Rita suddenly said to my mother.

"You must keep yourselves within eyeshot. I want to see you," replied my mother, but this time her voice sounded less resolute.

Seeing all those half-naked women in swimming suits, my mother was shocked at first. The scene was new to her. Sitting in her sun bed under the umbrella, my mother looked like an old black crow amid a flock of white pigeons. Most people ignored her, but some looked at her as if she were an alien landed on Earth from a remote planet.

For the first time in her life, my mother realized how outdated she was. Sicily had changed. The world had changed! She had been unable to follow the changes of time. By living in Enna from birth to old age, she had acquired a limited vision of life. So far, the world had been her house, the church, and the neighborhood. The daily routine never changed for her. She had worn black clothes since she was left a widow for the second time. At home, she used to spend the days washing dishes and clothes, ironing, cooking, and making the beds for herself and her children. Her only diversion was going to church in the evening.

Here, sitting in the sun bed under the umbrella, she pondered on her morals. She had mistaken appearances for reality. Only too late she realized that a woman can be honest and faithful even though she displays her bare legs. The boys and girls that played in the beach didn't behave badly. On the contrary, they seemed to be innocent. She had been too serious in her life. She couldn't recollect having ever played with somebody. Now it was too late to change her life, but there was something she could still do as an act of love. She could do the first good action in her life: allow Rita and me to spend our beach day freely.

She lay down on the sun bed and pretended to fall asleep. Rita and I were free finally.

Rita cast a handful of sand at me and ran to the sea. I followed her and walked in the water until it reached the height of my shoulders. I didn't feel like going into the deep water. I had tried to swim a few times in Lake Pergusa and had succeeded in remaining afloat in the calm water of the lake for a short while, but in the sea things went different. Now and then a wave skimmed my face, scaring me. I was afraid that if I tried to swim in the deep water I would drown, but love can work miracles!

"Come over here, Pasqualino. The deep water is clean and transparent. The Sicilian sea is amazing! Come on."

I placed myself in a horizontal position on the water and swam toward her. When I reached her, my tongue was hanging out. I could hardly breathe. I needed support, so I put my hand on her shoulder. It was as if we both caught fire. She hugged me and brushed my lips with hers.

"I love you more than my life. Would you marry me?" I asked Rita instinctively.

I felt like I had a fire burning inside me while waiting for Rita's answer. If she had said no, I would have drowned. Rita opened her black eyes wide but kept hugging me. She didn't expect my proposal. Feeling that my words had left her cold, I turned pale.

"I love you too, Pasqualino. I would be the happiest woman in the world if we got married. I need to inform my parents in America. I am sure they will approve of our marriage."

"I must get my mother's permission too. This evening at dinnertime let's talk to her."

When we returned to our umbrella, my mother was sitting on the sun bed. She waved the fan Rita had brought her from America with her hand and tried to cool her face. She smiled at us. She looked like another woman. Even her nose looked less aquiline now.

At dinnertime, my heart was pounding harder than a drum when Rita nodded to me to start talking. My legs quaked under the table, but I had to find the courage to talk to my mother about our intentions. Finally, I took a deep breath and opened my mouth to speak.

"Rita and I want to get married. What do you think about that, Mum?" I asked while shaking like a leaf.

Contrary to what I expected from her, she answered calmly. She liked Rita and would be happy to have her as her daughter-in-law.

"I won't oppose your marriage, on the condition you ask your brother and sister for permission to get married to Rita," my mother answered with a large smile.

I was happy. My sister and brother had no reason to object to my marriage. As usual, I obeyed my mother.

Filippo lived with his wife, Filomena, and his little daughter, Francesca, about seven years old, in a house on Via Monticello, a steep street near the Church of Saint Mary of the People. When Rita and I were still some distance from my brother's house, he was watching us from the terrace. Due to the slant of the road, I looked like a dwarf and Rita like a flagpole.

When we were about to enter the living room, Rita hit the top of the door frame with her head and hurt herself. She was too tall to pass easily through the doors in my brother's house. The drops of blood on her head were a bad omen!

We took a seat in the lounge without saying a word. Rita smiled at Filippo, at his wife, and at his young daughter, but they didn't return the smile. My brother tightened his lips and had a quick look at his wife and daughter.

Filomena was a short and plump woman who loved tidiness and cleanliness in her house. She had a demure character like her husband, but she was less shy. Her house was full of beautiful flowering plants. There was not a single speck of dust in the lounge. Even the leaves of the plants had been carefully cleaned. Being a bit more talkative than my brother, she was the one who spoke, just as Aaron spoke instead of Moses. By giving a quick look at her husband's face and eyes, Filomena was able to make out his thoughts and feelings. Overall, she was the kind of woman who loved good manners, but her heart was colder than ice. She didn't mind hurting others with her words, which were more biting than bee stings.

"Would you like a cup of coffee?" Filomena asked with an affected smile.

"Yes, please," said Rita not to displease her.

While Filomena was preparing coffee, Filippo and little Francesca kept their eyes fixed on Rita as if she were a giraffe runaway from a zoo.

After Filomena served coffee, Filippo didn't say a single word, but the expression on his face was eloquent. He didn't approve of my marriage with Rita. Filomena interpreted his feelings and began her harsh speech.

"An old proverb says, 'Choose your wife and oxen from your own town.' My husband and I agree with the proverb I have just quoted. You are not Sicilian, Rita! Try and understand it. Even though your ancestors are Sicilians, you were born and grew up in America, a different country with a different culture. Therefore, you'll never get used to our traditions. Apart from this problem, which might be surmountable, there is an insurmountable obstacle that prevents Filippo from expressing his consent to your marriage with Pasqualino. You two look ridiculous when you walk down the street. Don't you see that people laugh at you? You two look like a giraffe that takes her little cub for a walk. Can you understand, Rita?"

Filomena's words were like a hail of stones. They hurt Rita deeply. I think what surprised her was that I didn't say a single word to defend her. Apparently, she thought I agreed with the opinion expressed by my sister-in-law.

The coffee in the cup cooled. Rita turned pale. It was a bad moment for her. She felt humiliated.

Then, she jumped to her feet. "I will never set foot in your house again. You don't need to serve coffee to your guests. It is more bitter than poison. Let's go, Pasqualino!" Rita said coldly.

We left my sister's house with our tails between our legs, like two dogs chased away by their master. Rita and I were terribly upset, but there was still hope. If my sister approved of our marriage, my mother would probably consent.

We entered a cafeteria to have a cup of coffee and take a rest. Meanwhile, my little niece, Francesca, swifter than a gazelle, ran to my sister's home and informed her that her brother Filippo was against our wedding.

There was nothing to do. My sister fell into line with Filippo. Moreover, she noticed some details that my brother had overlooked.

She introduced her husband to Rita. He was openly effeminate but good-natured. He tried to familiarize himself with Rita and put her at ease, but she sensed in the air that once again she would be rejected.

While her husband was chatting with Rita, Giovannina took me to another room and whispered in my ear, "She's too tall for you. Moreover, I don't like the dazed eyes of that strange woman. She doesn't look sane to my eyes. She hides something. She is American. She is different from us. She is accustomed to living in a big city. Forget her. She is not for you."

On the way home, we met my cousin Serafino, who pretended not to see us. I didn't ask his opinion about our marriage. It would have been superfluous. However, pretending not to have seen us was quite eloquent. He too was against our marriage.

When we arrived home, we informed my mother that my siblings had denied their consent to our marriage. Rita and I tried to convince her to give her assent, but she was unshakeable. I couldn't marry Rita without the approval of all the family members. Our love dream was over!

Rita packed silently and moved to Villarosa. She stayed at her aunt's house for fifteen days and then returned to America. The sandcastle we had tried to build had collapsed and was swept away by the sea waves. Fate had decreed differently for our lives.

The Second Engagement

After Rita left Sicily, the only person with whom I spent my free time was my cousin Serafino. I didn't have other acquaintances in Enna. He had completed his apprenticeship as a carpenter, but he didn't have a job. He hoped to open a shop to sell furniture. He was a handsome black-haired young man, tall, stout, and self-confident.

I used to meet Serafino after dinner in Piazza San Francesco, and then we strolled on Via Roma. One evening, a buxom red-haired woman approached him. She liked my cousin, but he seemed to ignore her. As soon as she saw the stripes on my uniform, she was dazzled by them. Serafino was out of a job and couldn't offer her anything but a life of privation. She kept fixing her eyes on the stripes on my sleeves, as if they were golden rings. I thought she liked my uniform, but she had other ideas in her mind.

"What do these stripes mean? Are you a captain?" she asked.

"No, I am not. My name is Pasqualino. I am just a master sergeant. Nice to meet you!"

"Nice to meet you too! My name is Luisa. Does the army give you a good salary? I heard that troops are not well-paid. Is it true?"

"I am a noncommissioned officer. My situation is different from that of ordinary troops. Before long, I'll be promoted to the rank of warrant officer, and then my salary will be increased."

"Very good! I like military life. I'd like to talk with you sometime."

"I'd like that too. Let's meet here tomorrow evening at seven thirty."

"Okay, I'll be here."

After Luisa left us, I kept strolling with my cousin on Via Roma.

"What do you think about Luisa? In your opinion, is she the right woman for me? What do you advise me to do? Should I meet her tomorrow or not?"

"Yes, you should. She is an attractive woman. You will make a good impression when you walk with her on the streets of Enna. Everyone will be surprised to see you with her. You can love her. I think she is the right woman for you. I am sure she will become your wife," Serafino answered.

I followed my cousin's advice and met her at the appointed time. Then we met every day for five consecutive months. I liked her red hair. Overall, she looked very polished. She had very basic schooling, for she stopped studying after the third class of elementary school, but she boasted about being educated, and sometimes she used difficult terms in our talks. I couldn't figure out who had taught her those refined words typical of scholars.

After we had talked enough to know our characters a little, I asked her to marry me. I wanted to find a wife different from my mother, who had always been very harsh and rude to me. Luisa looked submissive and sweet. She accepted my proposal of marriage, and we set the wedding date for August 1—that is, in three months.

Following Sicilian tradition, I introduced Luisa to my mother and my siblings. They were pleased that I was marrying her.

I rented a house far from my mother's. I wanted to change my life with my new wife. I wanted to forget all the suffering I had endured in my mother's house and in the army during the war. At long last, I would have a taste of happiness. I deserved it! Now, the sun, moon, and everything were smiling at me. I felt like I was the happiest man in the world. I bought the furniture on installments. Since I was a noncommissioned officer in the army, all sellers gave me credit.

The day before our wedding, everything was ready for my new life. I had bought a ceremonial dress for my mother and a wedding dress for my bride-to-be. We had been presented with gifts from our relatives, and the church had already been decorated with flowers.

According to Sicilian tradition, the day before the wedding relatives and friends come and visit the bedroom of the newlyweds in the house where they are going to live. That evening, my house was swarming with visitors. Many were the friends of the bride. Obviously, there was also the bride-to-be who welcomed the visitors, but unexpectedly, just before going home, Luisa came close to me and whispered something in my ear.

"Let's go to another room, I want to tell you something important," she said.

I followed her to the kitchen smiling, full of joy. "Do you want to give me a kiss?" I asked.

Her face grew serious. "If you want to marry me, you can. I'll not oppose. But you have to know that I am pregnant."

"What are you talking about? I have never made love with you. You haven't even allowed me to give you a kiss! You said you wanted to be a virgin until the wedding."

"Stupid, I am expecting a baby from another man, not from you!"

At that moment, I felt like a wild animal that had fallen into the hunter's trap. I was upset. My eyes were bulging out of their sockets and moving swiftly. I couldn't find a way out of the cage where I was trapped. I didn't know what to do, what to answer. On the one hand, I didn't want to leave her with a baby in a city full of prejudice. She would have been exposed to public condemnation as if she were a prostitute. On the other hand, I didn't want to parent a child who was not mine. My whole body was perspiring.

Then, I opened my mouth with trembling lips. "See you tomorrow. Right now, I need to ponder on what you have just said to me. I'll go out for a breath of fresh air. You can stay here and see to the guests."

I left home, headed for the tobacconist's, and bought a carton of cigarettes. It was the first time I had bought tobacco. With the carton of cigarettes in hand, I walked to the Castle of Lombardy and then to the Monastery of Montesalvo. From there, I moved to Belvedere Marconi and walked back and forth like a madman. Then, I stopped walking, leaned over the handrail of Belvedere Marconi, and looked at Calascibetta and the other faraway towns that were lit up by the streetlamps. Mount Etna was erupting, and lava was pouring down its sides. I lifted my eyes to the starlit sky and to the moon over the Madonie Mountain range. I hoped that the sky and the moon would give me a piece of advice about what to do on the morrow, but they kept silent!

I got home late at night with that goddamn carton of cigarettes under my arm. That night, I started smoking, and that horrible vice didn't leave me until almost the end of my life.

There were no ashtrays at home, so I took a plate and put it on my night table. Sitting on the bed and smoking cigarettes, I pondered my predicament. There were two people inside me who were discussing my case.

One of the two said, "Deep down, Luisa has been honest with you. She could have kept her relationship with the other man hidden. You wouldn't have known anything about it until the baby was born. She could have pretended that the baby was yours. Women are masters in the art of shamming. Furthermore, you are a gullible man. It is not difficult to cheat you. Once the baby had been born, she could have said to you, 'Look at the baby! It resembles you: the same eyes, the same mouth, the same nose, and so on.' Hence, you have to appreciate her sincerity and marry her."

The other person inside me disagreed completely. "You stupid idiot! Except for your mother and sister, you shouldn't trust women. They are more venomous than serpents and as wily as foxes. This woman, Luisa, whom you want to marry, has deceived you. She confessed her unfaithfulness to you before the wedding artfully. She wanted to give you the impression that she was a sincere and honest woman. Don't you know that to be a cuckold is a tremendous dishonor for a Sicilian? Are you a man? Are you a true Sicilian? If yes, go and kill both the bride-to-be and her lover. Italian law considers the killing to preserve one's own honor as a mitigation. Your murder will remain almost unpunished!"

"Are you crazy?" replied the other. "I am not even able to kill a fly. I am too meek."

"You took part in the war against Russia. When you were on the frontlines, didn't you open fire on the Russians?"

"No, I didn't. I served in the support area."

The dialogue between the two people inside me continued until dawn, without either of them prevailing over the other in convincing me to take this or that decision. Then, I lay down on the bed and tried to sleep, hoping that a restorative sleep would bring me new ideas about what to do.

The wedding had been set for eleven o'clock in the morning. I slept for a few hours. At the appointed time, the wedding guests and the bride-to-be in wedding dress were waiting for me in front of the Church of San Cataldo. As I didn't go there, my brother came and knocked on my door. At that moment, I was sitting on my bed, staring into space with a cigarette in my lips. I didn't feel like going and opening the door.

"Open the door soon or I'll beat it down!" shouted my brother from behind the door.

Slowly, I stood up and went to open the door.

"What are you doing here? Everybody is waiting for you in front of the church."

"Please, Filippo, go and tell the priest that I have changed my mind. Then send away all the guests, including the bride-to-be. Find an excuse, whatever you like. I won't marry that woman anymore."

My brother went back to the church and informed the priest about my decision. Within an hour, the staircase of the Church of San Cataldo, which before teemed with guests in ceremonial dresses, emptied. The priest put the sacred vestments back in the sacristy. The florist removed the flowers from the altar and took them back to his shop. In Enna, people gossiped for a few days about the missed wedding, but then everything returned to normal.

A few months went by, and in the same Church of San Cataldo, another wedding was celebrated, this time between Luisa and the father of the child she was carrying in her womb. He was a teacher of the Italian language and literature at the high school in Enna. It was then that I understood why Luisa, a woman with little schooling, sometimes talked in a mannered language when she strolled with me.

Deep down, he acted as an honest man. He didn't want to put Luisa in the pillory. So, in spite of the huge difference of social class and culture between the two, he kept loving her and crowned his dream of love.

I rescinded the rental agreement with the owner of the house I had rented. The lawsuit with him took some time. At last we reached an agreement. I sold him the furniture I had bought at a giveaway price, and he dropped his claims. Finally, I returned to my mother's home. Although harsh, she was at least sincere and honest with me.

The Marriage

Eleven years had gone by since I split up with Rita. I heard from my mother, who kept exchanging letters with her sister in America, that Rita had a job at an employment agency in Harlem and had been in a relationship with an official at the Consulate General of Italy in New York. Later, on his recommendation, she got a job in Rome. She was hired as an English teaching assistant at an English academy.

The Atlantic Ocean couldn't part us now. It would have been possible for me to meet her, but I was still completely under my mother's thumb. I didn't have enough courage to tell her that I wanted to take a train to Rome to meet Rita. For my mother, the Rita affair was long dead and gone. It couldn't be unearthed.

Two years later, my mother passed away at the age of ninety-four. In her will, she bequeathed me with her house and the little tomb she owned at the cemetery. She had inherited that burial place from her father, but she had asked her children to bury her in another tomb, for she wanted to rest next to her first husband. She also bequeathed my siblings with the land she owned near Lake Pergusa.

Once in a while, Rita came to Villarosa and stayed for a few days at her aunt's. She detested me and seldom came to Enna.

One day, my brother told me that he thought he had seen her in the park around the Tower of Fredrick with a man as tall as her. Based on his height and his way of dressing, my brother inferred he must have been an American.

On hearing my brother's words, my heart skipped a beat. The passing of time had strengthened my love for Rita. How stupid I had been at the time! Why was I incapable of making decisions with my own will? Why did I follow others' opinions as gospel truth? My siblings had been wrong to oppose my marriage to Rita. Because of them I had lost the woman I loved.

Sometimes, Rita appeared in my dreams. We walked arm in arm in the pinewood near Lake Pergusa. I was a bit taller than her in the dream. Unfortunately, reality was different from illusion. Upon my awaking, Rita disappeared. Now she was in Rome, far away from me. Maybe she was in a relationship with another man, who knows!

Until my mother died, I followed her orders passively. It was a blunder. After she passed away, I became a free man. Living alone in my gloomy house, I was getting more and more sad and depressed, but I could hold my head up, for my mother was in another world, in another dimension. She couldn't control my movements from up there. Feeling free, I wanted to change my life radically.

Going back and forth from Enna to Caltanissetta every day was becoming a burden to me. I led a routine life. I always got up at the same time, and every day I took the same bus. My job at the recruiting center in Caltanissetta was always the same. Loneliness weighed heavily on me.

One day I put my military uniform into the closet and never wore it again. I quit my military job. I got severance pay and a small pension from the army, which would have been enough for me to live on, but I was not a person who idled all day. I wanted to get a job.

I asked the tailor with whom I had trained as an apprentice before I joined the army to give me a job. He hired me. I started making my own suits, which were not bad at all. My siblings could hardly believe I was their brother. My suits were really elegant. I had a strong propensity for manual work. Furthermore, I had a sense of aesthetics. Within a year, I became an excellent tailor.

My employer didn't give me a great salary, but having no expenses except buy food, I could live well. I was even able to put aside some money. I was a free man, but freedom and money are not enough in life! Humans want to love and be loved. I felt a void inside myself. I longed for love, for Rita's love. I felt I couldn't live without her. I needed Rita just as a plant needs water to flourish.

In Via Roma, the main street in Enna, a cloth seller had gone bankrupt. His shop was for sale by order of the court. With the gratuity from the army and the money I had put aside, I participated in the auction and won the shop, with the clothes and fabric inside, at an extremely low price.

When I entered the shop for the first time, I found it messy and covered with dust. The clothes and fabric were piled on the counters higgledy-piggledy. There were two rooms in the shop. I cleaned them, and then I selected the best clothes and fabric, for I was able to recognize the quality of a good fabric just by touching it. I displayed the clothes in the room that overlooked the street, while I used the other room to make new clothes.

Customers started buying items in my shop. In the back of the shop, I sewed tailored suits for both men and women. My business thrived. I had so many orders for tailored suits that I hired two more tailors to help make the clothes. Within three years, I was rich. I got my driver's license and bought a Fiat convertible sports car.

I used to spend my free time by driving my car. Sometimes I drove on the streets in Enna, and sometimes I drove to Calascibetta or to Villarosa. The more I drove my car, the more I felt alone. My car was useless if I didn't have Rita beside me. I needed to see her, but she lived in Rome!

One day, I went to Villarosa and parked my car in the main square. Then, I walked to Rita's aunt's home. The old wizened woman, Aunt Giuliana, was always dressed in black and used to sit in front of the door of her house knitting or chatting with some of her neighbors. I approached her.

"Good afternoon, Aunt Giuliana, I haven't seen you for a long time. How are you doing?"

"No complaints!" she replied coldly.

"Do you have news about Rita? When will she come to Villarosa again?"

"I don't know. I can just say that she lives in Rome."

"Could you give me her address in Rome?"

Aunt Giuliana didn't reply. She just kept her mouth shut. She had a good reason for doing so. Her niece had come home in shock after we had split up. I begged her on my knees, with tears in my eyes. Finally, she gave in to my pleadings and gave me the address of Rita's workplace.

The English academy where Rita worked was near the Basilica of Saint John in Lateran. I was sure that if she saw me waiting for her in front of her school, she would have strong emotions and realize that I loved her really, and then she would reconcile with me.

I took a train from Enna to Rome. I travelled all night and arrived at Termini Rail Station at dawn. From there I walked on Via Merulana up to Saint John in Lateran Square. Rita's school overlooked the square. It was not difficult for me to spot the academy's sign.

I waited for her all afternoon. While I was waiting, I paced on the sidewalk in front of the English academy like a madman. Now and then, a passerby looked at me and wondered whether I was someone who had escaped from a mental asylum. Actually, I was very anxious.

After I waited for five hours, I saw that the lights of the school were turned off, but Rita didn't come out. I asked the last person who left the academy about her. He was the school keeper.

"Today is Rita's day off."

"Will she come to school tomorrow?"

"Yes, she will be here in the afternoon until her last class, which will end at seven o'clock in the evening."

I found accommodations near Rita's workplace and spent the night in Rome. Even though Rome had many attractions, I preferred not to go around the city. I only had Rita on my mind.

In the morning, while waiting for the passing of time, I visited the Church of the Lateran that had been built by Emperor Constantine. It was the oldest in Rome. I entered the small church, knelt down, and prayed to God to soften Rita's heart and let me have her as my wife.

At five to seven, I stood in front of the academy and waited for Rita. Not far from me there was another man who also waited. The sight of this man made my heart beat harder in my throat and in my temples. Perhaps he was waiting for Rita too.

At five past seven, Rita came down the school stairs. She was with another woman. I moved forward and stood in their way. I smiled and strove to keep calm. Rita parted with the other woman and smiled at the man that was waiting for her. She couldn't help meeting me, because I was standing just in front of her.

"What are you doing in Rome?" she asked.

"I have come here just to meet you. What about having a coffee together?"

"Sorry, I can't. The man standing on that corner is my boyfriend. I have to go with him. You had better go back to Enna," she said coldly.

"I need to talk to you, Rita. I still love you."

"Don't say nonsense!"

Rita moved forward, but I grabbed her by the arm. I was without dignity by then.

"Please, stay with me, Rita. Let's go together somewhere, to the cinema, to the theater, or wherever you like."

Rita beckoned to that young man to come to us. He was tall and uncouth and had the typical face of a Roman bully, with black hair and a muscular build similar to that of a mastiff.

"What does this person want from you? Is he harassing you?"

As Rita nodded, the bully grabbed my lapel, lifted me up, and gritted his teeth. "If you dare to harass my girlfriend again, I'll kill you," he said in his marked Roman accent.

"Okay, put me down. I didn't know Rita was your girlfriend."

"Now you know. Go away immediately or I'll slap your face."

I remained in front of him and looked him in the eye. Surely his slaps would have been less painful than Rita's refusal. He also stared at me.

"This evening I don't feel like fighting. You are lucky!" he said. Then he put his arm on Rita's shoulder and walked away with her.

I had no choice but to return to Enna with a broken heart.

My business went well. I bought a splendid house with a garden at a bargain price near the sea of Taormina. I knew that Rita loved the sea. I was sure that if she saw my gorgeous house in Taormina, her grudge against me would vanish.

I had no idea how to contact her. I didn't have her telephone number. On the other hand, if I had gone to Rome one more time, her boyfriend wouldn't have allowed me to approach her, so I took three photos—one of my shop, one of my car, and one of my house in Taormina—and then I wrote the following letter to Rita:

Enna, December 2, 1974

My beloved Rita,

I apologize for the pain I caused you in the past. I hurt you because I was very weak. I had no personality at all. If I had been as strong as I am now, things would have taken another course and we would now be happily married.

These days, my situation has changed. My mother passed away. I don't wear a military uniform anymore. I am now a strong and rich man. My business thrives.

What can that Roman bully give you? Nothing! You said he was your boyfriend. He's not the right person for you. You deserve a better man.

I can make you happy. I can give you everything you want: gold jewelry, expensive clothes, and so on, whatever. My splendid house in Taormina will be yours if you marry me.

And finally, I love you very much. It is the reason why I want to marry you.

I will be waiting for your reply.

With all my heart.

Much love and kisses,

Pasqualino.

I thought I had made another mistake. I had the feeling that my letter was the seed of a tragedy for both of us. I should have written a love letter to her instead of a business letter. The photos in the letter suggested that I wanted to buy her love. I just wanted to show her that I had changed and was not the submissive person of before, but I had treated her as a prostitute, a woman who sells her love to get a material reward. I had to rethink my offensive letter and ran to the post office to block it, but when I arrived there, it had already been dispatched. *With that letter, I've lost Rita forever!* I thought.

One week later, peeping into my mailbox I saw a letter lying there. I saw from the postmark that it was from Rome. *It must be a letter from Rita!* I took it in my hand and opened the envelop with a knife. My hands were shaking. I felt Rita would rebuke me, but it was not like that.

Dear Pasqualino,

Congratulations on your success in life!!! You are a strong man now. I am very happy to hear it.

I want you to know that the Roman bully you saw in front of my school is not my boyfriend anymore. He was too violent. Once he even dared to slap me.

I also quit my job. I don't like living in a big city. I love Sicily and its sea. I love Taormina, the pearl of the Mediterranean Sea.

What a beautiful house you have in Taormina! It is by the sea! We can go to the beach from your house directly. I adore swimming. Can you swim well now? The garden of the house is also nice. I love plants and flowers.

I will come to Villarosa next week. I have already informed my aunt, who is waiting for me. What about coming to Villarosa and picking me up in your car?

Yes, you are the only man I have loved in my life. Of course, I have had a few love affairs since you left me, but they were just diversions. The men I met couldn't make me forget you. You are always in my heart.

What about celebrating Happy New Year together in Taormina? After dinner at the restaurant on New Year's Eve, we can visit your house. I am sure our love will blossom again.

I love you, Pasqualino! See you soon.

Much love and kisses,

Your love, Rita

Rita had drawn a small heart on every corner of the letter and had imprinted the lipstick on her lips at the end of the page.

After reading the letter, I hopped around my house like a little boy. I was living an instant of happiness like a little mouse that, lured with a small tasty piece of cheese, enters a mousetrap and starts gnawing the delicacy. Suddenly, the trap snaps shut, and it remains trapped, with no hope of getting out of the trap alive.

When one week later I pulled to the curb in front of Rita's aunt's house, everybody looked at me. There was even a young man who caressed my car and said, "This car is the dream of my life!"

I honked my horn. Rita immediately came out and got into my car. She wore a black skirt and a green blouse. The lipstick on her lips and her makeup made her more attractive than ever. She looked like a star. A small crowd of onlookers soon surrounded us. We were an attraction in that small town. That afternoon, I took her to Enna to show her my shop, then I took her back to her aunt in Villarosa.

I was looking forward to New Year's Eve and spending the night with Rita at my house in Taormina. At long last, the eagerly awaited New Year's Eve arrived. We had dinner at the best restaurant in Taormina, and then we went and danced at a nightclub. We danced for a couple of hours and then headed for my house. It was a unique, wonderful night. It was the first time I had slept with a woman in the same bed.

Two months later, she told me that she was pregnant. We had no alternative but to get married. Even my siblings couldn't oppose our marriage. In my hometown, it was considered immoral to refuse to marry a woman that was expecting your baby. I didn't feel like leaving Rita and her child to their fate.

The wedding was celebrated in the Church of San Calogero. The wedding guests were my sister and her husband, my brother and his wife and daughter, my cousins, Rita's aunt, and the employees in my shop. Rita wore a long white dress that I had made with my own hands. Both Rita and I seemed to be happy at that time, but our happiness was just an illusion.

We went to France on our honeymoon. I noticed there was something strange in her eyes. She didn't look happy. Maybe her mind went to her past lovers for whom she had felt attraction. We didn't talk much. We just visited the monuments and took some photos, nothing more.

When we returned to Enna after a ten-day honeymoon, Rita realized that she had made a terrible mistake in marrying me. She didn't marry me for what I was. She just married the rich man I looked like. After all, I wasn't as rich as she had imagined and as I had led her to believe. She wanted to go to the most luxurious and expensive restaurants. If she saw a necklace or a ring in a jewelry shop window, she wanted me to buy it for her. If I refused, she became sad. She was insatiable. The more jewels I bought for her, the more she wanted.

When I returned home after a long day of work, I always found her nervous. Nothing could calm her down. Every now and then, I took her to the theater, the cinema, or to a restaurant to make her enjoy herself, but in vain. She was always sad.

She didn't usually cook at home. I often found there was nothing to eat for dinner, so I'd go out again to buy some ham, bread, a salad, and some fruit.

After a few months, our firstborn daughter arrived. Rita wanted to give her an English name, so she named her Sharon. She didn't speak with her baby girl in Italian, but in English, a language I didn't know. So, I spoke with my baby in Italian. The result was disastrous. Sharon had such confusion in her mind that at the age of three she didn't speak at all. We thought she was a deaf-mute. Later, Sharon started to articulate some words in Italian, the language I spoke to Rita daily.

Our second born was another girl. She was named Lucy, like Rita's American mother. Although Sharon didn't speak a single word of English, Rita, more stubborn than a mule, continued to talk to Lucy in the same way.

Rita and I were continuously fighting. It was always Rita who prevailed. I gave in for the sake of peace. Maybe it was another mistake. I should have divorced her, but I didn't for the sake of my children. At that time, I didn't realize that it would have been preferable for my daughters to grow up in a more peaceful environment, even if with only one parent, instead of living with their parents who hated each other. Yes, little by little, I started hating Rita, and that was the same feeling she had toward me.

"Why are you so bad?" I asked her one day.

"You were the one who made me an evil woman," she replied.

"How can you say that?"

She didn't reply. Indeed, she seldom answered my questions. She remained silent. What I hated most about her was that she didn't reply to my questions. She just kept silent. There was no dialogue between us anymore.

The oddities of that evil woman were innumerable. Once, my wife left Sharon, who was just one year old, alone at home and took a stroll in the city. The neighbors rushed to the baby's cries. The doorbell rang but nobody answered. Then they came to my shop and informed me that Sharon had been left alone. I left my work and my customers to rescue Sharon, who was trapped at home. I took her to my shop and kept working with her in my arm.

When the babies cried at night, Rita never got out of bed. I had to get up and look after them. Consequently, I felt drowsy all day long while in my shop. She also never collected the children from school. I had to close the shop and pick them up.

At home, we lived in semidarkness. Rita never opened the windows to let in the sunlight. Only pale rays of light filtered through the closed shutters.

Her hobby was painting. A nice hobby indeed, if done in moderation, but she used to paint from morning till night. If the girls or I called her, she didn't answer.

The house was always dirty. Once in a while she cleaned the house, but she wanted me to pay her for the chores. I never did. How could I ever pay my wife for doing housework!

She also stirred up the girls against me. They didn't respect me and considered me an idiot.

I hired a maid to clean the house, but Rita made her only clean the windowpanes while the rest of the house remained dirty.

When the girls grew up, things turned worse. Both my wife and daughters always asked me for money. My daughter Sharon once sued me because I didn't give her enough money. Another time, the police summoned me. This time Lucy had reported to them that I had induced her into prostitution. I was appalled to find that my daughters had turned into my enemies. Fortunately, the police chief knew both me and my family well. He knew that I was unable to commit such a crime, while my wife and daughters were widely known for being liars.

At home, Rita and my daughters screamed continuously. They made a hell of a racket. Rita yelled at her daughters. Sharon and Lucy yelled at each other and at their mother too. I put my hands on my ears not to hear them, but to no avail. I felt like I was going crazy.

The idea of committing suicide once flashed into my mind, but I immediately turned that horrible thought away. Killing myself would have been an act of cowardice and an insult to God, who had given me the gift of life.

In the business world, you can never rest easy. A competitor can pop up. In a town near Enna, Valguarnera Caropepe, a factory of ready-made clothes was born. The clothes they made were much cheaper than mine and also of good quality. I could no longer sell the clothes and fabric I had in stock. I was forced to close down my shop for fear of going bankrupt.

The pension I received from the army was enough for my family's basic needs, but my wife and daughters were insatiable. So, I sold both the car and the house in Taormina.

My wife said that I was a good-for-nothing and that, from then on, she would manage my money. Actually, she was a miser. She managed family money well. As for me, I scarcely had the money to buy cigarettes.

My health started declining. I couldn't walk well. To go to the library, I needed a stick. My wife didn't give me enough food, so I grew weaker day by day, until I finally stopped even going to the public library. I couldn't write my diary anymore.

I feared that if my wife or my daughters found the diary at home, they would throw it away, so I entrusted it to Primo, the only friend I had.

The End of the Story

"I finished reading Giuseppe Chiarello's diary, alias Pasqualino Butera. Now you can put away the desk, the chair, and the magnifying glass. I really enjoyed reading the diary. I think it will give me inspiration for my new book. Today, I want to purchase a book by one of our local authors." I said.

"I see you are getting rid of your ingrained habit of buying books through the Internet," said Primo, smiling from ear to ear.

"Yes, you have guessed right. By staying in your bookstore for one month to read Giuseppe Chiarello's diary, I have realized how important friendship is. We are friends, Primo. From now on, I'll buy books only at your store."

"I am happy to hear your words. Which book do you want to buy today?"

"Let me think. Umm, yes, I've got an idea. Let's go to the local author's shelf. I'll pick up a book at random, and then I'll purchase it."

"Okay, let's go!"

I closed my eyes, touched the books on the shelf, rested my fingers on one in hardback, and picked it. It was *Il Capopopolo* (*The Rabble-Rouser*) by Nino Savarese, a great author from Enna.

"I'll purchase this," I said with a decided tone.

"You chose well. It is one of my favorite books."

Primo looked pensive while we were walking to the counter. I had a feeling he wanted to tell me something but was reluctant to speak.

"Is there anything wrong, Primo?"

"No, everything is okay, but I want you to know something more about Giuseppe Chiarello. What I want to tell you is not written in his diary. I've hidden a secret inside me. You are the only person whom I talk to about it. I just want to know your opinion. I think I've done well not to respect the will of my friend Giuseppe, but I'm not one hundred percent sure about that."

"Tell me what happened. I am all ears."

"As I told you before, every evening after I closed my bookstore, I went to Giuseppe's home and stayed with him for a while, usually for about half an hour. When his health worsened, sometimes the three hyenas pretended not to have heard the doorbell and kept me waiting at the door. Apparently, they wanted me to get tired of waiting and give up visiting Giuseppe. But I was more stubborn than the three women. I kept ringing the bell and knocking on the door. At last, the ugly beanpole came and opened the door. I just said to her, 'Good evening,' and then I walked quickly to Giuseppe's room.

"I was very sad on seeing that Giuseppe had turned weaker and weaker day by day. The three jackals didn't give him enough food or water. I couldn't do anything for him. I just stayed at his bedside to solace him as much as I could.

"One evening he looked weaker than usual. He hardly had the strength to talk."

"Primo, could you do me a favor please?" he asked.

"I'll do whatever I can for you, Giuseppe. Tell me."

"Last night I had a strange dream. I saw some snow-white lambs grazing the grass in a green meadow. A ravenous black wolf watched them from a knoll. It howled and gnashed its

teeth. Its fangs were as terrifying as those of a lion. It was ready to leap on them, but all of a sudden, one of the lambs turned into a gigantic monster with seven heads that spit fire that devoured both the other lambs and the wolf. The dream made me think that the epitaph on my tomb is wrong."

"Which epitaph? I don't understand you, Giuseppe."

"His breathing became more and more labored, his lips got dry, and his head fell on the pillow. I wanted to give him a glass of water, but I didn't feel like going to the kitchen and confronting the three witches. Then he sat up again and kept talking to me."

"Let me explain. I have inherited a little tomb at the cemetery in Enna from my mother. After I die—it will not take long—I will be buried there. It will be not difficult for you to find the tomb. It is located about one hundred meters from the entrance to the cemetery, on the right. The tomb is empty by now. The bones of my grandparents were moved to my uncle's tomb long ago. No one, except you, will visit my tomb to lay a flower or light a candle after I die. I am sure about this. My wife and daughters can't wait for me to die. Right now, I am just a burden to them."

"I was convinced that Giuseppe was telling the truth, so I asked him, 'I feel that your wife and daughters hate you. What do they give you to eat?'

"Giuseppe replied, 'I eat just a small dish of zucchini once a day. My wife says that zucchini detoxifies my body. At first, I was always hungry and thirsty. I called her all day long to have some water, but she didn't come. Now my body has become accustomed to hunger and thirst, and I feel good.'

"I was tempted to go to the filthy spindle-shanks and slap her face, but Giuseppe asked me to keep calm. Then he kept talking. 'There is an epitaph engraved on my tomb. I wrote it two years ago. A stonecutter carved it on the tombstone. I ask you to remove that tombstone and replace it with another one with a different epitaph, please.'

"Now I had clear ideas about what Giuseppe wanted me to do for him. I would have done for my friend Giuseppe whatever he asked me, but before going along with his wishes, I wanted to be sure that I was doing something right for him."

"Why do you want me to change your old tombstone with a new one?"

"Because it doesn't tell the truth about who I was. In the epitaph, I look like a good and meek man, but that is not the truth."

"I thought the fever was making him delirious, so I put my hand on his forehead to check whether he had a fever. His body temperature was normal. I said, 'What are you talking about, Giuseppe? You are a good man. You are an angel. However, give me the new epitaph and I'll ask a stone mason to change the old one with the new one.

"Giuseppe took a crumpled sheet of paper from under the sheets and reached out to hand it to me. His hand trembled and his voice became weaker and weaker. Then he clasped the piece of paper in his hand and sank into the bed motionless. Finally, he got rid of his earthly trouble. I opened his fingers one by one and took the sheet. I gave him a kiss on the forehead and then left the house."

"Did you change the epitaph in his tomb?"

"No, I didn't."

"You made a mistake, Primo. You should have indulged his wish."

"You don't know what Giuseppe wrote in the sheet of paper he handed to me before dying. Read it aloud, please, and then you'll understand why I acted that way."

I spread the sheet on the counter and deciphered it with the magnifying glass. Besides being tiny, the writing was tremulous.

"Read it, Mario," insisted Primo.

My voice rang in the bookshop while I read aloud the epitaph that should have been set in Giuseppe Chiarello's tomb:

Here rests Giuseppe Chiarello,

A man who lived an unhappy life.

He didn't love anybody, for he didn't know love.

From birth to death, he kept his heart locked.

Can you live without heart, o passerby?

His mildness was false goodness.

He was a wicked and malevolent man,

A devil disguised as a lamb,

A rotten apple that infected those around him.

How can one love the devil, o passerby?

"Why didn't you change the old epitaph with the new one, Primo?"

"I didn't do it because I am still convinced that Giuseppe Chiarello was a good man, as pure as the driven snow. He lowered himself due to the humility of his heart. I didn't feel like putting this ugly epitaph on his tomb. In your opinion, did I do well?"

"No, you didn't. You were wrong. You should have changed the epitaph, because the latter better shows what Giuseppe Chiarello was. He was a dangerous and malicious man who made those around him grow wicked."

"How can you say that?"

"I speak with good reason, because I am the only one who has read his diary from start to finish. First of all, he lured his wife with his money. This was one of his many bad actions. He foresaw that his marriage, based on interests, would turn into hell sooner or later. He wasn't stupid. He married Rita for mere egoism—that is, to get rid of his loneliness."

"I don't think so. There are marriages not based on love at the beginning. Then love springs naturally in the course of the life of the married couple. It especially happened in the past when families arranged marriages and the bride and groom even didn't know each other before the wedding. By living together, they ended up loving each other."

"The case you have just quoted is different. In your example, the couple didn't know each other well. In our case, Rita disliked Giuseppe from the beginning of the wedding and didn't respect him. How can love be born from repulsion? Don't you think so?" I asked.

"I didn't read his diary, so I don't know these details about the lack of love you have just mentioned. But as far as I know, Giuseppe was a victim of others. You said he did many bad actions. Can you list some of them?"

"Yes, I'll tell you his main bad action that is the basis of the others. He was too submissive and cowardly."

"Ha! ha! ha! This is new for me! Is cowardice a bad deed? It is a state of mind. What are you talking about?"

"No, acting as a coward is a harmful action to oneself and to others. I am convinced that submissiveness, meekness, and cowardice may turn into very bad actions, because they encourage bullies and offenders to overcome the weak. The victim is as guilty as his aggressor!"

"Can you give me an example?"

"Yes, of course. If an extortionist comes to you and asks you for some money or he will set your shop on fire and you cowardly give him what he requires, is that a good or a bad deed?"

"I think it is bad deed, for yielding finances criminality."

"You hit the mark, Primo. The same happened to Giuseppe Chiarello. Being extremely meek and cowardly, he spurred those around him to grow bad and violent."

"Tell me another bad action by him," asked Primo.

"He didn't have a mind or a heart of his own. He found it easier to act with others' minds and hearts. It was his cousin Serafino who spurred him to love Luisa, the woman to whom he got engaged for the second time. He didn't love her with his own heart but with his cousin's heart! Furthermore, he followed his mother's and siblings' opinions passively. These were insults to God who had created him with a mind to think on his own and a heart to love on his own. He was an adult and had a salary from the army when he asked Rita to marry him the first time. He could afford to maintain a wife. Why didn't he follow the voice of his heart? The answer is quite clear. He was an opportunist who shunned responsibility and made others decide his future."

"Do you think we shouldn't accept the good advice somebody gives us? Should we ignore others and always decide for ourselves?" asked Primo.

"I think it is absurd not to accept good advice. Yes, we should accept it, but we should take the initiative in doing what concerns our future, our feelings, and our life instead of following others blindly. As far as I know, Giuseppe Chiarello let himself be led by others and by circumstances."

"Mario, you've heard of Giuseppe Chiarello through his diary, while I knew him, his wife, and his daughters personally. Sometimes direct experience make us see reality better and more clearly than through reading books or a diary. Based on my knowledge of the real facts, I confirm that Giuseppe Chiarello was a good man. However, who can ever know the ultimate truth about him? Nobody but God."

Chapter Four
The Limiti Family Tomb

Not far from my grandmother's tomb there is one of the noble Limiti family. It is one of the biggest in the cemetery. It has four spires that seem to touch the sky. The room is quite large and has both niches in the walls and a tombstone in the floor that covers an underground room, so the dead can be buried either in the niches or under the floor. Opposite the entrance to the tomb, there is an altar with a lacy linen cloth on it. On the altar are a few framed photos, while three old oil portraits, one portrays a man and the others two ladies, all of them in nineteenth-century clothes, stand in the middle of the room. A parchment on the right wall shows the family tree. In fact, the Limiti family belongs to the old Sicilian nobility.

On November 2, the Day of the Dead, the Limiti family tomb is adorned with flowers both on the floor and on the altar. In front of each photo and portrait are lit candles. Overall, the tomb is kept clean and is well preserved. The following inscription is engraved on the tombstone:

Here rests:

Alessio Limiti, duke of Sferravalle, a brave man who died in the Battle of Calatafimi in the defense of the Kingdom of the Bourbons.

The noblewoman Countess Angela D'Alcontres of Biancavilla, exemplary mother and wife.

Alessandro Limiti, baron of Cannavò, an erudite and highly intelligent man.

Letizia Bonafede, duchess of Cannizzaro, a noblewoman of extraordinary beauty and exemplary virtue.

Bernardo Limiti, count of Castrogiorgio. The sun never set in his fiefdoms.

Gianmatteo Limiti, prince of Saint Matthew, a great businessman. He owned ten sulfur mines.

Amedeo Limiti, marquis of Alimena, the last scion of the Limiti noble dynasty, an excellent university professor.

The number of the portraits and photos on the altar didn't match the number of names engraved on the tombstone. There was an extra photo on the altar. I knew the reason. A nonblue-blooded man had been stealthily buried in that noble tomb.

Professor Amedeo Limiti was a client of my Uncle Beniamino's law firm. They had known each other since their school days.

Beniamino Ribaldi was one of the best criminal lawyers in Enna. After my eldest brother, Vincenzo, received a degree in law, he did his qualifying period with him. Now, Vincenzo had a law firm of his own.

Uncle Beniamino was my mother's brother. Being a bachelor, he used to live with us. He was a reserved man, shorter than average. To make up for his short stature, he used to walk with his chest out. His stentorian voice and gesticulations were highly effective when he pleaded cases. Judges were pleased to listen to him, even though his defensive arguments were sometimes too long.

At the table, he never talked about the cases he pleaded. He taught Vincenzo to behave in the same way—that is, never to spread what the clients confided in him. During our meals, Uncle Beniamino used to chat with my father. He rarely spoke to the other family members who were sitting at the table. Uncle Beniamino sometimes talked with my father about the Masonic lodge that they both belonged to, sometimes about the weather, and other times about my father's business.

Contrary to his habits, one day, on November 2, after visiting the cemetery in the morning as he usually did every year, while we were eating peacefully at the table, he unexpectedly started telling my father about the strange lawsuit Professor Amedeo Limiti had been involved in years ago. There was no reason to keep it secret, because the lawsuit had been public and had been closed for a few years.

My father, who was very curious by nature, wanted his brother-in-law to tell him the lawsuit in the smallest details. The case was this:

Professor Amedeo Limiti's great-great-grandfather had built a family tomb for himself and his offspring in Enna's cemetery. The lineal heirs of the tomb were Amedeo and Angela Limiti, his sister.

Angela was two years younger than Amedeo. She didn't look like his sister. While Amedeo was good-looking, tall, and stout, Angela was not attractive at all; I dare say she was ugly. She was angular and had a convergent squint. Moreover, her black eyes trembled continuously. It was a mystery that she could see objects clearly. Her bushy eyebrows met at the upper nose. She had a gap in her front teeth that made it seem as if she had a tooth missing. Finally, she had a cleft in her lower lip that sometimes bled a bit.

It was ironic that, in spite of such ugliness, she had sophisticated tastes. She liked handsome men. It seemed impossible that she would someday find a husband, but she had a gift that other women lacked. She was blue-blooded. Although peerage had been abolished in Italy after the fall of the House of Savoy, there were still people that were susceptible to the charm of nobility. After all, she was Angela Limiti, duchess of Pasquasia and Geraci, a good catch.

According to tradition, a nobleman should marry a noblewoman and vice versa. In fact, Professor Amedeo Limiti had married a countess. But in the case of Angela Limiti things were different. No nobleman wanted to marry her. For most people, appearance is very important when one chooses a partner! She was much too ugly and repulsive. It didn't matter that she had a warm heart and a noble and gentle soul. It didn't matter that she was very clever and had a degree in mathematics. She seemed to be doomed to remain unmarried.

At long last, a handsome, high-flying manufacturer named Oreste Tantillo, who aimed at entering the world of the Italian aristocracy, after a year-long engagement, offered to marry Angela, who accepted. Who knows! Maybe it was not a marriage of convenience. It cannot be ruled out that Oreste loved Angela. There are men who prefer the beauty of the soul to the beauty of the body. Even Aphrodite, the goddess of beauty, was sometimes outshined by Psyche, the goddess of the soul.

Professor Amedeo Limiti had been against his sister's marriage, but she had been unshakable, for she loved Oreste. Eventually, Amedeo consented to the wedding. Family tradition was broken. For the first time, a plebeian got his space on the Limiti family tree.

Amedeo didn't enjoy Oreste's company, because he was convinced that he had married Angela because she was a noblewoman, not because he loved her, but for the sake of family peace, whenever he met Oreste, he strove to keep up appearances. He was a professor of ancient Greek at the University of Turin, a city in the north of Italy, and used to come to Enna twice a year: for one week on the occasion of the Festival of the Dead, and for about ten days during the Christmas holidays. On these occasions, the two families— that is, Professor Limiti and his wife, and Angela Limiti and her husband—went to Mass and had dinner together.

Since Amedeo had to meet Oreste only on these two occasions, he was able to endure his uncouth brother-in-law's manners. What Amedeo could hardly stand was the sight of Oreste cleaning his plate with a piece of bread. But what to do? He also accepted this for his sister's sake.

One day, something tragic happened in the Tantillo family. Giacomo, Oreste's younger brother, was involved in an accident on his motorbike. He hovered between life and dead until he passed away one week later.

Oreste hadn't thought about death until then. He didn't have a family tomb. Angela had the keys to enter the Limiti tomb and allowed Giacomo's body to be buried there. For that purpose, she transferred the property of a walled niche to Giacomo's father on the condition that no more relatives of her husband be buried there.

Angela didn't take into account the impulsive and despotic character of her brother. The Salic law, which decreed that no land could be inherited by a woman because it belonged only to a male heir, was still in force in Amedeo's mind. He was the male heir of his father. Any decision regarding the property of the tomb should have passed through him.

On October 31 of that year, Amedeo returned to Enna to celebrate the Festival of the Dead on November 2. The day before the feast, he went to the cemetery to clean up his family tomb. He had gotten up earlier than usual, and when he arrived at the cemetery, he found it deserted. The keeper had opened the gate only a few minutes earlier. On the way to the cemetery, Amedeo had bought some chrysanthemums, cockscombs, and candles to adorn the tomb. He had also brought a new, well-ironed altar cloth from Turin.

He opened the door to the tomb with his key and aired out the room, threw away the withered flowers into a plastic bag, filled a pail with water from the nearby drinking fountain, and mopped the floor. Then he cleaned the panes of the door, dusted off the four chairs in the room, and wiped the flower holders clean. He also dusted off the three oil portraits of his ancestors with a feather duster and put the flowers he had brought into the flower holders. He was removing the photos from the altar to replace the old altar cloth with the new one, when his eyes fell on young Giacomo's photo. It was as if the photo of the stranger had taken a poke at him. Amedeo stepped back, blushed to the roots of his hair. His eyes grew round and his hair stood on end. He couldn't control himself.

"Who is this man? Who dared put a picture of a stranger in my family tomb unbeknownst to me?" he cried out.

He was upset, but he continued to tidy up the tomb. He changed the cloth on the altar with the new one he had brought, wiped the photos clean, and put them back on the altar, except for that of the stranger, which he put away.

He checked the names on the tombstone to see whether somebody had been buried under the floor and reassured himself that there were no other names besides those of his ancestors. Then he looked up and saw something carved on one of the marble niches: "Here rests Giacomo Tantillo, a purple bud picked by the gardener before it could bloom, born in Catania on 18 December 1988, and died in Enna on 10 January 2008."

Amedeo took a close look at the photo he had put aside on a corner of the floor and noticed a certain resemblance between the features of the man and those of his brother-in-law, even though the person in the photo looked much younger than his sister's husband.

This must have been my sister's work! I have to talk to her soon, he thought to himself.

He locked the tomb and ran to his sister's home. He rang the doorbell, but Angela was not at home. Her husband came and opened the door.

"Where is my sister, Oreste?" Amedeo spoke out.

"You look upset, Amedeo. What happened to you? Why didn't you greet me? When did you arrive in Enna?"

"I arrived yesterday. I am in a bad mood. I want to talk to my sister. Where is she?"

"She's not here. She went shopping this morning."

"Do you know who the stranger buried in my tomb is?"

"He's my younger brother. He died tragically in January."

"Who gave you permission to bury him in my tomb?"

"The tomb is not only yours. It belongs to my wife too. Your sister allowed my father to bury my brother in your tomb. We didn't have a tomb of our own, so we had no choice but to bury my brother in a niche in the Limiti family tomb."

"I give my condolences to you and your father. I didn't know about the tragedy that had happened in your family. However, you have to know that your brother cannot remain in our family tomb. You have to find another place for him."

"Why do you think my brother should get out of the tomb that you say is yours?"

"Because the Limiti family tomb is reserved for the burial of only family members. Since you are my sister's husband, you can be buried there upon your death—but only you, not your brother or other relatives of yours."

"My father paid some money to your sister and bought one of the walled niches in the tomb. It is the one you have seen with the name of my brother carved on the marble. Angela also signed a deed to transfer the property of the niche. We made a copy of it for you."

Oreste went to the rear of the house and came back holding two handwritten sheets of paper; one was the original and the other a copy. He showed the original and gave the copy to Amedeo, who perused it.

"This contract is not valid!" Amedeo exclaimed.

"Why not?"

"First of all, there is no mention in the deed about your father giving money to my sister to buy the niche. Second, my sister was not allowed to transfer the property of the niche without my consent, for the tomb belongs to both of us. Third, the contract needs two signatures to be valid: mine and that of your wife. Forth, according to Italian law, the changeovers of property must be drawn up by a notary and then transcribed at the Real Estate Registry. These rules were not applied to the deed you are showing me now. It is evident that your brother has been buried in my tomb against the law. To put it simply, you brother must be removed from the noble family Limiti tomb. Otherwise, I'll evict him from there. Understood?"

"Calm down and don't be silly, Amedeo. Listen to reason! How can you ever evict a corpse? Is a dead body able to walk? Of course not. Let him rest in peace, please. Have mercy for his soul. Surely, he cannot spoil or debase your and my wife's tomb."

"The law is the law. No one is allowed to alienate an asset if he is not a hundred-percent owner. My sister and I have inherited the tomb from my father. We are both owners, fifty percent each. Therefore, the contract had to be signed by both of us to be valid. If you don't take your brother out of my tomb right away, I'll file a lawsuit against your father and my sister and ask that the court declare this deed null and void."

"Do as you like. I won't take my brother out of his tomb."

"What are you talking about? The tomb is mine!"

"No, you own just half of the tomb. The other fifty percent belongs to my wife, and to my father too, for he purchased a walled niche."

"I'll go to my lawyer this afternoon. He will enforce the law."

"That's ridiculous!"

Amedeo snatched the deed out of Oreste's hands, slammed the door in his face, and went away in a fury.

At home, Amedeo had a quick lunch. While eating a sandwich, he pondered on what to do. On the one hand, he didn't want to sue his sister. In fact, a lawsuit between a brother and a sister would cause scandal in Enna and bring dishonor to his family. On the other hand, Amedeo couldn't allow a stranger to be buried in the noble Limiti family tomb. In his opinion, Angela had made a big mistake.

After long reflecting on what to do and balancing the pros and cons of his actions, Amedeo made the decision that was the right one for him. He would sue Angela and her father-in-law. In fact, there was no other way but to resort to the law to remove the intruder from his tomb.

In the afternoon, Amedeo rang Lawyer Beniamino Ribaldi's doorbell. He had known him for a long time. They had been classmates for thirteen years, from elementary school to high school. Beniamino Ribaldi was a criminal lawyer, but he had civil lawyers that worked in his firm.

At the entrance, a beautiful secretary behind a desk welcomed Amedeo with a large smile. She wore silver-framed glasses and sat in front of a computer. She asked him to tell her his personal details and the reason for his coming. She filled out a form with the personal details Amedeo had given her, and then she took the form to Lawyer Beniamino.

Hearing from his secretary that the new client was his old school friend Amedeo Limiti, the lawyer got out of his room and ran to hug him. He was really happy to see his old friend.

"How are you doing, Amedeo. I've not seen you for at least thirty years. You've not changed much. You are just a bit plumper, aren't you?"

"You look the same as when you were a student. You have just grown a belly."

"I heard you are a professor of ancient Greek at the University of Turin."

"Yes, I live in Turin, but once in a while I come back to my hometown. I can't stay far from Enna for too long. Enna is a second mother to me."

"What brings you here?"

"Beniamino, I have a big problem."

"I am here to help you. Let's go to my room."

A bookcase with law books covered two walls of the room. Opposite the entrance was a wide desk and a young man sitting behind it.

"This is my nephew, Vincenzo. He is a trainee of mine. You can talk freely in front of him. He is discreet and smart."

"Nice to meet you, Vincenzo."

"Nice to meet you too, Professor Limiti."

"What bothers you, Amedeo?" Beniamino asked.

"My sister and I own a tomb at the cemetery. My father remodeled it, but the tomb dates back to the time of the Bourbons. As is well known, my family comes from noble Spanish lineage.

"This morning, I went to my tomb early to clean it up, put some flowers in the flower holders, and change the altar cloth. To my unpleasant surprise, I found out that a stranger by the name of Giacomo Tantillo had been buried there, unbeknownst to me. The photo on the altar showed a young man similar to my brother-in-law, Oreste. I inferred that my sister had to be in the know about the burial of that man in our tomb. I went to her home to get a full explanation from her, but she was not there. I found my brother-in-law, Oreste. He gave me a copy of this deed. He said—"

"Sorry to interrupt you, Amedeo. May I have a look at the deed?"

"Yes, of course."

"What do you want me to do for you?" Beniamino asked after reading the deed.

"I want you to evict that stranger from my tomb, because he was buried there illegally. As you can see from the deed, my sister transferred the property of one of the walled niches in our tomb to her father-in-law—that is, to Giacomo Tantillo's father. Of course, along with the ownership of the walled niche, she passed the key of our tomb to the family members of the dead man. It follows that the Limiti family tomb now also belongs to another family. I won't allow it! In my opinion, my sister couldn't transfer the property of the walled niche because she was not one hundred percent the owner of the tomb. Furthermore, I don't think an immovable asset can be transferred through a private agreement. An official registered document is needed. Don't you think, Beniamino?"

Lawyer Beniamino looked into his old friend's eyes and recalled the time they had spent together playing in the street and alleys in Enna. When they were children, there was no television, and cars in the streets were rare. They used to play with a wagon Beniamino had made with planks and bearings.

They had different characters. Beniamino was joyful and humorous, while Amedeo was prickly and too serious for his age. He used to boast of his noble lineage and was so sensitive that if somebody dared to tease him, he broke the friendship. Evidently, time had not softened his rigid character. When Amedeo and Beniamino did their homework together, their ideas clashed. Beniamino had left-wing tendencies, while Amedeo was a conservative. Nevertheless, they were inseparable friends.

On the one hand, Beniamino didn't want to disappoint his old friend. On the other, he didn't feel like pleading a case that was difficult and, in his opinion, absurd. It seemed to already be a lost case. No judge would evict a dead man from his resting place. Beniamino made an excuse.

"Amedeo, I am a criminal lawyer. Your case can be better treated by a civil lawyer. I can recommend a good one to you."

"Yours is a big firm. You have many lawyers under you," replied Amedeo promptly.

Realizing that the excuse had had no effect, Beniamino thought it better to expose another of the reasons why he didn't want to take the case.

"I don't want to disappoint you, my old friend," said Beniamino, "but you must know that lawyers have a heart. Pleading a case like the one you propose clashes with my moral code. We lawyers abide by two laws: one is the written law that comes from lawmakers, while the other is the natural law—that is, the moral code humans have engraved in their hearts since birth. This latter law doesn't allow me to take your case. I don't feel like evicting a dead man from his resting place. Try and find another lawyer. Perhaps a young lawyer still little known who wants to acquire new clients and make a name for himself will accept pleading this strange kind of case. Sorry, I can't accept it."

Amedeo's face turned white, and his lips quivered. He jumped up from the chair and headed for the exit door, but suddenly he turned back, raised his arm, and pointed his finger at Beniamino.

"You are a liar! You have defended many criminals. You never asked yourself if it was honest and moral to defend mafiosi, murderers, and rapists. On one occasion, you had a rapist acquitted. You knew he had raped a girl!"

"In any case, the moral code of a lawyer is to defend his clients. Everyone has the right to defense, including the worst criminals. I treat my clients equally and do my best to protect their rights," replied Beniamino promptly.

"So why do you have scruples about pleading my case? I don't understand you. I will not come to your office anymore. You are no longer my friend!"

Young Lawyer Vincenzo, who was sitting next to his uncle behind the desk, was an honest and sincere man. He disapproved of his uncle's behavior. He felt he had treated his friend harshly. Vincenzo couldn't say that Amedeo was right and embarrass his uncle, but he felt he had something to say on the matter.

"I will plead Professor Amedeo Limiti's case, if you don't mind, Uncle," Vincenzo said.

Hearing his nephew's words, Beniamino ran to Amedeo and grabbed him by the arm before he slammed the door in his face.

"Let's talk! Let's discuss the matter! Don't be prickly like in old times! I thought your character had changed over the years, but I see you are still the same. Keep in mind that friendship is more important than anything else. I don't want to break our friendship, so sit down and relax. I'll do whatever you wish."

Amedeo calmed down and took his seat again in front of Beniamino's desk.

"Do you know how much this case will cost, Vincenzo?" Amedeo asked his nephew.

"No, Uncle, I have no idea," replied the young lawyer.

"This lawsuit will cost Amedeo a lot of money, because we need to research the land register to find the original owner of the land on which the tomb was built. If the opposing party questions Amedeo's title deed, we need to prove his ownership by witnesses. Is it worth it?" asked Beniamino.

"Yes, it is. This lawsuit is a point of principle. That plebeian cannot remain in a tomb of nobles. He must stay with those of his own lower social class," replied Amedeo.

"I have a good civil lawyer in my office. He knows what to do. He and Vincenzo will lay out the case, but I will give them a hand. They are young and in search of fame. If they win the case, everyone will talk about it. In the newspaper there will be banner headlines: 'Dead Man Evicted from His House.'"

Attorney Beniamino tried not to laugh, but he couldn't help himself. On the other side of the desk, Amedeo stared at his friend with a serious look.

"There is nothing to laugh about!"

"I am sorry, Amedeo. I apologize to you. I didn't mean to make fun of you."

That said, Beniamino picked the phone and dialed a number. A young man who could be about twenty-five entered the room from a side door and got near Beniamino's desk.

"Please, sit down, Angelo. This is Professor Amedeo Limiti, an old friend of mine since we were children. He wants our firm to deal with a very unusual case. My nephew, Vincenzo, will work with you. You both can start working on the case while Professor Limiti and I have a walk to the cemetery. I want to see the tomb and take some photos. In the field of law, we must prove everything. Judges don't know the places. Their judgment will be based on the documents we'll provide them."

Lawyers Angelo and Vincenzo worked on the case eagerly. Now and then, Beniamino joined them to discuss the thorniest points together. The three lawyers were sure of winning the case. The only problem was how to execute the sentence. Giacomo Tantillo would be removed from the Limiti family tomb, but where would the corpse be placed? Since Giacomo Tantillo didn't have a grave on his own, the body would be placed in the public ossuary, which was in disuse. Everybody in Enna's cemetery had a tomb or at least a grave. There was a small area allotted by the municipality to the poor that didn't have a grave, but this was not the case of Giacomo Tantillo, who belonged to a rich family when he was alive.

The day of the discussion of the case came. The courthouse was located in an ancient palace that had belonged to Andrea Chiaramonte, one of the most powerful noblemen in Sicily who lived in the fourteenth century and fought against the Spaniards to preserve the independence of Sicily. But he was allured into a trap and captured. After the Spaniards captured him, they beheaded him in front of Palace Steri, his prestigious residence in Palermo.

The ceiling of the courtroom was frescoed with figures depicting the glories of the Chiaramontes. The judge's bench was carved with the motto "All Men Are Equal Before the Law" and the figure of the blindfolded goddess of justice holding a balance in her hand. The tables for the defendant and the plaintiff were in the center of the courtroom. Behind them was a wooden barrier beyond which the public stood.

As soon as the judge in black cap and gown entered the courtroom from a side door, everybody stood up. After him came the clerk of the court and the bailiff, who called out the names of the parties.

Professor Amedeo Limiti and his three lawyers, Beniamino, Angelo, and Vincenzo, took a seat at the table of the plaintiff, while Angela and her father-in-law, Alessandro, sat at the table of the defendants. With them was a lawyer from Catania, a good lawyer indeed. Beniamino would have met his match!

"This judge is well known for his leftist tendencies. This is not what we needed today, but we'll do everything we can," Beniamino whispered in Amedeo's ear.

The hearing lasted for about two hours, and then the judge retired to his room to examine the documents that had been produced by the parties and to write the sentence.

After no more than ten minutes, the judge returned to the courtroom. Everybody stood up to listen to the verdict, but he didn't have any paper with him. He just stared at Amedeo and said an old Latin adage aloud: "*De minimis non curat praetor*" (The judge does not care about trivial things).

"Do you understand, Professor Amedeo Limiti?" the judged asked him.

"I see, Your Eminence. Today, I have learned a new thing: Justice depends on the judge one comes across. Perhaps a different judge with more conservative ideas would have issued a different verdict," replied Amedeo coldly.

The judge didn't get angry. Instead, he smiled at Amedeo. After all, he was a good man as well as an expert judge.

"Let the dead rest in peace, Professor Limiti. You will never find a judge who will agree with you," said the judge before leaving the courtroom.

Amedeo appealed the sentence, but the Court of Appeals of Caltanissetta confirmed the initial judgment. He then appealed to the Supreme Court of Rome, but he lost the case one more time.

Ten years had elapsed since the case began. Amedeo had spent a lot of money for nothing. A few years later, Amedeo died.

Although ugly, his sister, Angela, was endowed with a beautiful soul. She mourned Amedeo's death and cried bitter tears for him. She forgave her brother for the ten-year lawsuit against her. After all, he was still her beloved brother.

On the day of the funeral, a small procession of families, relatives, and friends followed the coffin to the Limiti tomb. The tombstone was raised and put aside. The coffin containing Amedeo's body was lowered into the room under the floor. The tombstone was then put back in place. The funeral was over.

Everyone gradually left the tomb, except Angela. She kept standing there, tears streaming down her face. The pain of her brother's death had made her uglier and bonier. She took a photo of Amedeo from her bag and laid it on the altar next to that of her brother-in-law, the plebeian Giacomo Tantillo. Amedeo and Giacomo looked like two old friends, happy to meet again after a long time. *In paradise there is no time, no space, no age, no ugliness, no beauty. All souls are angels of light*, Angela thought.

It was getting late. The keeper of the cemetery came and kindly asked her to head for the exit. Angela nodded. She took a sheet of paper from her bag and handed it to the keeper. It contained the epitaph she had written:

> *Death is a melter.*
>
> *He gathers souls here and there.*
>
> *Souls of the rich, souls of the poor,*
>
> *Souls of the noble, souls of the plebeian.*
>
> *Then he put them into its crucible where*
>
> *All souls become ONE.*

"Tomorrow, would you mind giving this sheet of paper to the stonecutter, please? He has already been informed. He will carve this epitaph on the marble wall above the altar," Angela said.

The keeper of the cemetery bowed his head and answered, "It will be done, my fair lady."

Chapter Five

Visiting More Tombs

On November 2 of that year, after visiting the Limiti family tomb, I kept roaming the cemetery, which was crowded with people all afternoon. I saw pictures of some old schoolmates of mine embedded in the facades or placed on the altars of their tombs. They had arrived at the last resting place before me. I was aware that I would follow them sooner or later, but leaving this life without understanding much of its meaning didn't appeal to me much.

After a while, I left the central avenues and walked on narrow paths lined with tombs. Cypress trees were scattered here and there. Some tombs had funeral wreaths both inside the room and in front of the tomb. Moreover, the family members of the dead person were dressed in black, and their eyes were red with weeping. It meant that somebody in the family had been buried there recently.

Katia's Tomb

I stumbled upon a tomb of a friend of mine. We had been classmates in middle school. Her name, Katia, was quite uncommon in Enna. Her voice sounded like the chirping of a chick. I'll never forget her. She had short black hair. Her eyes were as black as coal, but her complexion was as white as snow. She had been quite tall and buxom for her age. Maybe she loved me, but I considered her just a dear friend.

We were both thirteen years old back then. Every time we went home after school, she took me by the hand and asked me to accompany her home. She said that a young man used to harass her, and she felt safe with me holding her hand. She was the best student in the class. Her desk was in front of mine. I too was a good student, but I wanted to achieve maximum results with minimum effort and always chose the easiest way to avoid straining my brain. So, during schoolwork, I gently knocked on Katia's arm and motioned her to move her body a bit to the side. Then I craned my neck, narrowed my eyes, and copied the classwork from her, especially the translations from Latin. She let me copy. How lovely she was!

Sometimes Katia and I sat on a bench in the park that surrounded the octagonal and, according to some, the esoteric Tower of Frederick, and she read some passages from her diary aloud. In fact, Katia had kept a diary since she learned to read and write. Once, she even handed me the notebook where she used to write her diary, and I leafed through the pages. It was written in clear, large letters. In the diary, besides her writing, were some green or red pen drawings of flowers and hearts. I was enchanted by her diary. It was very clean and tidy. Katia's writing had evolved since she attended elementary school, but although a little different from when she was an elementary school student, her penmanship was impressive. I couldn't spot even the slightest cross-out or scribble in her notebook. According to some, the way we write reflects our character and personality. I agree with such an opinion. As for Katia, I felt that her tidy writing reflected her noble, fine, and sensitive soul.

"Why do you keep a diary?" I asked her one day while we were sitting on a bench.

"By writing a diary, I can record my daily life and my feelings. I can talk to myself and tell myself whatever I want to express. I can freely express my anger, my joy, and my emotions," Katia answered.

I didn't understand Katia's words at the time, but now, while standing in front of her tomb, I realized how huge the cultural gap was between us when we were teenagers. Her words: emotions, feelings, talking to myself, etc., belonged to a lexicon unknown to me.

Katia and I followed different destinies in our lives. I was always looking for my soulmate, without being able to find it, while Katia married a doctor soon after she earned a degree in modern literature at the University of Catania. Her marriage didn't last long, for she divorced her husband two years later.

After graduating, Katia got a job as a middle school teacher. She also wrote a book of poems. Unfortunately, at the age of fifty, while driving her car on a foggy road, she ran into a truck and died after slipping into a coma for a month. The tombstone in her tomb had been engraved with a poem of hers:

> Love is a wandering knight.
> He appears to you only once in your life.
> Don't let him go.
> When he goes away, it is too late.

Eraldo's Tomb

From Katia's tomb, a staircase led to the lower part of the cemetery. Not far from the boundary wall, the avenue was lined with tall cypress trees. The tombs stood beyond the trees. In one of these, my former business partner, Eraldo, had been buried. With him, we had created a shop for the sale of art objects. Since I was a lawyer and couldn't run the shop personally, I entrusted him with the task of managing it.

We lived different lives. I was a traveler and had some love affairs. He got a girlfriend when he was sixteen. She was the only woman in his life. He married her and lived with her happily. He loved his wife to such an extent that he even endured her flings with some of his best friends. It was unusual for a Sicilian to put up with his wife's love affairs. For Eraldo, perhaps it was real love, or maybe it was blind passion. Who knows! We cannot know what feelings a human soul harbors.

After a few years, my partnership with Eraldo ended. I felt that he had been unfair to me. Apparently, his love was focused only on his wife; as for the rest of humanity, his heart was harder than a stone. Only his interests mattered.

Looking at his photo on the altar, I also looked inside myself. It was as if his picture was a mirror on which I was looking at myself. Had I behaved well in my life? Of course not. While Eraldo was greedy for money, I was eager for women. More than once I went to bed with married women. A friend of mine once told me this proverb: "Women are like bottles. Empty them and then throw them away." I treasured this wrong saying. After I succeeded in having sex with a woman, I left her as if she were an empty bottle. I kept behaving immorally for a great part of my life. We all have skeletons in the closet; no one is immune from blame.

I said a prayer for Eraldo's soul, and then I took an uphill path lined with humble tombs. I passed through the small area allotted to the poor who couldn't afford to build either a grave or a tomb. Near there were the tombs of the Franciscan Sisters and that of the Carmelite Sisters. I paused in front of their tombs for a few minutes and then continued to walk uphill.

Gerlando Sferrazzanetti's Tomb

I arrived at the tomb of a man who, when he was sixteen years old, killed a boy of his same age with one punch. The killer's name was Gerlando Sferrazzanetti. He remained in jail for fifteen years. During that time, he learned to paint. His oil paintings depicted sacred images and Enna traditions: the procession in honor of Our Lady of Visitation, the Good Friday procession, the Church of Valverde, and the like.

Seeing his photo on the altar in his tomb, I felt that he must have been a good man, the murder aside. His features were gentle and his eyes sweet.

An epitaph had been engraved on his marble niche:

As a rosebud becomes a rose,

And a seed becomes a tree,

So the soul grows and evolves

Up to the last stage, the light of love.

Antonio Colinari's Tomb

About one hundred meters away from Gerlando Sferrazzanetti's tomb was that of Antonio Colinari, who was reputed to be a Mafia boss. He was killed in an ambush while on his way to his farm. In the world of criminals, even the bosses cannot feel safe. He had a gun in the glove compartment of his car, but he didn't have time to pull it out. Two masked men on motorbikes came abreast of his car and shot him dead. According to the investigators, he was killed by order of another faction of the Mafia hostile to him.

Was he a mafioso? Was he killed by the Mafia? I cannot know. I'll only say that there is an official truth, which comes from the authorities, and the real truth. The two truths do not always match.

To say that the Mafia killed him is equivalent to saying that nobody killed him. The Mafia doesn't have a name like a person. It is something indistinct. With the alibi of the Mafia, criminals go unpunished! It would be more honest for the authorities to say, "We are unable to find the killers," rather than say, "It was the Mafia that killed him."

The Mafia recalls the myth of Odysseus and Polyphemus. When Polyphemus's friends asked him who had blinded him, he answered, "Nobody." The same goes for the Mafia. When the authorities are unable to detect a culprit, they say, "The culprit was the Mafia"—that is, nobody.

Italian public television once interviewed a mafioso from Corleone, a town in the province of Palermo. He served his life sentence in a prison in Sardinia. During his captivity, he produced oil paintings. Seen on the small screen, his paintings looked beautiful. The interviewer asked him if it was true that he was still a Mafia boss and wielded power from prison.

"Every time a Mafia murder occurs, the authorities charge me as the mandator in the murder. This is absurd! I have been locked in this prison for many years. Do you think I can keep control over the Mafia from my cell?"

In my opinion, he was right. If a lifer can still have influence over a criminal organization while he is locked in a prison, it means that the prison administration is inefficient.

Actually, some murders were charged to that convict from Corleone. I can assume the reason. When serious bloodshed happens, the general public wants a culprit. Why not give people an easy-to-find culprit, the indistinct Mafia that has neither name nor surname, or a lifer?

What is the Mafia? In my opinion, it is nothing more than an alliance among some business groups, politicians, and common criminals. This does not happen only in Sicily. Politicians and financial lobbies get along well everywhere.

In past centuries, bankers pushed governments to declare war so that they could borrow the money from them. If this was not the Mafia, what was it? What about the lobbies of arms manufactures and arm dealers? Don't you think they push governments to war too?

Italian public television once spread the news that the choice of the foreign ministers in the Italian government had always been imposed by an important multinational firm. How can you define such behavior if not the Mafia?

All over the world, some businessmen, politicians, and criminals are joined together. This is the reason the Mafia can never be defeated. I am aware I am pessimistic on this topic, but this is the truth, in my opinion.

I stood for a few minutes in front of the tomb of the Mafia boss from Enna. I said a prayer for him and asked the Lord to forgive him and his murderers. After all, all crimes are caused by ignorance and error. Evil doesn't exist.

Gioacchino's Tomb

I kept walking uphill and headed for the top of the hillock of the cemetery. In front of me was a long stairway between two lines of tombs and cypress trees. While I was climbing the stairs, the sky suddenly clouded over, a few drops of rain came down, and a thick white fog covered the tombs, the stairway, the cypress trees, everything. Visibility was very poor. Within minutes, people left the town of the dead and headed for their homes.

I continued to go up to visit more tombs. I arrived at the tomb of Gioacchino, a friend of mine with whom I had acted on the stage. He had died last year while he was sleeping at night. He died peacefully, passing from sleep to death, but he was just seventy years old when he passed away. In life, you cannot have everything!

His tomb stood near the hilltop. Three families shared it. On the top of the facade were written three family names: Cammarata, Baiunco, Costanzo. Gioacchino's family name was Baiunco. Originally, the tomb had belonged to only one founder; later, his children and sons-in-law remodeled it and added two more family names. On the altar, Gioacchino's photo stood out. He looked like a movie star. In the picture, he wore a fedora aslant like Frank Sinatra. They resembled each other indeed.

When Gioacchino died, his beautiful wife, sixteen years younger, was desperate. At the funeral, she was dressed in black and wore dark glasses to conceal her eyes, which were red with tears. During the funeral procession, two women held her arm in arm, for she felt dizzy and couldn't stand. Six months later, I saw her walking in Via Roma hand in hand with another man. This time she had a smile on her face and wore a colorful dress. Apparently, nobody is irreplaceable!

Romualdo Fischietti's Tomb

As I kept strolling in the cemetery, I came across Romualdo Fischietti's tomb. It stood at the beginning of an avenue. He was a lawyer renowned all over Sicily. His framed photo dominated all the others on the altar. In the photo, he was smiling and wore a black cap and a black gown. I did an internship in his law firm in Catania at the beginning of my career. Although he spent his life in Catania, he was buried in the cemetery of his hometown, Enna, when he died.

He was a conceited man. When we were in the court of law, he sometimes talked to me about a judge, sometimes about a colleague of his, sometimes about somebody else. He almost never said a good thing about anybody. He particularly badmouthed a judge and a colleague of his. He conditioned me quite a lot. In fact, whenever I met someone whom he had backbitten, I had prejudice against them; it was a very big hindrance in my career. After some time, I realized that his opinions on others were wrong. Those whom he had described as ignorant or incompetent were good people of great value. Once, he even lost a case against a lawyer whom he considered a good-for-nothing.

In my opinion, one of the worst sins a human being can commit is backbiting others. If I were a priest, I would talk about this sin in my homilies every Sunday. Many people don't know anything about the vibrations of words. Speaking ill of others creates harmful vibrations that harm not only the backbitten person but also the one who slanders.

I considered as gospel truth what Lawyer Romualdo Fischietti told me. Now, standing in front of his photo on the altar of his tomb, I realized how harmful it is to follow others' opinions passively, whether they come from your teacher, your doctor, or even from the pope.

My Parents' Family Tomb

My parents' family tomb was not far from that of Lawyer Romualdo Fischietti. It was a tomb of classic cut. Two travertine marble columns with Corinthian capitals supported a triangle-shaped architrave. At the center of the triangle had been carved another smaller triangle with an eye inside. It must have been an esoteric symbol that the founder of the tomb, my grandfather, inserted in the architrave. I couldn't make out the meaning of that symbol.

When my Uncle Ugo remodeled the tomb, he enlarged the walled niches, in order that husband and wife could be placed in one niche next to each other upon their death, as if the niche were a double bed. Obviously, Uncle Ugo had the illusion that death was a continuation of life. Was he right? I can't know. What happens after death is a mystery!

The altar in my parents' family tomb was crowded with framed photos. At the center of the altar, the picture of my Uncle Ugo's first wife stood out. She was a beautiful woman, always smiling. The other photos portrayed my parents, my uncles, and my aunts. My grandparents' photos had been put in the background of the altar. It is normal that after a few generations not only are our photos removed from the altar of the tomb, but our memory also vanishes. From nothing we came and to nothing we will return!

Looking at the photos of my parents, I relived the years I had spent with them until the age of thirty. I had been strongly conditioned by my parents' opinions of others. My father ran a business in partnership with his brothers. At home, he used to boast about being the only one capable of running the business. According to him, his brothers were not as able as he was. He used to tell me that if it had not been for him, the family business would have gone bankrupt a long time ago. I believed blindly in what my father told me. How can a child think that his father tells him lies?

My mother conditioned me a lot too. Her opinions about others changed, depending on her good or bad mood. She used to give me pieces of advice about everything I should do in my life. In hindsight, I realized that I should have listened to the voice of my heart instead of following her advice passively, but I didn't. The biggest mistakes I made in my life happened when I followed others' advice and opinions. Later, when I started to act with my brain and my heart, I succeeded in life.

Napoleone Colajanni's Tomb

One of the most important things to visit in Enna's cemetery is the grave of Napoleone Colajanni, a great statesman and a good writer. He was born in Castrogiovanni on 27 April 1847 and died in Castrogiovanni on 2 September 1921.

His grave stands on the upper avenue of the cemetery and is similar to the grave of John Fitzgerald Kennedy, though on a smaller scale. There is no flame always lit on Napoleone Colajanni's grave. While John Kennedy rests next to his wife, Jacqueline, Napoleone Colajanni's grave only houses his body. With the due distinctions of proportions, the two graves are similar.

Napoleone Colajanni was a clear example of an honest and incorruptible politician. After he was elected to the parliament of the Kingdom of Italy, he unmasked the scandal of the Banca Romana, which minted banknotes illegally. The scandal also involved members of the government. Following the precise denunciation of corruption by Napoleone Colajanni, the government was forced to resign. This great son of Enna was also a professor of statistics at the University of Palermo and an author of books on the Mafia and the problems of southern Italy.

I read a book written by him entitled *Nel Regno della Mafia* (*In the Kingdom of the Mafia*). It tells of Emanuele

Notarbartolo, marquis of San Giovanni, an eminent nobleman who was stabbed to death while traveling by train in a tunnel on the Messina Palermo railway line. Strangely, he was killed a few days after he had accused the general manager of the Banco di Sicilia, one of the most important banks in Italy, of financial improprieties. The book by Napoleone Colajanni is one of the first on the issue of the Mafia. It denounces the collusion between magistrates, police, politicians, and mafiosi.

By standing in front of the grave of Napoleone Colajanni, I realized one thing: It is incorrect to tar everybody with the same brush. Even though I don't like politicians much, I cannot exclude that there may be some politicians like Napoleone Colajanni who are honest and aim at the well-being of citizens.

Giulio Sperlazzari's Tomb

From Napoleone Colajanni's grave, I moved to a tomb of a friend of mine, Giulio Sperlazzari, who was born into a wealthy family. He was seven years older than me. His father started his business by buying an autobus to carry passengers from the railway station on Piazza Armerina to Aidone. In fact, the town of Aidone stood on a plateau, while the railway station was located in Piazza Armerina, about ten kilometers away from the city center of Aidone.

The business went well from the start, for the bus was always overcrowded. That first bus his father bought was the seed that gave birth to a big company with tens of buses that carried passengers throughout Sicily.

When the founder of the bus company died, his sons Giulio and Michelangelo inherited the business. The two brothers had different characters. Michelangelo had a knack for business, and Giulio was a sincere, ingenuous man that trusted his brother blindly. Consequently, Michelangelo managed the bus company, while Giulio used to spend his time in the countryside, for he loved nature and animals. He sometimes invited me for a horseback ride in the countryside.

After a few years of good management by Michelangelo, the company grew further. Now, hundreds of buses ran throughout Sicily. But human greed has no limit! *Why do I have to share my business with my brother? I am more able than him. He is a wimp!* Michelangelo thought one day. So, he set up another bus company on his own, unbeknownst to Giulio. Later, Giulio came to know that his brother had become much richer than he was, thanks to the new business he had created. Michelangelo's new bus company grew more every day, while the old company the two brothers owned together didn't develop. When it was too late, Giulio realized that he had wrongly placed his trust in his brother.

I once met Giulio on the street. We walked together, and he confided in me his feelings towards his brother. Even though Michelangelo had betrayed him, he was unable to hate his brother. Giulio's heart was too innocent. He just blamed himself for having put his trust in the wrong person.

"The world hasn't changed since the days of Cain and Abel!" Giulio said to me one day. He felt bitter about the way Michelangelo had treated him.

"I agree with you, Giulio. We are born in a contaminated world. Ignorance is the basis of all evils. Evidently, your brother doesn't know that all his buses are useless in getting him the respect of others. Let him wallow in luxury! He will 'never have a true friend or a true love, for greed for money has made his heart harder than a stone. As for me, I wouldn't change my friendship with you for all the gold in the world. You can be proud of yourself, for you have at least one true friend, while your brother has no one to love him."

Standing in front of Giulio's tomb and looking at his picture on the altar, I recalled the many cases between family members I had dealt with when I was a lawyer: sisters versus sisters, brothers versus brothers, and even daughters against fathers. If I could start my life over again, I wouldn't be a lawyer! I would do a quieter job, as far as possible from the quarrels caused by man's greed. But we cannot live twice. There is only one life with one path. The steps taken cannot be retraced, and the errors we've made can't always be fixed!

My Great-Grandfather's Tomb

Also in the upper part of the cemetery was my great-grandfather's tomb. He was my grandmother's father by the name of Tanino. I didn't know him. His tomb was almost the same size as Giuseppe Chiarello's. There were no photos of the people who rested inside. The only difference between the two tombs was that my great-grandfather's housed three bodies: his, his wife Carmela, and his daughter Venerina, while Giuseppe Chiarello lay alone in his tomb.

Tanino was a unique man. My father, who was one of his neighbors, told me that my great-grandfather was able to memorize all the traditional Enna proverbs. When he talked with someone else, he often expressed himself in proverbs or through maxims he had invented. My father also told me that Tanino liked drinking a couple of glasses of good wine during meals. When he drank more than usual in an evening, he went out on the balcony, leaned out with his hands on the railing, and spoke his maxims out loud. His neighbors listened to him from the nearby balconies and windows of their houses and chuckled with fun.

His maxims were roughly the following: "He who pays no taxes is a nobody!", "The generous will become rich!", "The miser will lose all their money!", and the like. I wish I had known him; he must have been an interesting guy.

At first, I didn't recollect his daughter, Venerina, and I had even forgotten that my grandmother had a sister. Then, thinking, I remembered her. When I was a child, my grandmother quite often asked me to go to her sister's house and then keep her informed about her health. I don't know exactly why my grandmother never visited her sister, but I suppose there was bad blood between her and her sister's daughter.

Venerina always sat in an armchair with a blanket over her legs. Maybe she had had a stroke or was suffering from another disease I didn't know about. I can only say that she looked like a piece of furniture. She always sat in the same armchair in the same place, next to the wall opposite the entrance.

I often went to Venerina's home, not only to please my grandmother but also because I was attracted by her house, which shared a garden with another house where a friend of mine lived. I used to play with him and Venerina's grandchildren whenever I went there.

Venerina had one daughter, Liliana, and one son, Renato, who studied medicine at the University of Milan. Liliana was married with two sons. They all lived in the same house, except Venerina's husband, Domenico, who had migrated to America.

Liliana was a muscular and grim woman who was always angry with her mother, whom she insulted continuously. She sometimes screamed at her mother like a hysterical crazy woman. I never understood why she was so disrespectful to her mother. The only plausible explanation was that Liliana had so much malice inside herself that she had to vent it on someone. On the other hand, her mother always kept silent. She absorbed her daughter's insults like a sponge absorbs muddy water. I don't remember ever hearing her saying a single word.

Whenever her brother Renato returned home from Milan for winter and summer holidays, Liliana also insulted him and screamed at him and his mother.

Finally, Venerina died. When Domenico was informed of his wife's death, he immediately returned from America to take part in the funeral. Venerina was buried in the tomb with her parents. Fifteen days went by, and her husband soon consoled himself by getting married to a woman twelve years younger than he was.

Since death doesn't discriminate, twenty years later it took Domenico to the kingdom of the dead. A few years before he died, Domenico gave a handwritten will to his daughter Liliana, for her and for her brother. He handed another handwritten will to his new wife. No one knows whether he acted in such a singular way on a whim or for some other reason. Of course, the two wills clashed and a lawsuit between Liliana and Renato against their stepmother ensued. Since Liliana trusted no lawyer but me, she asked me to plead her case. I was loath to have her as my client. The memory of her hysterical outbursts against her mother was still alive in me, but in the end, I agreed to defend her. The lawsuit lasted for years until we came to a compromise.

As for Renato, after he earned a degree in medicine, he returned to his old house in Enna and stayed with his sister. Since Liliana used to insult him and scream at him in the same way as she had done with her mother, Renato got tremendously depressed and couldn't work as a physician anymore. He finally got a job at Enna's hospital as a nurse.

The story of Venerina and Liliana is nothing more than human misery. Liliana was a domineering woman that used to subjugate those around her. She was certainly not the first case on earth of an aggressive and hysterical woman, nor will it be the last.

If I had been with my great-grandfather Tanino when he leaned out over the balcony of his house a bit drunk and let out his maxims, I would have suggested he include a new one in his collection and then shout it out at the top of his voice: "Never give in to bullies who pretend to be hysterical or crazy. Otherwise, they will eat your soul!"

Giacomino's Tomb

It was getting late in the cemetery. Before long, the darkness of the evening would follow the dusk. I kept walking uphill a little longer until I arrived at the last tomb I intended to visit for the year. It was the tomb of Giacomino, a dear friend of mine who died young due to an error made by the doctors who treated him.

While he was changing a bulb in the chandelier in his house, he fell off the ladder and broke one of his ribs. His father took him to the orthopedic ward of the hospital. The doctors who treated him discharged him from the hospital after three days, even though he was still feverish. Once at home, the fever didn't go down, so his father took him back to the hospital, but this time his son was put in the lung disease ward. He stayed in the hospital for a month and eventually died. Oddly, a trivial rib fracture caused his death.

Giacomino's father came to my office and entrusted me with the task of lodging a complaint against the doctors who had treated his son. Following my precise complaint, the prosecutor ordered Giacomino's body be exhumed and appointed a forensic expert to ascertain the causes of his death.

I was full of hate against the doctors who treated Giacomino the first time, but hate never generates good things; it poisons the mind.

I attended the exhumation of Giacomino's body in the cemetery mortuary in Enna. Six months after his death, his body was unrecognizable. The flesh was still attached to his bones, but it was swollen, his eyes were almost out of their sockets, and his body, obviously being in an advanced state of decay, smelled terribly. The forensic expert dissected Giacomino's body from head to toe and later wrote a very long and detailed report.

After I had a copy of the report in my office, one of my colleagues advised me to have it read by a doctor. I followed my colleague's advice and asked a doctor who was a friend of mine to give me his opinion about the report. He said the ones responsible for my friend's death were the doctors who treated him the first time. It was a blunder of mine to trust him. I should have read the report myself. How could I win a case without having read the report? Moreover, I was blinded by hatred against the doctors of the orthopedic ward that had treated Giacomino the first time. If I had been serene and read the report, I would have found that, according to the forensic expert, it was actually the fault of the doctors in the lung disease ward. They had made mistakes in his therapy. I lost the case, and Giacomino's father couldn't recover damages. It was one of my biggest mistakes in my career as a lawyer.

I said a prayer for Giacomino's soul, asked him to forgive both me and the doctors who caused his death, and then I took the stairway to the exit.

Chapter Six
Meeting My Cousin Luigi

The cemetery was still shrouded in thick fog. The shadows of the incoming evening seemed to describe ghostly figures amid the tall cypress trees. I didn't feel comfortable at all. Although I was an old man of eighty, the fear of ghosts I had when I was a child had never left me.

I quickened my steps down the stairs. Suddenly, I thought I saw a figure looming up through the mist. I had the start of fear. I couldn't go back. It was too late by then. I could take a side path, but I had no idea where it would lead me. I had no choice but to face the ghost.

The specter was walking toward me without faltering. He had a stick in his hand and wore a blue jacket and white trousers. If it had not been for the stick in his hand, you couldn't say he was an old man. His gait was firm and elegant.

When the figure got close to me, I recognized it. It was not a ghost but my cousin Luigi, two years and two months older than me. He lived in Catania, but he used to come to Enna every year on November 2 to visit his parents' tomb. I felt relieved and ran to hug him.

I hadn't seen him for a few years. He moved to Catania with his parents long ago. His father had his vocal cords operated on. After that difficult surgical operation, which left him almost unable to speak, he could no longer endure the cold and fog in Enna, so he was forced to move to Catania, a city with a mild climate, with his family. It was his fortune, because in Catania, a commercial city much larger than Enna, his sons, Sandro, Valerio, and Luigi, were able to fully express their skills as businessmen. They became rich in a short time.

Luigi had a knack for selling cars. He was rightly considered the best car dealer in Italy. He was not a very good student in school, but he was number one in the field of business. When we were kids, we were inseparable friends. His hair was blonder than mine, and he was light-skinned. Obviously, his ancestors must have been the Normans. After he failed twice, we happened to be in the same class. After he failed one more time, his father made him leave the school in Enna and enrolled him in a technical school in Leonforte, a town near Enna. Finally, he earned qualification as a building surveyor, a profession he worked in until he moved to Catania.

"What are you doing here? You scared me! I thought you were a ghost," I said.

My cousin laughed. "Don't you know I come to Enna on November second every year?"

"Yes, I know, but your parents' tomb is on the main avenue. What are you doing here at the top of the hillock at this hour? Didn't you hear the siren announcing the closure of the cemetery?"

"Yes, I know the cemetery is about to close. I've already visited my parents' tomb, so I am going to see a special tomb on the top of the hill facing Calascibetta. Do you want to join me?"

"Are you crazy? If we don't get out soon, we will be locked inside the cemetery. Do you want to spend the night here?"

"Don't worry. I know a side exit. It is near the graveyard for the poor. There is a hole in the fence near there. We can go out through it. Now, let's go up. I want to show you the photo of the man buried in a tomb. Maybe you'll recognize him."

"Okay, let's go!"

We climbed up the stairs up to the hilltop. Due to thick fog, the visibility was low. We arrived at a tomb near a cliff. The name on the facade was Antonio Reggiani. The small gate at the entrance to the tomb was unlocked. Luigi pushed it and we entered inside. Two lit candles allowed us to have a look at the tomb. On the altar was a framed photo that showed a man who must have been suffering from a skin disease, for he had eczema in his red and rough nose. I didn't see a niche inside. He had evidently been buried under the floor.

"The man you see in the photo was one of the richest men in Latin America. Let's meet again tomorrow, Mario. I want to tell you his life story. He was Antonio Reggiani from Calascibetta," said my cousin.

"Don't you return to Catania tonight?"

"No, I want to spend a week in my house in Enna where I was born. Come to me tomorrow anytime. I'll be happy to have dinner with you at my house."

"Okay, I'll come tomorrow at ten o'clock in the morning, but now let's go out of this sinister tomb, please. I can't wait to get out of the cemetery. It is dark by now. Do you remember well where the hole in the fence is?"

"You haven't changed at all since we were children. I enjoyed pretending I was a ghost and scaring you back then. Don't worry! We can get out of the cemetery easily."

We passed through the graveyard of the poor. There was a cross on each mound of earth and a small wooden board with the name of the person buried there. Then we passed through the hole in the fence and got out of the cemetery. I breathed a sigh of relief.

The following day at about ten in the morning, I knocked on Luigi's door. He was waiting for me.

"Come in. Would you like to have a cup of coffee?" he asked.

"I'd love to! I haven't been to this house for almost seventy years. It's been so long, yet it seems like yesterday. We played hide and seek here. Time flies like an arrow!"

Luigi's house was originally part of a larger building. It had belonged to our grandfather. There was an upper floor and a ground floor. A staircase in the yard led to the upper floor. In his will, my grandfather bequeathed the first floor to my father and the ground floor to Luigi's father. The yard remained a common area.

The kitchen in Luigi's house was in the basement. A wooden, steep staircase connected the ground floor to the basement. In the kitchen was a bread oven and a wood-burning stove. The blazing wood kept the room warm. After the water in the coffee machine boiled, Luigi turned it upside down. The water dripped through the coffee grounds into the other part of the coffee machine. When coffee was ready, Luigi poured it into two china cups.

"We were inseparable friends when we were children, but I realized that you were too selfish and unfair to me. For this reason I cut off our friendship," I said while we were sipping that delicious coffee.

"When was I unfair to you? Tell me," Luigi asked me calmly.

"Once, when we were children, you asked me to take part in the Good Friday procession. You told me where I could get the procession alb and the cloak. I got them, and then I took part in the procession wearing the clothes of the Confraternity of Our Lady of the Sorrows. You had already been admitted in the confraternity, while I was not a member. My participation in the procession was occasional. Later, even though I asked you many times how I could become a member of the confraternity like you, you never told me. If I had joined the brotherhood, I could have had the privilege of carrying the litter with the statue of Our Lady on my shoulder when I became an adult. I wanted that a lot, but you didn't do anything to help me. You were selfish and envious of me. I couldn't forgive you for your egoistic behavior against me."

"You are right. All children are selfish. Once at school, our teacher told us 'The Fable of the Two Bags' by Aesop. He said that man was created from clay with two bags hanging on his neck. The one in front of him was full of his neighbor's faults, and the other on his back was full of his own faults. The teacher said, 'The meaning of this fable is quite clear. Man can recognize his neighbor's faults quickly, but it is difficult for him to see his own.' You were more egoistic and unfair than I was, Mario."

"How can you say that?"

"We were classmates. You never helped me at school. You were a good student, but I wasn't. You could have encouraged me. You could have done homework with me and helped me to understand the lessons, but you never did! What do you think about your behavior? Wasn't it also egoistic?"

I didn't retort. I nodded silently. Luigi was right. I was as selfish as him, maybe more. Like the man in the Aesop's fable, I saw only Luigi's faults, not mine. For seventy years, I had closed the door of my mind to him. I should have talked to him and cleared the misunderstandings up instead of harboring a grudge against him.

"Let's not talk about the past anymore," continued Luigi. "What matters is the present. We both are old men. Now we don't have any reason to be envious of each other. The past is past, and it is dead and gone. I want you to be my guest today. Do you agree?"

"Of course! Let's be intimate friends like when we were children."

"I've always loved you, Mario. Now sit in this rocking chair. While I am preparing the dough for bread, I'll tell you how I came to know the story of the man in the tomb we visited yesterday. Do you remember him?"

"I've never heard about that man."

"When I was seven years old and you were five, a young man with a long American car called a limousine passed by us while we were playing in Via S. Agata. I ran and waved at him. You also ran and followed me. The man in the car saw us through the driving mirror and pulled over. He was kind to us. He got us into his car and took us for a ride to Calascibetta, his hometown. He wore a gold watch that must have weighed half a kilo or so. He told us that he lived in Mexico and used to visit his land by plane, for it was vast. Do you recollect him now?"

"Oh yes, I remember him now, but I've just a vague memory of him. Seventy-five years have passed since then!"

"He told us his name, Antonio Reggiani. He gave us two chocolate bars and dropped us back at Via S. Agata. Then he disappeared. I heard no more about him until a few years ago when I stumbled on his tomb on November second while I was hanging out in the cemetery. The photo on the altar was undoubtedly his. I recognized him from his eczematous nose."

"It could have been another person's photo. Surely he was not the only one to suffer from a skin disease."

"No, his nose was unmistakable. Furthermore, I remembered his name!"

"You have a good memory, Luigi! How can you remember his name seventy-years later?"

"There are things in life that you forget easily and things that you can't forget. That name, Antonio Reggiani, remained engraved on my mind because he looked very rich. I'd never met someone like him in Enna before."

"Your tale is intriguing, Luigi. Go on with the story."

"I found it quite strange that one of the richest men in Latin America had been buried in so humble a tomb. It was unusual for a citizen of Calascibetta to be buried in Enna. In Calascibetta they have their own cemetery, indeed. There must have been something mysterious in his life."

"It is not unusual for a rich man to be buried in a humble tomb. For instance, Robert Francis Kennedy lies under the bare earth," I said.

"In our Sicilian culture, such a thing is unthinkable. Moreover, I wanted to know how it was possible for a poor emigrant to become one of the richest men in Latin America in a short span of time. I was not convinced at all about that.

But who knows? Sometimes life hides surprises, mysteries, and miracles. Everything is possible!

"I was eager to know about him more. It was said that Father Giordano, the parish priest of the Cathedral of Calascibetta, knew everything about the history of his hometown, so I decided to ask him about this man.

"In the morning, I kept strolling in the cemetery. Then, in the afternoon, I went to Calascibetta, where I hoped to meet Father Giordano. It took no more than fifteen minutes to get there. I passed Piazza Umberto, the main square in Calascibetta, and the narrow streets up to the upper part of the town. Then I parked my car in the square in front of the Royal Palatine Chapel.

"On the left, facing the church, was an iron railing that overlooked the valley and Enna. The majestic facade of the Royal Palatine Chapel towered above the square and the surrounding houses.

"Before entering the church, I walked toward the railing to admire the landscape, which was amazing. I lingered there for a while, enchanted by the green of the valley and the mountain ranges that stood out in the distance. Seen from there, Enna seemed to be a gigantic natural castle, and the houses on the edge of the plateau looked like battlements. The valley between Calascibetta and Enna was uneven. It must have been a hard task to walk through it to reach Enna from Calascibetta.

"A large limestone staircase led to the entrance of the chapel. I entered the church, dipped my finger in the stoup near the entrance, and made the sign of the cross. I felt peace and sacredness inside the chapel.

"The parish priest was celebrating Compline. I sat on a pew waiting for the end of the function and had a look at the chapel. I saw some bas-reliefs at the base of the columns. One of them was enigmatic. When Compline was over, I headed for the sacristy to meet the parish priest. A few old ladies dressed in black were helping him put his vestments back into a closet

145

made of black wood embellished with patterns typical of the baroque period. The priest was short, black-haired, and about fifty years old. His black eyes were bright like those of a sparrow. The old ladies called him Father Giordano.

"Good evening, Father Giordano! My name is Luigi Chiaramonte."

"Good evening, sir!" replied Father Giordano, looking at me with inquisitive air.

"He knew all the citizens in Calascibetta, but I was a stranger to him."

"May I ask you a question?"

"Of course! If I know the answer, I'll be happy to tell you what I know,' the priest replied with a kind smile.

"The old ladies in black left the vestry, and I was left alone with Father Giordano. 'Please have a seat! What can I do for you?' he asked. I got right to the crux of the matter."

"When I was just a child, about seventy years ago, I had the chance to meet in Enna a man from Calascibetta. He got my cousin and me into his car and drove us to Calascibetta. Then he took us back to Enna. He was a kind man and looked very rich. He said that he lived in Mexico, but this morning I saw his photo on the altar of his tomb in Enna's cemetery. The name on the tomb was Antonio Reggiani. Have you ever heard about him? If so, I'd like to learn something about his life."

"Father Giordano seemed to be delighted with my question."

"Yes! I've heard about the man you are talking about. Calascibetta is a small town, and everybody knows everything about others. It is said that a man called Antonio Reggiani emigrated first to Guatemala and then to Mexico. He amassed untold riches!"

"Is this man the same man buried in the cemetery in Enna? It is unusual for a citizen of Calascibetta to be buried in Enna. You have your own cemetery here. Nevertheless, looking at the photo, I was sure he was the man I had seen seventy years ago."

"Father Giordano knew Antonio Reggiani's story only by hearsay. He didn't want to give me wrong information, so he said, 'To verify whether such a man called Antonio Reggiani really existed in Calascibetta, we have to search in the baptism register. If he was born in this parish, we'll find his name here. Otherwise, we must broaden the search to other parishes. I hope we'll be lucky."

"I think it is easier to consult the birth register in the town hall," I replied.

"No! In the town hall, it is very difficult to consult old documents dating back almost one hundred years ago. In our parish, we can search his birth easily, because our baptism register has been kept since 1340, the year of the erection of the Royal Palatine Chapel. I am interested in your question because I love history. Come here tomorrow in the early afternoon. We'll try to learn something about him.'

"Didn't you live in Catania at that time, Luigi?"

"Yes, I did, but my curiosity prevailed over the trouble of driving my car from Catania to Calascibetta. So, the next day, it took more than three hours to cover the distance from Catania to Calascibetta. Thick fog made me drive very slowly. When I entered the sacristy, Father Giordano seemed to be a bit annoyed by the long wait, but as soon as he saw me, his face lit up with his innocent smile.

"I thought you wouldn't come!" he said, smiling.

"Sorry, I'm late due to the fog. On the winding road to Calascibetta, visibility is down to a few meters!"

"Okay, let's start our work right now. I have to celebrate Mass pretty soon!"

"Then, he opened a drawer, took out a parish register of about one square meter, and put it on the table at the center of the sacristy. He turned over the yellowish pages until he stopped on a page that had been handwritten in 1926."

"Oh yes, here he is!" he cried.

"Did you find his name?" I asked.

"Yes, I did! In this record are written the name of the priest that baptized the twin brothers, the godfather's and godmother's names, the parents' names, and of course the names given to the twins, who were Antonio and Nunzio, born from Filippo Reggiani and Lucia Bruno. There is no doubt!"

"Could you tell me more about Antonio Reggiani? What did he do before emigrating to Latin America?"

"I don't know his life's story. Anything that I know is hearsay, but there is a person that can help you. You need to go to the monastery of the Capuchin Franciscan Friars near the entrance to the cemetery in Calascibetta. You'll find a very old monk there. It is said that he knows everything about Antonio Reggiani's life. He is ninety-four years old and his sight is not good at all."

"What is the name of the monk?" I asked.

"Father Massimiliano D'Antoni. I will call and inform him about your visit."

"The monastery of the Order of Friars Minor Capuchin was at the beginning of Via Giudea, in the ancient Jewish quarter of Calascibetta. It was a very large building with an attached chapel. A large adjoining gate was at the entrance to the cemetery. I rang the doorbell and waited for a short while. A long-legged, tall friar came and opened the door. His light eyes were covered with a whitish veil. A white stick on his hand helped him to move from room to room in the labyrinthine monastery, which appeared to be deserted at first glance.

"Kindred souls recognize each other at first sight! I had the feeling of meeting an old friend."

"Please, come in," he said, shaking my hand.

"Are you Father Massimiliano?"

"Yes, I am. Father Giordano has already informed me about your coming. I can tell you something about the Reggiani family, but we have plenty of time to talk. First, let me show you

the place where I have spent almost all my life," he said, smiling with his protruding lips.

"He led me to the large dining hall on the ground floor. There were about twenty tables, but only one had a cloth on it. Then, we passed through a corridor with cells on both sides. I looked into one of them where the door was open. It was furnished with a bed, a night table, a desk, and a statue of Saint Francis of Assisi standing on a small column. Inside, everything was clean and tidy. It seemed that those empty cells were waiting for new friars to come and stay there, but in vain! These days, people can't endure living a Franciscan life. Father Massimiliano said, 'Once this monastery had many monks, but now only two are left. I live here with another friar a bit younger than me. Let's go to the monastery library now.'"

"We passed a long corridor before arriving at the library."

"These volumes," he said, "are ancient and precious. We keep more than seven thousand volumes here. Some of them date back to the sixteenth century. They are mainly related to religion and medicine. Among the volumes you see, there is a small manuscript written by me. It contains information on the history of both Calascibetta and Enna, but it also has a few references to the Reggiani family.

"It is handwritten, but the writing is clear. When I wrote it, my hand didn't tremble as it does now. You can come here anytime if you want to read it, but it doesn't contain the whole story of Antonio Reggiani. If you want to know more details about him, you can ask two of his relatives that are still alive, although they are of advanced age. I will tell you their names and where you can find them, but for now, let's put aside Antonio Reggiani's life story. I want to show you our chapel, which contains a seventeenth-century altarpiece depicting the nativity scene with Maria holding the baby Jesus. It is an invaluable work of art."

"I liked the quiet and peaceful atmosphere of the monastery. I felt that monastic life was a doorway to get near God. Suddenly, the desire to become a Franciscan friar flashed in my mind. I wanted to ask Father Massimiliano to accept me as one of his monks, but soon I gave up such a thought. I felt I couldn't endure a secluded life. I thought life in a monastery was too boring and hard for me. On the other hand, the founder of the Franciscan order, Saint Francis of Assisi, didn't live a secluded life. He was a traveler and didn't only fix his mission in one place.

"Father Massimiliano seemed to have read my thoughts."

"I didn't always stay in the monastery. Besides being a monk, I was a teacher at the primary school in Calascibetta for about ten years, then I taught ancient Greek and literature at the high school in Enna for thirty years. Every day, I traveled from Calascibetta to Enna with my car. Teaching was like a mission for me. I wanted to hand down to my students what I had learned in many years of study. Even though I was a teacher, I kept abiding by my vow of poverty."

"Didn't you get a salary when you taught high school?" I asked.

"Yes, I received a good salary! But I always poured all my wages into the monastery's coffers. These days, I spend my old-age pension to maintain this cloister. With my pension, we pay the cleaners, maintenance men, and the bills for water, telephone, electricity, and gas. We spend the surplus to help needy people who knock on our door now and then."

"We then entered a large kitchen where a short and chubby monk was cooking something on one of the many stoves. 'Today you are our guest!' Father Massimiliano said. 'Friar Angelo will prepare a delicious dinner for us. Let's take a seat in the dining room and wait until dinner is ready!'

"The fog outside and the half-light in the empty dining room made me feel a bit gloomy. Surely, I wouldn't live in such solitude, but I admired those two monks who managed the monastery steadfastly.

"While we were sitting at one of the many tables in the dining room, Friar Angelo came to us with a large pot of steaming soup. 'This is a Franciscan soup!' he said, proud of himself. He poured two or three ladlesful of soup with stirred raw eggs and thin spaghetti divided into small pieces into the bowls. Father Massimiliano said it was a special Franciscan dish.

"Before starting our meal, he asked me to keep silent and meditate for a few minutes, giving thanks to God for the food we were about to eat. Then we made the sign of the cross. Father Massimiliano and Father Angelo seemed to enjoy the soup, but I found it disgusting. I had never eaten such a soup seasoned with raw stirred eggs, but I ate it all just not to displease them."

"Now, you had better return to Catania, because the weather is increasingly hazy. From tomorrow on, feel free to come here anytime and read the book that contains some pieces of information about Antonio Reggiani's life."

"The following day, early in the morning, I left Catania in my car and arrived at the Capuchin Franciscan Monastery about ninety minutes later.

"It took half a day to read the little manuscript about Antonio Reggiani's life. After I finished it, I thanked Father Massimiliano, who accompanied me to the exit of the monastery. 'To get further information about Antonio Reggiani, ask Ferdinando Bruno and Alessandro Buscemi. They are good Christians and relatives of Lucia Bruno and Antonio Reggiani. They know details about him that are not recorded in my manuscript,' said Father Massimiliano, who also handed me a sheet of paper with the addresses of the two persons he had mentioned.

"It was not easy for me to find them. One, Ferdinando Bruno, lived in a humble, small house partly inside a cave with a wide garden grown wild. As for Alessandro Buscemi, his condition was a bit better than Ferdinando's. He lived near the Royal Palatine Chapel and had a good relationship with Father Giordano. They were both very old, but their memories were still good. I met them four times and talked with them at length. They were very helpful. Thanks to them, I came to know a lot of details about Antonio Reggiani's mother, Lucia Bruno.

"Based on the manuscript written by Father Massimiliano and the information I got from Ferdinando Bruno and Alessandro Buscemi, I reconstructed Antonio Reggiani's life, and then I typed it. I bound the typewritten sheets and made a small book of about seventy pages. I have entitled it *The Wheel of Fortune*. I keep it in the lower drawer of this cupboard. Sometimes I reread it, for I find Antonio Reggiani's life adventurous and unique."

"Every life is unique. You cannot find two lives that match perfectly."

"Yes, you are right, but some lives are highly symbolic. As for that of Antonio Reggiani, it symbolizes the caducity of human achievements. Do you want me to read his life story for you?"

"Yes, I'd like to hear it."

"I want to have you as my guest for one week. I'll read ten pages a day of the book between one meal and another. Do you accept?"

"Yes, of course. Start reading it aloud right now. I am all ears."

Chapter Seven
The Wheel of Fortune

The Reggiani Family

Antonio Reggiani and his twin brother, Nunzio, were born into a family of small hardware dealers in Calascibetta. Their father, Filippo Reggiani, owned a store in Via San Michele, not far from the town center. He sold many kinds of goods: hardware, gas cylinders, articles for carpenters and bricklayers, and even coffins. Their home was above the store, to which it was connected by a spiral interior staircase. It was not a spacious house; it had two bedrooms, a bathroom, a kitchen with a table and a few chairs, a wood stove, a wood-burning oven, and a sink.

Even though his family was not needy, Filippo Reggiani couldn't afford to rent a room for his children to continue to study at the middle school in Enna. He had made many sacrifices to build his house, and he still had a lot of debt to pay off. Moreover, while building his house, he accidentally caused damage to the adjacent neighbor's property. Now he was in a dispute with them, who exaggerated the damage and wanted to profit from the incident. He needed money to pay the lawyer and make up for the actual damage. He just hoped that his financial situation would improve before his children finished primary school. Otherwise, there would be no hope for them to progress in their studies.

Filippo stood out for his stern look and thick mustache. He was tall and dark-skinned. His black eyes resembled those of a wolf and gave him an aggressive appearance. He was a resolute and short-tempered man with an iron will. He didn't like being contradicted by either the children or his wife.

However, sometimes he was capable of acting with great generosity.

While drinking a glass of good wine during meals at home, he loved to talk with Lucia about what had happened in his small store during the day. He had the bad habit of eating and speaking with his mouth full. Whenever he ate spaghetti with tomato sauce, he sucked it noisily and spread the sauce on the table and on the others' plates. This provoked Antonio's pent-up anger, who couldn't endure that bits of food and tomato sauce landed on his plate from his father's mouth, but he couldn't tell him that his way of eating was disgusting; he feared his father too much.

His wife, Lucia, had a completely different character from that of her husband. She was submissive to him and rarely spoke, for she was not happy with him and harbored a grudge against her relatives who had arranged her marriage to Filippo.

Conversation with her irascible husband was impossible, and her big emerald-green eyes often moistened with tears. Sometimes, she vented her frustration by telling her pains to Antonio and Nunzio, who were too young to know about unhappy marriages. They patiently listened to their mother's sad stories, which were full of resentment against her relatives, just so not to displease her.

Lucia used to spend her days cooking and doing the housework. Whenever she felt a bit relaxed, she knitted a sweater for her sons. On Sundays, she couldn't help going to Mass with her children to the chapel in the Capuchin Franciscan monastery. She had tried to convince her husband to accompany her to church, but all her efforts had failed, for he was a tremendous anticlerical.

When she was a girl, she used to attend the convent of the Franciscan sisters. She had learned to play the organ, and she dreamed that someday she would be able to accompany the lauds with this musical instrument. In fact, she wanted to become a nun.

The boys in Calascibetta vied with one another to have her as a girlfriend, but she was not interested in them. She considered sex a sin. Even now, her mind had not changed. Before having sex with Filippo, she made the sign of the cross, unseen by him in the darkness.

She was one of the most beautiful girls in her hometown. Her green eyes looked like two emeralds. She wore plain clothes, but her loose-fitting jackets and skirts couldn't completely hide the voluptuous curves of her gorgeous body. To appear more serious, she wore her hair bobbed.

Although she repressed her feelings and emotions, she couldn't help liking a handsome and cheerful boy called Silvano. He was chubby and loved playing football in Piazza Umberto. He was an incredible player. One day she saw him dribble past all his playmates. However, Lucia and Silvano never met. Silvano was younger than she was. On the other hand, she was also too involved with her religion to care about mundane relationships.

Silvano liked Lucia too. He wanted to approach her and reveal his love for her, but it was impossible. Lucia almost always walked the streets with her mother. On the rare occasions he saw her alone, she covered the distance from her house to the Franciscan convent as speedily as a hare, her eyes fixed on the street as if she wore blinkers. He was also too young for her. It seemed impossible that Lucia would become his girlfriend one day.

When he was a young adult, her voluptuous figure and sensual lips very often appeared to him in his dreams. He hugged and kissed her. She seemed to like him too, but it was just a dream! Reality was a different thing. By the time he was ready to propose to her, she was already engaged to Filippo. Their relatives had arranged the engagement.

Whenever he saw Lucia walking arm in arm with Filippo in Calascibetta's main square, he greeted him while at the same time casting a glance and a smile at her. In fact, Silvano fostered the secret, vain hope that sooner or later Lucia would leave Filippo. Such a thought was absurd! The marriage had already been set.

He noticed that Lucia blushed whenever she saw him. In his mind, it meant that she felt something for him. She actually did find him attractive, but she suppressed her emotions.

Although Lucia was already engaged to Filippo, Silvano would have continued to court her indefinitely, but one day he saw Lucia, her parents, Filippo's parents, and other relatives at the exit of the Royal Palatine Chapel. They had all been in the church to talk to the parish priest who would publish the banns. Now, Silvano's last hope was really gone! Fifteen days later, Lucia married Filippo.

At primary school, Antonio and Nunzio were two of the best students. They excelled in mathematics and always sat side by side at the same school desk. If the teacher separated them, they didn't like the change. They were undisciplined and inattentive to such an extent that the teacher made them sit at the same desk again.

Even though they were twins, their appearances were different. Antonio was of average height. His hair was uncommonly red, and his eyes were so blue and bright that they looked like seawater. Nunzio's hair was dark like his complexion, but his eyes were beautiful olive green, a bit similar to those of his mother. He was the tallest boy in the school, but his character was extremely mild. Whenever Antonio took the initiative, Nunzio followed him because he loved and esteemed his brother so much.

They finished elementary school with good marks. Two doors then stood before them: either helping their father at the store or going to work as apprentices of a carpenter or a builder. It was impossible for them to continue to study. They needed a considerable amount of money to stay with a host family in Enna. Their father wanted to help them, but he had no way out; he couldn't afford to enroll his children at the middle school in Enna. They were doomed to remain in their hometown until the end of their lives. But one day something unexpected happened. After dinner, Filippo told his family members to stay in the kitchen for a while, because he had important news to share.

"A few days ago," he said, "an old friend of mine came to my store. I hadn't seen him for decades. He moved to Enna a long time ago, but from time to time he comes to Calascibetta. His old house is still here, for he didn't sell it when he moved to Enna. I don't know who informed him, but he knows I have two smart sons. He would like my children to continue their studies, but he too finds it difficult to support his family. He is a carpenter, but his work is not continuous. Sometimes he has no job at all.

"'My dear old friend!' he said to me, 'I want to help you! I can host one of your sons in my family, but not both of them. Honestly, I can't afford it! At your choice, either Antonio or Nunzio can come and stay with us in Enna to continue to study. My wife and I will treat him as if he were our son. We have no children, and your son will be our joy. You don't have to pay for our hospitality. I know that my proposal is heartrending for your sons; they are twins and they don't like to be separated, but something is better than nothing! It is preferable that at least one of them goes on in his life instead of both giving up study.'

"I was quite hesitant about accepting his proposal. After having pondered on it, I came to the conclusion that my friend was right. I agree with him. Therefore, I want at least one of my sons to continue his studies. After middle school, he will be able to go to commercial technical school. I want him to become an accountant in the future. Obviously, I cannot say who of you will remain in Calascibetta. You are my children, and I love you both equally. Therefore, it is up to you to decide what to do," Filippo said.

Even the evilest and harshest man has a soul and a heart which harbors emotions and feelings of goodness! Filippo's eyes moistened with choked-back tears. A hot lump in his throat prevented him from continuing to talk. His wife, not accustomed to thwarting her husband since their wedding, sat motionless, repressing her emotions. Antonio and Nunzio looked at each other for a few moments. Then Nunzio turned up his eyes to the ceiling as if he wanted to get his inspiration from heaven. Nobody in the room felt like opening their mouth to say something.

"Antonio will go to Enna! He will study there, and I am sure he will become a good accountant! I'll continue to live in Calascibetta. I am strong and sturdy, so I will go to work at a bricklayer," Nunzio said, looking his father in the eye to show him that he was more mature than him.

A few minutes of absolute silence followed. Antonio was torn by two opposing feelings. On the one hand, he was happy to be allowed to move into the host family in Enna and continue his studies. On the other hand, he didn't like the idea of leaving Nunzio in Calascibetta. He didn't say anything, nor did he counter Nunzio's proposal. It seemed that he had accepted what Nunzio had said.

"Okay, Antonio will go to Enna!" said Filippo with a voice broken by sadness. "Tomorrow I'll write a letter to my friend, and I will tell him that we were unanimous in deciding that Antonio will move to Enna."

The family meeting ended. Everybody went to bed with a bitter taste and the feeling that an injustice had been committed.

That night, Antonio could barely sleep. He tossed and turned in bed. Whenever he dozed, the generous figure of his brother appeared to him in a dream. Nunzio's clothes seemed to be spattered with mud, his hands were chapped from handling lime and cement, and his shoulders were bent by the weight of the bricks. How could he opt for such an awful choice! Suddenly, he woke up and found himself sitting on the bed. He was perspiring all over and breathing heavily when an idea flashed through his mind. He found the solution to get out of the dark tunnel!

He jumped out of the bed and ran barefoot to wake his brother.

"Wake up! Wake up, Nunzio!" he said, shaking Nunzio's shoulders with his little hands.

"What happened to you? Why do you wake me up in the middle of the night? I was sleeping peacefully!"

"I don't want to move to Enna without you. Let's go and study together there!"

"How is it possible? Didn't you listen to what our father said? There is no room for both of us. Unfortunately, only one of us can stay with the host family. We have no choice!"

"I have got the solution to our problem! We'll walk along the valley and then take the path that leads to Enna. It is so easy!"

"Are you joking? Our father will never allow us to go to Enna on foot by ourselves. It is dangerous. We are just children! How can we?"

"Nunzio, keep in mind that I'll not go to school if you are not with me!"

At last, Nunzio yielded to his brother's insistence and agreed to discuss the matter with their father the following day.

It was lunchtime. While eating, Antonio worked up the courage to talk with his father.

"We'll go to middle school together. Nunzio and I will walk from Calascibetta to Enna!"

Father opened his eyes wide and then exploded. "Are you crazy? You will go nowhere without my permission! I have already decided! Only you will go to Enna! As for Nunzio, he will find a job in Calascibetta or will help me in the store! The issue is closed!"

His voice thundered so loudly and furiously that it made the children's blood run cold.

Silence, disappointment, and frustration pervaded the dining room. There was nothing to do! The twins were doomed to be separated. Undoubtedly, it was unjust that Nunzio had his wings cut, but what to do? This is life! To some it brings good gifts and to someone else it gives just disappointments.

All of a sudden, a voice never heard before with such determination resounded in the room. "The children will both go to Enna!" Lucia burst out with a grating, loud voice. She banged the table with her fist so hard that the glasses and dishes on the table rattled, making the wine spill over.

Years and years of submission to her husband had not been able to quell her willpower, which now was fueled by the love for her children. Suddenly, she exploded like a pressure cooker.

Filippo was caught off guard. He could never have imagined that his submissive, silent, religious, chaste wife would burst with such anger. He felt paralyzed. It was as if a devastating earthquake was upsetting his mental rigidity, his pride, his beliefs, and his role as a father-leader. Then a sudden flash lit up his mind. For the first time in his life, he thought about love. Yes, it had been the love for her son Nunzio that had triggered such an unexpected reaction in his wife. Nunzio was the son Lucia held dearest. She was crazy about him. How could she allow him, the best student in his class, to go work with the bricklayers?

Filippo was tempted to slap her and stood up, but the children ran toward her mother to shield her with their bodies. Lucia and her sons stood stock-still on the opposite side of the table, hugging one another. Antonio and Nunzio shivered with fear, while Lucia stood firmly, determined to hold her stance. She fixed her cold eyes on those of her aggressive husband, denoting that she could do anything for her children, like a tigress that protects her cubs.

Filippo went purple with rage; his eyes were bulging out of their sockets. He felt paralyzed. He didn't have the strength to move forward. At last, he bent his knees and sat down again. He realized that an act of violence against his wife and children would bring him dishonor. They would hate him for the rest of their lives. He couldn't take the chance of losing everything he had—that is, the love of his family. He inevitably had to admit defeat.

Suddenly, Antonio and Nunzio, sensing that victory was in hand, ran to hug their father, took him by the hand, and led him to their mother. Hot tears of joy flowed down their cheeks. Love blossomed in the home!

Back to sitting at the table, they tried to discuss the issue calmly.

"It snows in Enna in the winter, and once in a while in Calascibetta too. Whenever it happens, the valley and the trails to Enna are icy. How will you protect yourselves from the cold?" Filippo asked his children with a worried look.

"I'll knit sweaters, woolen socks, gloves, and mufflers, so that the children don't feel cold," Lucia said, beaming with excitement.

"What will they do if they come across stray animals? Especially in winter, packs of hungry wild dogs attack sheep pens. Children also are exposed to danger."

"I am strong," said Nunzio, "and I'll make mincemeat of wolves with my staff!"

Filippo burst into belly laughter. "Listen to me, Lucia! You have been a housewife for too long. Now the time has come for you to change your life radically. You will be a businesswoman instead of a housewife!"

Lucia looked at Filippo incredulously. "I will be a businesswoman? What do you mean?" she asked.

"I will walk Nunzio and Antonio up to Enna. You will take charge of our store!"

Lucia couldn't imagine such a sudden metamorphosis of a man who had been harsh until a few moments ago and now was sweeter than honey. Her courage and determination to stand up to the dictatorship of her husband prevailed at last. Now she would no longer be a housewife. Before today, her feelings, opinions, and creativeness had been quenched by her own cowardice. A new wide road with many unfathomable and unpredictable branches was opening before her eyes.

Enraptured, she gazed at Filippo as if he were the shining sun that was defrosting and bringing her abilities back to life. Since she'd been a little girl, she had always been conditioned by her father and then by her husband. Now she wanted to get rid of her old suppressed personality.

I want to change myself! I want to begin a new life!

Lucia the Businesswoman

"The school will open in ten days," said Filippo.

"You must begin your training right away. You'll have to run the store with the opening of school."

"Yes, I am ready to start right now," said Lucia, who looked as thrilled as a charged wind-up doll.

"No, let's start tomorrow. There is a fair in Calascibetta. What about going there? While we hang around the booths, Antonio and Nunzio can play with other children there."

"Hurray! Hurray!" cried out Antonio and Nunzio. It seemed to be the best day in their lives.

Lucia spent the whole night tossing and turning in her bed. She couldn't sleep because she was so thrilled! At dawn, she got dressed, ready for her new life. After breakfast, she ran down the internal staircase, opened the door, and reached her husband in the store.

"First of all, you have to study the whole range of products we deal with and what each item is used for. Keep in mind that the secret to being a good seller is to know well the items you sell. If a customer asks you something about the item he is going to purchase, you have to answer well. Nobody buys anything blindly," said Filippo.

Lucia hung on her husband's every word. It was as if she were back to being a schoolgirl, eager to learn everything soon.

"After you know the products and the prices, we will pass to the second stage. You will learn how to make payments to suppliers and keep the accounts. This will not be difficult for you," continued Filippo.

Lucia placed a desk near the counter and sat there to study the information sheets attached to the products.

Entering the store, the customers looked at Lucia with surprise. At that time, most women spent their lives at home. Lucia was one of the few women in Calascibetta to work outside the home. She was thirty-five years old by then, but her beauty, and above all her buxomness, had not faded at all.

As the days went by, the customers in the store got used to seeing her sitting behind the counter. They asked her directly, instead of Filippo, for information on the articles they intended to purchase. Some items were exhibited in front of the counter; others were placed on the shelves in the back of the store. Lucia managed to get the customers the articles they needed, regardless of where they were placed. In fact, after a few days of apprenticeship, she knew almost everything about the placement of the items in the store. Ten days later, Lucia was able to take over the business from her husband.

It was October 1, the first day of school! Filippo and his children set off when it was dark. Nobody walked in the street. Calascibetta was asleep. The lights in the streets were dim. It was a starry night, and the half-moon was like a lamp over the valley that separated Calascibetta from Enna.

Walking through the deserted streets in Calascibetta made Filippo feel more comfortable. If his fellow citizens had seen him and his children walking towards Enna before dawn, they would have thought he had gone out of his mind. Gossip from person to person would have annoyed him more than the difficulty in finding an easy path through the valley. No one had ever done such madness before!

They walked towards the countryside. The valley spread out before their eyes, and Enna appeared covered with low clouds in the distance. They had to find the shortest way to cross the valley and then reach Enna. Walking the wrong path would have led them astray. Olive groves gleamed under the half-moon light. The densely overgrown ground didn't let them catch sight of any path to follow. They could have walked on the road, but it would have taken hours. They needed to find a shortcut.

Filippo was about to give up this absurd venture, but his children spurred him to go on. Then he recalled that an angel in human form had always appeared to rescue him in his life whenever he had to confront an obstacle that seemed to be impossible to overcome. He had gotten over many difficult situations in the past. Even this time, he would succeed. All he needed was to just wait calmly and trust Providence.

He held hands with his children and kept looking for the right shortcut to follow, but he couldn't find it. Hot beads of sweat dripped from his forehead. The undergrowth of weeds and brambles was too thick. It was really impossible to go on.

All of a sudden, they heard a sound of heavy, slow footsteps. They turned back to see the source of that sound. An old white-haired man appeared as if by magic. He was coming down from Calascibetta on his donkey. His eyes were half-closed. The reins were loose in his hands. He swung on the ass, which seemed to know where to go. Suddenly, the animal pricked up its long ears and let out a bray, which aroused the farmer from his slumber. At the unusual sight, he started in fear. Calascibetta was full of ghost stories. He thought that those figures were maybe ghosts.

The frightened farmer's body stiffened. He would have changed his way if it had been possible, but his donkey, accustomed to treading the same path, walked straight. Now it was too close to those he had mistaken for ghosts to change direction. In the twilight, he rubbed his eyes to see better and was stunned to see some familiar faces.

"What are you doing here with your sons at this ungodly hour, Filippo? I thought you were evil ghosts!"

Filippo knew the old man. From time to time, he came to his store to buy shoes for his she-ass or tools for his work in the countryside. He was known to his fellow citizens under the nickname Farmer Peppe. He was serious and taciturn. Unlike most customers, he never asked for a discount on what he bought, nor did he linger in the store to chat with Filippo. He always hurried away after purchasing something. People in Calascibetta said he was under his wife's thumb. Whenever he went back home from the countryside, his wife waited for him in front of the doorway with a broom in hand, ready to strike her husband if he didn't bring enough food.

Filippo considered him a godsend.

"I am looking for a shortcut to Enna. I am walking my children to school there. I have enrolled them at middle school. This is their first day at school," Filippo answered.

"You are a lucky man. I own a patch of land next to the slope of Enna. I know a passage to get there safely. You are very lucky!" said Farmer Peppe, stressing Filippo's good luck.

The children and Filippo let out a sigh of relief.

It's true! God never forsakes those who have even a bit of faith! Filippo said to himself.

Farmer Peppe dismounted and ordered his she-ass not to move. The communion between the two was astonishing. Apparently, Farmer Peppe loved his she-ass more than his wife. He stroked Caterina—this was the she-ass's name—and chatted with her as if she were his girlfriend.

"Let's put the children on Caterina! We will walk behind them. She knows the path to get to my land and doesn't need reins. She knows what to do, even if I don't say anything to her. She can read my thoughts and figure out what I want from her. Now, let's go to Enna right away. Otherwise, the little boys will be late for school!" said Farmer Peppe, gently patting Caterina on her back.

While Caterina was walking amid rustling shrubs and bushes with Antonio and Nunzio on her back, Farmer Peppe and Filippo were getting acquainted with each other.

"Why are you walking with a little limp? Do you want to mount Caterina's back as well?" asked Filippo.

"No, I don't! I am okay. My limping is a mark of the First World War. In those days, we soldiers kept our legs dipped in the Piave River for a long time, so as not to allow the Austrian army to invade the Po Valley. The cold water of the river froze my legs. At first, I couldn't walk at all, but then I gradually regained the use of my lower limbs. I am fine now, although I have a limp.

"I go to my land every day, except on Sundays, which I devote to resting and attending Mass at the chapel of the monastery of the Franciscan friars. A very young friar named Father Massimiliano celebrates Mass. Whenever he preaches, he touches my heart. I have the feeling that he knows what happens inside me. Do you want to join me? We can go to Mass together this Sunday."

"I don't know. I have never been into a church except for my baptism, my wedding, and the baptism of my children. Once in a while, I go to church to attend the funeral of a friend or a relative of mine. I believe in God, but I don't follow any rites," answered Filippo, puzzled by Farmer Peppe's words.

Filippo was about to say that religion is matter for women and weak people, but he held his tongue for fear of hurting Farmer Peppe's feelings. Then he realized that their encounter had not been by chance. Maybe heaven had arranged their meeting to help him and his sons. Farmer Peppe would have been disappointed if he had declined his invitation. Filippo couldn't afford to lose his help to get his sons to school.

"Okay, I'll come with you to Mass. What time does it start?" Filippo asked

"At ten o'clock in the morning!" answered Farmer Peppe, with his eyes beaming with joy.

"I'll pick you up at your home at nine thirty. Let's go together to the Franciscan monastery chapel," said Filippo.

Farmer Peppe, who was used to spending his time alone except when he stayed at home with his shrewish wife, was grateful to Filippo, who gave him the chance to be with someone.

"After school," he said with a smile, "you can eat something in my humble little house, and then we will go back to Calascibetta, the children on Caterina's back and we on foot. We can do so every day until the end of the school year!"

Filippo could not believe his ears! That lonely old farmer, who seemed to be a useless man, was like an angel who had come down from heaven to help him.

"By the way," asked Filippo, "what about your wife? Does she go to Mass as well?"

"Unfortunately not! She is an atheist. She is convinced that religion is opium for the masses."

"My wife will make her change her mind! I will ask her to meet your wife. There is no Catholic more eager and authentic than my wife. As a little girl, she used to attend the Franciscan convent. She would have entered a convent for sure if she had not met me. Every night she says her prayers. If you pay me a visit someday, you will see all kinds of statues and portraits of saints in my home. Now she manages our store. I trust her very much. She is an honest woman who loves me and her children immensely. She would do the impossible to make us happy."

"Don't you think that a rude customer, seeing her alone in the store, may harass her? She is a good-looking lady!"

"I don't think so. My wife is very serious when she works. Nobody dares to molest her. Furthermore, everyone in Calascibetta knows I am a bad-tempered man. I would react badly against whomever showed disrespect to her."

Even though Farmer Peppe had been in a state of solitude for a long time, he could sometimes perceive real life clearer than those who were plunged in worldliness. In his opinion, Filippo trusted his wife too much. He should not give her so much freedom. Anyway, it was none of his business!

Within half an hour, they arrived at Farmer Peppe's plot of land. The children dismounted, Farmer Peppe took Caterina to the stable, and then he tied her to the manger.

"Now we can go!"

"Where?"

"To Enna!" answered Farmer Peppe. "Today, I will walk you there to show you the way. From tomorrow on, you will go there by yourselves."

Farmer Peppe's farm was near Enna. They followed a narrow path that led to the upper town, and in the space of fifteen minutes they caught sight of the first houses. The school was not far away.

At that very moment in Calascibetta, Lucia was behind the counter of the store to serve the customers. Builders and farmers used to go to work at daybreak, so she had to start working early in the morning if she wanted to sell something to them. She would settle the accounts late in the morning, because after nine there were no customers in the store.

She had got up very early to make breakfast for Filippo and the children before they set off towards Enna, but she was not sleepy at all. On the contrary, she felt livelier and more alert than ever. Today she was the store manager and wanted to show her husband that she was a good seller. She had lived as a slave for more than ten years of marriage. Now she smelled the scent of freedom. She felt self-confident and strong.

She dressed in a simple way: a wide skirt and purple blouse. Her clean, beautiful face showed no makeup. Her turgid lips were reddish naturally. Her harmonious body smelled of freshness and innocence.

I am a woman capable of running a business! I am not a slave! she said to herself, clenching her fists.

Her first day of work was not going bad. In the early morning, she had sold many items: nails, hoes, pickaxes, and so on. Now she was going to start to work on the accounts.

Everything looked calm and peaceful in the store, but a young mason was standing on the corner of the street waiting for the right moment to enter the store when there were no customers inside. He was Silvano, the only boy for whom Lucia had had some liking when she was a girl. Everybody in Calascibetta called him by his nickname, Fimminaru, which means playboy. They nicknamed him that because he liked women and easily conquered their hearts. Almost every month he was seen in Piazza Umberto with a new girlfriend.

Eleven years had gone by since Lucia had married Filippo. The young mason Silvano had grown handsome. His hair was black and curly like a ram's head. He wore a clipped mustache. His features made the girls in Calascibetta go crazy for him. He was tall, his legs were as strong as two pillars, and his arms were like two boughs.

In the early morning, he had seen Filippo and his children walking towards Enna. Therefore, he was sure that Lucia had been left alone in the store.

He kept standing in a side alley inconspicuously. At the right time, when there were no customers in the store, he entered the store.

Taking off his hat, he greeted Lucia with a deep bow. "Good morning, Mrs. Lucia! I have never seen such a beautiful lady in a hardware store!"

Hearing his words, Lucia had a sudden blush, but she was too much involved in her work to respond to the young man's flattery.

"Don't you go to work today, Silvano? All masons and farmers are at work at this time!"

"I am working too. I just left my building site for a few minutes to buy a special tool at your store."

"I am here to serve you! Tell me which tool you need."

"I want to buy a handsaw to cut a few planks." Fimminaru knew that this tool was kept in the back of the shop and Lucia would meet with some difficulties to find it.

"Wait a moment here. I'll go to the rear to get the handsaw for you."

The back of the shop was separated from the counter area by a thick, brown curtain that Filippo had set there, though no one knew why. Maybe by doing so, he wanted to prevent customers from seeing the wares he kept in the back of the store. The curtain was always dusty and dirty. More than once, Lucia had asked Filippo to remove it, or at least to wash it, but he always had postponed that.

Lucia rummaged through the items scattered on the shelves and on the floor to no avail. As Fimminaru had foreseen, she couldn't find a handsaw. So, she returned to the counter with empty hands.

"I cannot find it! It is probably sold out. However, as soon as I see Filippo, I'll ask him to look for this item. If he finds the handsaw you need, I'll keep it here under the counter and tomorrow you can get it. Okay? Now, it is time for you to go to work."

"I know where it is kept. I once went to the rear of the shop with your husband. I remember exactly where he keeps handsaws. Please, let me go inside and I'll point it out to you."

Lucia looked at him waveringly. Her husband had ordered her not to allow anybody to go to the rear of the shop, because there were shoplifters in Calascibetta. Sometimes customers stole small tools whenever he allowed them to get in.

"It is very easy to find the handsaw. I know precisely where it is! It will take just one minute to get it," Fimminaru insisted while his heart was racing.

"I cannot allow you to get into the stockroom. My husband forbade me to let customers in!"

"Let's go together!"

Lucia was more and more hesitant. The rear of the store was a bit dark, and it would be easy for him to steal something. All her concern was for a possible theft, not for anything else.

Then Fimminaru knelt on one knee with his hands folded and kept begging Lucia. "I cannot work today without a handsaw. I really need it. Please, help me!"

He was such an actor that his eyes even moistened. His countenance was so beautiful and sincere that he looked like an angel.

Lucia was a kind and simple soul. She wanted to please everyone. Once again, she looked into his moistened black eyes. They had something magnetic, like those of some species of snake that immobilizes its prey with its stare before darting on it, but his overall look didn't give her the feeling he was a bad man. On the contrary, Fimminaru seemed to be a nice guy and an honest worker. He was definitely not a thief. He was too innocent.

I can trust him! However, when we are in the rear, I will be alert, to prevent him from stealing something, Lucia said to herself.

"Okay, if you know where the handsaws are kept, let's go inside together. You go first. I will walk behind you," she at last naively said.

Fimminaru rubbed his hands and licked his lips, pleased with himself for convincing Lucia. Before going through the curtain, he had a quick look at the street to make sure it was deserted. Then he stepped over the curtain, followed by Lucia.

They passed through two rows of shelves and walked up to the last shelf near the back wall. It was the place where Filippo kept the tools for carpenters.

"Look! The handsaw is on the upper shelf. Now, I'll lift you up and you can take it."

He didn't give Lucia the time to get a ladder, because he quickly lifted her with his powerful arms.

"Can you see the handsaw?" he asked.

"Yes, I already have it in my hand. Now put me down immediately!"

As soon as Lucia put her feet on the floor, he abruptly hugged and kissed her, sealing her lips with his and moving his tongue around hers.

Lucia was taken aback. At first, she tried to hold back the young mason. She put her hands against his chest, but as he continued to kiss her and kept his tongue stuck to hers, Lucia's arms gradually loosened. Her hands dropped, and she finally let him kiss her. Seeing that Lucia was about to lose her self-control, the bastard, swifter than a bird of prey, put his arm round her waist and lifted her. Then he pulled her skirt up, took off her panties with the other free hand, and immediately inserted his penis into her vagina. Lucia felt short of breath. Now she was at Silvano's mercy. He tossed her up and down until his warm sperm flooded her vagina. At last he lowered her, still kissing her for a while. He had already satisfied his desire to make love to her. Silvano had finally conquered her!

Lucia felt as if that sudden, unexpected accident led her to a dark, unexplored planet full of traps. Now it depended on her not to fall into further pitfalls. Her mind was clouded and confused. She had the sensation of wandering in the clouds. Black storm clouds enveloped her head, but she had not completely lost the light of reason.

"Remember this. If you tell anybody what happened to us, I'll kill you with my hands! We keep a revolver at home. If my husband and children come to know about our sexual happening, I'll shoot you dead. Now, swear that you will keep silent, and then leave this place immediately, because a customer may come and see you here!" Lucia said in a tremulous yet firm voice.

"I swear, Lucia! Nobody will come to know about our love! Give me one last kiss!"

He gave Lucia a kiss that seemed to be interminable. Their hearts pounded one close to the other, as if they were a drum beaten from both sides. Lucia put her arms around his neck, but suddenly she disentangled from him.

"I love you, Lucia!"

"Don't talk nonsense! I am a married woman with two children. You should have proposed marriage to me before I got married. Now it is too late."

"I wanted to talk with you then, but you refused to even look at me. Your intention was to become a nun, but I love you still."

"It is impossible! Please go away immediately. If a customer enters the store and hears that we are talking about love behind the curtain, I am ruined."

"Okay, I am going, but keep in mind that I'll return to you."

"No, please! Don't come anymore!"

After Fimminaru left, Lucia should have gone back to the counter to finish settling the accounts, but she couldn't. She was badly upset. Her eyes, lips, and face were swollen and clearly showed that something unusual had happened to her. What to do? She decided to close the store for a while and go home through the inner staircase.

She went to the bathroom to wash her vagina. That irresponsible, mad Fimminaru had ejaculated inside her! What would happen if he had made her pregnant? What if the baby were the spitting image of Fimminaru? The thought of being pregnant with his child shook her like a reed amid strong wind. Would she pretend that Filippo was the father of the newborn? Her husband trusted her a lot, and she had repaid him with adultery!

What a thoughtless woman she had been! But how could she resist Silvano's kisses? His lips were sweeter than honey, his arms and chest vibrated with passion, and his whole body spurred her to enjoy that unique moment of real pleasure. It was an irresistible temptation!

Arabs know well how weak a woman's heart is. That is why they make their wives stay at home and cover their faces whenever they go out! she thought bitterly.

Everything had happened so suddenly. Her first day of work unexpectedly turned into her adultery day! She would never confess the sin to a priest, not even to Father Massimiliano, whom she esteemed and trusted. She was too ashamed of what she had done.

Now it was time to find a remedy. She had to keep calm, hoping that Silvano would keep silent. She had to open the shop again as soon as possible so as not to arouse suspicion. Filippo, Nunzio, and Antonio would come back home in the afternoon. At that time, everything should appear normal and ordinary, as if nothing had happened to her. Her face looked disturbed now, but she would be relaxed on their arrival.

Supposing that she was not with child, everything would be resolved, but there was a big issue left. If Silvano came to the store again under the same circumstances, would she be able to resist the temptation of having sex with him? Of course not! Now she was under his spell. On seeing him crossing the threshold of the store, she would soon head for the rear, even beckoning him to follow her, and then let him do whatever he liked with her body.

That young mason bewitched her. He penetrated into her mind like a worm and gnawed at it continuously. She couldn't help thinking of him, his strength, virility, and paralyzing gaze.

Some time ago, a happening similar to hers had happened in Calascibetta. A young couple, Raffaele D'Alessandro and Filomena Perticaro, had opened a bar on a square in Calascibetta. The husband ran the confectionery, while the wife minded the cash desk. The business went very well, but one day Filomena fell in love with a customer who was no good. They became lovers and met secretly. However, everybody in Calascibetta but Raffaele knew about their love affair. At last, she lost her head over her lover, to such an extent that she was willing to do anything to please him.

As he was a bad guy, he asked her to lend him money. Hence, she convinced her husband to lend a large amount of money to that scoundrel, who never gave it back. The unlucky couple fell short of money. They were forced to close down their bar, and then they emigrated to Switzerland to make a living.

At that time, the puritanical Lucia had stigmatized Filomena's immoral conduct. She had even occasionally chatted with Filippo about the shameful Filomena's adultery.

"Why doesn't Filomena go to church to confess her adultery?" she asked Filippo, who laughed at Lucia's question.

Ironically, she had fallen into the same sin.

Never be shocked at others' behavior! The chaste, Catholic Lucia, who was about to become a nun, has become worse than Filomena, an adulteress like her. This is life! Lucia thought disconsolately.

However, for the time being, she had to try to be cool and tackle the problems one by one.

Time flies very fast, and soon Filippo and the children would come back home. The first thing to do was to recover her serene look. She washed her face once more, put some lip balm on her lips, and went downstairs to reopen the store. Fortunately, no more customers came in, so she was able to finish settling the accounts.

Lucia and Farmer Peppe's Wife

In the early afternoon, Farmer Peppe, Filippo, and Antonio and Nunzio on Caterina crossed the valley to return to Calascibetta.

The kids had spent their first day of school getting acquainted with their teachers and new schoolmates. While they were at school, Filippo bought the textbooks for them. From the next day on, they would start studying earnestly.

Lucia closed the shop a little earlier to prepare dinner for her hungry children and husband. She cooked pasta with potatoes, garlic, and cabbage, a dish they enjoyed a lot.

When they ran home, they found the table already set. They hugged one another and sat down to dinner, as had happened every day in the past, but this time Lucia had not disposed the cutlery properly while laying the table. She had omitted putting a spoon next to Antonio's bowl, which had never happened before.

Antonio, without saying a word, stared at her mother, got up from the table, and headed for the cupboard to get his spoon. His mother looked a bit absentminded in his eyes, but neither Filippo nor Nunzio noticed any change in her look.

"Do you know Farmer Peppe's wife?" Filippo asked Lucia with his mouth full of half-chewed pasta.

"Yes, I know her. She is the most waspish woman I have ever known. I think she is the only woman in Calascibetta that never goes to church. She is a she-devil. Poor Farmer Peppe goes to church alone on Sundays. He sits on a pew near ours. He is a lonely man. I have never seen him talk to anyone, but when I see him, I greet him, and he responds to my greeting. He is really an earnest Catholic!"

"I promised him that you would try to convince his wife to come to church this Sunday. I will come to Mass too."

"This is really good news! I never ever expected that you would set foot in a church."

"Farmer Peppe has been very helpful to us. Without his help, it would have been impossible for us to cross the valley. The undergrowth was too thick. I tried hard to find a path to go on, but I couldn't. I was about to give up the attempt to reach Enna on foot when Farmer Peppe miraculously appeared to us and showed us the path to safely cross the valley. Although he was limping, he walked with me on foot through the path, while Antonio and Nunzio sat on the back of his she-ass. He also offered us a meal in his little house in the countryside and promised me that he would guide us through the valley for the entire school year. Don't you think he deserves a small favor from you?"

"Yes, of course! I'd be happy to help him; the problem is that his wife is a bit sour. It will not be easy for me to convince her to come to church, but I'll do my best to convert her to Catholicism!"

"You don't need to convert her. Just try and convince her to come to Mass on Sundays. That's all."

"Okay, tomorrow I will go to her house."

The following day, after the peak hour in the store had passed, Lucia left her workplace and headed for Farmer Peppe's home. As soon as she knocked on the main door, she heard a terrifying voice similar to that of an ogress.

"Who is there?"

Lucia shivered with agitation, but she soon pulled herself together and strove to keep calm. She answered with a conversational, affable tone, "I am Lucia, Filippo Reggiani's wife."

A woman with a muscular body, an aquiline nose, dark-haired, and wearing a chignon full of long hairpins came down the stairs with heavy and hurried footsteps and opened the door. If she had not worn an apron and a long skirt, it would have been quite difficult to recognize her as a woman. As soon as she saw Lucia, she made her irritation quite plain, for she was not used to having visits from strangers.

"I have a lot of things to do at home and have no time to lose! What do you want?"

Lucia didn't lose heart. Her face was relaxed and smiling. Her smile was her best bet.

"Good morning, wife Angelina! Your husband has been very kind to my children and my husband. This morning, he accompanied my children to Enna for their first day of school. If it weren't for him, my children and husband wouldn't have been able to cross the valley. I have baked and just taken out of the wood-burning oven this fruitcake. I want to give it to you just to return your husband's favor."

Angelina's face softened with the fragrance of the freshly baked fruitcake. The door she was about to slam in Lucia's face opened slowly, so Lucia entered the yard with the fruitcake in her hands.

"What did my husband do for you? Don't you know he is a good-for-nothing?"

"I don't think so! He was like an angel from heaven who came to show my children the way to go to school. Now they go to school every day, thanks to him."

"Thank you for your gift. I like cakes very much! I have no children; on the other hand, my husband spends almost all his time in the countryside, so for whom should I make cakes?"

"I very often bake cakes for my husband and children. From now on, whenever I take cakes out of the wooden-burning oven, I will put one away for you. By the way, do you like buns? I guess yes! I am sure we will become good friends."

Angelina seemed to be stunned by Lucia's gracefulness and by her smile; frankly, such an extraordinary encounter had never happened to her. It was as if a fairy from a distant Nordic country had come to visit her in the courtyard of her humble house in Calascibetta.

At that point, Lucia was about to ask her to go to church together this Sunday, but she held her tongue. She thought that such a hasty invitation addressed to an atheist could give rise to a curt refusal. Furthermore, Angelina could have thought that the gift of the fruitcake was not spontaneous but had been done for the mere purpose of getting something in exchange. In this case, the frail thread of liking that Angelina had for her would have been broken irreparably.

I have three more days at my disposal to convince Angelina to come to church. During that time, I'll try to get more acquainted with her and will come to know something more about her tastes, Lucia thought.

"I see you have nice hairpins. A few months ago I made a lot of laced hair clips. If you don't mind, next time I come here I'd be happy to give you one."

"You can come here anytime, Lucia."

Lucia had gotten to Angelina's heart! Now she had to find another gift that would be appealing to her new friend. She thought to present Angelina with a fine cotton apron that she had laced a long time ago.

The following day, after the frenzy of two days before, everything seemed to go smoothly in the store. Silvano had not come to upset Lucia. During the lunch break, Lucia put on her shawl and went to Angelina's home. This time, the front door was open. She stepped into the courtyard and called out, "Angelina! Angelina!"

"I am coming! Sit down on the bench," answered Angelina while hanging out the laundry in the backyard.

Lucia took a seat on the bench waiting for Angelina, who came after a few minutes.

"I have brought several laced hairpins of various colors and an apron. I laced them with my own hands. It took a year to finish the work. All these are for you. I hope you like them. If not, I can take them back home."

At the sight of what Lucia had brought, Angelina was speechless with joy. For the first time in her life, she felt affection and admiration for another woman. Hitherto, she had lived in a state of separation from the world and all humans; now she was tasting the pleasure of friendship.

"What a wonderful gift! How can I ever repay your sweetness! I am too excited!" said Angelina with a voice broken with emotion.

Lucia felt the approaching victory. In the following two days, she would bring more gifts to open Angelina's heart, and then finally she would ask her to come to Mass.

"I have enjoyed sewing since I was a little girl. I am so skilled that I can sew a dress. Let me take your measurements. I have good cotton fabric at home. I assure you that within two days you will have a wonderful dress."

Angelina exploded with joy and hugged Lucia tightly.

"I've always dressed in rags. I never imagined I'd wear a new dress."

"Life is changeable. Sometimes it brings us nice surprises. Let me take your measurements, Angelina."

Lucia took Angelina's measurements for the new dress and then hurried home to tailor it. She worked all night on it, and the following day she brought Angelina the basted dress to check whether it fit her or not. Moreover, she gave her a chiffon scarf.

When Angelina saw the scarf, and above all the basted dress, she quivered with joy. She had a fitting and went to look at herself in the mirror. The pale-blue dress lit her face and enhanced her faded beauty. Now she looked like a different woman. The grim, old, and manlike woman of three days ago had turned into a graceful figure.

Angelina hugged Lucia with her strong arms and whispered in her ear, "Today you have made me happy!"

Everything was going well, just as Lucia had planned. She was sure that Angelina, seeing the gorgeous dress on her body, would have had no problem whatsoever accepting the invitation to come to church.

On Saturday, the day that preceded their going to Mass, early in the morning, Lucia baked some biscuits. She would introduce the theme about going to church while drinking a cup of coffee and crunching the biscuits with Angelina.

"Your dress is ready. Let's munch these biscuits first, and then you'll try it on," said Lucia as soon as she entered Angelina's home.

Angelina laid a cloth on the stone table in the courtyard and then headed for the kitchen.

"Let's have a cup of coffee with the biscuits. I made coffee while waiting for you," Angelina said.

While they were eating the biscuits and sipping their coffee, Lucia thought it was the right moment to ask Angelina to come to church.

"Tomorrow, your husband, my children, my husband, and I will go to Mass in the chapel of the Franciscan monastery. Will you join us? Shall we meet there or here?" asked Lucia with a perky voice, expecting that Angelina would say yes.

"No! Not at all!" said Angelina as furiously as if a swarm of bees had stung her. Hearing the word Mass was as if holy water had been sprinkled on a she-devil.

"Never and never! Priests will not see me attending their rites. Religions have been invented to deceive people. Religion is a poison. You can find God in your heart, not outside. The priesthood is the richest class in Calascibetta. Didn't you know that? They preach chastity and say that sex is a sin, but as everybody knows, all priests have their own illicit relationships. Don't believe in what priests say, Lucia. They are deceivers! Ask me anything except going to Mass! I am sure that my stupid husband asked you to convert me. This evening, when he comes home, I will beat him with that broom; I swear I'll do it!" said Angelina, pointing her finger to a broom leaning on the wall of the courtyard.

Lucia turned pale. She hadn't expected that her friend was against religion to such an extent. Fortunately, Angelina had no suspicions about the reason why Lucia had given her so many gifts. If she had gotten an inkling that the gifts were given just to allure her, she would had given them back to Lucia, except for the fruitcake and biscuits she had already eaten.

Lucia stopped eating and drinking. She had a bitter taste in her mouth. After a few minutes of absolute silence, she stood up and silently headed for the front door. Her house of cards had collapsed! Her hope of helping Farmer Peppe had vanished. He was doomed to go alone to Mass. His wife would never sit in the same pew in the church. Lucia didn't care about the two sleepless nights she had spent to tailor Angelina's dress. What hurt was her wounded pride. She had failed. Angelina's refusal weighed on her like a granite block. Her attempt to persuade her to come to Mass hit an unshakable wall.

Lucia put on her shawl and left Angelina's house brokenhearted. She was making her way home, when she heard, "Lucia! Lucia! Come over here!" It was Angelina, who had rushed to the threshold and called her before she entered an alley.

"Let's finish drinking our coffee," Angelina continued, "and then we can discuss the matter quietly."

Lucia turned back, and a feeble ray of hope rose in her heart. They sat again at the stone table as if nothing had happened.

"I will come to church just for you, Lucia. I don't want to lose the only friend I have. However, keep in mind that I will never change my mind about priests, monks, the Vatican, and so on. I cannot understand why priests blame sex while the Vatican is full of homosexual—"

"Let's change the subject," Lucia interrupted. "Let's talk for a while about our families. Do you promise me that you will not beat your husband? He has nothing to do with my wish for you to come to Mass."

"Okay, I promise! What time shall we get ready to go to Mass?"

"It starts at ten o'clock in the morning, I'll come here with my husband and my children at nine thirty. Then, we'll all go together to the Franciscan Monastery chapel."

"People in Calascibetta will be surprised to see us going to Mass. 'What happened to Filippo Reggiani and Farmer Peppe's wife?' everyone will whisper to one another. 'They were deep-rooted anticlerical! Now they are Catholics. It's a miracle!'"

"You don't need to care about what others may think. Just confide in yourself and in our friendship. All the rest is vanity," said Lucia.

"I would be happy if after Mass our families could gather at my house and have lunch together. For me, it would be the first lunch with others since I got married. I've never cooked anything for my husband, but I have not forgotten how to cook. I'll make a mouth-watering lasagna."

"Yes, we'll have dinner together after Mass. My husband and my children will be happy too. I'll bake an apple pie."

"Okay, see you tomorrow at nine thirty in the morning."

The Two Families go to Mass

On Sunday, Lucia dressed her children up to the nines. Having no formal clothes, Filippo put on the suit he had worn for his wedding. At 9:30 sharp in the morning, Filippo knocked on Farmer Peppe's front door. He found him in the courtyard wearing a black suit and a traditional Sicilian flat cap.

The night before, although Farmer Peppe had slept well, he had had a strange dream. He had dreamed of his wife standing naked in front of him. Another man massaged her all over her body. Then he touched her all around her pelvis. At last, Angelina and that man entered a room while he remained outside, speechless and motionless like an ice block.

When he woke up, he went over the stages of his unhappy marriage to find an answer to the many mysteries in his life. Why had his wife always refused to go to Mass with him but now accepted to go to church with Lucia? Why, every time he returned home, did his wife scream like crazy and hit him with a broom?

There was just one answer: their marriage had not been founded upon love. Theirs had just been a marriage of convenience. Farmer Peppe had married Angelina to have sex, while she had married him to flee her indigence.

Since the early days of their marriage, Angelina had realized her mistake. How could she ever live with a man she didn't love. Money cannot make a union happy! As a little girl, she had dreamed of meeting Prince Charming. Actually, she had had a boyfriend, Turiddu, a young blacksmith. His hair was light brown and thick, like a tail of a fox. He wore a drooping mustache similar to that of Stalin. Overall, he was a handsome boy. Girls in Calascibetta liked him. He was tall and stout. Angelina was madly in love with Turiddu, but after a year with her, he left her and got engaged to another girl. It was a blow to her. From then on, she never trusted men, but she didn't despair of the future. Who knows? Maybe someday she would find a man whom she could love.

Unfortunately, she lived in a poor family. Farmer Peppe was a safe refuge, but after she got married to him, all her dreams vanished. She would never meet a man like Turiddu again. Her beauty also faded like a rosebush in a harsh winter.

She didn't like Farmer Peppe's physique. He was seventeen years older. Furthermore, their tastes and trends were dissimilar. Day by day, living together made her more and more wicked. Her heart hardened. She felt that her home had turned into a golden prison.

Farmer Peppe was a well-off farmer. He owned a house and many plots of land. Little by little, he sold almost all his properties to meet the repeated requests for money from Angelina and her relatives, but despite everything, his wife was insatiable. She wanted more and more money from him.

Until the age of forty, Farmer Peppe couldn't find a woman to marry. He was too shy, introverted, and unable to open his heart to others. Moreover, he was suspicious of everyone and couldn't speak calmly. Whenever he happened to meet and talk to somebody he knew, his mind whirled as if a hurricane were swirling inside him, stirring and confusing his ideas. What annoyed him most was the feeling that the person he was talking to could perceive his inner disorder; therefore, he took good care to show a peaceful face, but his speech also became too calm, slow, and artificial.

He tried to understand why others seemed to live peaceful and extroverted lives while he lived separately from the rest of the world. Despite his efforts, he couldn't find an acceptable rational answer.

Over time, looking inside himself, he found that the cause of his social maladjustment might lay on his feeling of being useless and subnormal. His inability to understand that he was not the only one in the world to face inner problems was at the root of his separation from the world. If he had realized that every human being has their own inner hurricane, he would have looked at the others differently. Now he only lived within his limited world made of his she-ass, Caterina, and the only one plot of land he had left.

Lucia had enlivened Angelina's heart, and now he was going to enter the church arm in arm with his wife, even though she detested him, despising priests, monks, and anything that sounded clerical.

The friendship between Angelina and Lucia was evidence that Angelina was not a bitch by nature. It had been the marriage with Farmer Peppe that had turned her into an aggressive, bad, and unfaithful wife. She had committed adultery a few times, not only with Turiddu, but also with other men while her husband worked in the countryside.

Angelina came down to the courtyard wearing the dress Lucia had given her. Filippo and Farmer Peppe were both dazzled by her figure. She looked like a new being. She was smiling and had regained a little of her former beauty.

"I have brought you a veil, for you are not allowed to enter the church bareheaded," said Lucia.

Angelina hated formalities and ritualism, but she accepted the gift so as not to disappoint her friend. Finally, they all walked to the Franciscan chapel together.

They entered the church and sat on a pew in one of the central rows. It was nearly ten. There were still a few empty pews in the church. Lucia was taking her rosary from her purse when her heart started pounding like the clapper of a ringing bell.

Silvano entered the church with his new girlfriend and took a seat on the other side of the aisle in the same row as Lucia, who couldn't help feeling uneasy. She felt as if she were about to collapse. Nobody noticed the fire that was flaring inside her.

As soon as the altar boy rang the bell, Father Massimiliano came out of the sacristy and walked to the altar. You could have heard a pin drop in the church.

Father Massimiliano read a passage from the Gospel of John: "At that time, a young woman guilty of adultery was taken to the square to be stoned to death. Jesus was nearby, and seeing him, the Jewish questioned him. 'Our fathers taught us that according to the Mosaic law, every woman that commits adultery must be stoned. According to you, was Moses right or wrong?'

"The question was tricky, but Jesus did not get upset. He drew signs on the sand and replied to them calmly: 'If any of you is without sin, let him be the first to throw a stone against this woman.' Hearing Jesus's words, those who had come to kill the adulteress one by one dropped the stone from their hand. In fact, nobody was free from blame. 'Nobody condemned you, and neither do I. Go home, but don't sin anymore!' said Jesus to that woman."

Father Massimiliano's homily followed the reading of the passage from the Gospel.

"You have to know," said Father Massimiliano to the congregation, "that this passage from John's Gospel cannot be found in the oldest original manuscripts that were written in Greek. To be clearer, this passage was subsequently added to John's Gospel. We don't know who added it and why he did so. However, the one who inserted it got it from Christian oral tradition, I think. Very likely, these are Jesus's real words.

"Jesus absolved the adulteress, but he said to her, 'Go home, but don't sin anymore!' It means that adultery remains a mortal sin. The congregation must know that both adultery and all kinds of illicit sexual intercourse are mortal sins."

Sitting on the pew, Angelina was quivering. *This priest is a liar! Doesn't he know that most priests have sex?* she thought to herself.

This monk must have a heart of stone! He has lived all his life within the walls of a monastery. He doesn't know the world! He does not know anything about love. I'd like to see him in my shoes. I love Silvano. If he comes to my store again, I will not be able to resist him, Lucia thought with her gaze fixed to the pulpit to avoid unwittingly turning her eyes towards Silvano.

"I know what some of you are thinking now," said Father Massimiliano, still sermonizing from the pulpit. "According to some, I am a liar or a naïve man," he said, as if reading Angelina and Lucia's minds. Every now and then, he turned his blue eyes, now toward Angelina, now toward Lucia, and then addressed the congregation again.

"Is a human being different from an animal? If someone believes that a woman in love is like a bitch in heat, there is no reason why they should come to my church. Whenever I say Mass, I don't confine myself to performing empty rites. Instead, I want to elevate the soul and spirit of my parishioners. I want them to understand that animals are unable to control their instincts, while humans have a soul inside themselves, a soul that illuminates their way and points to them the right path to follow to live a spiritual life. Have you ever seen a dog controlling its instinct of mating? Surely not. But I have seen some men and women control their instinct of copulation. Therefore, man is different from animals. Always keep this in mind!" thundered Father Massimiliano, staring at Lucia.

This preacher is just a Christian theoretician. He cannot understand how powerful my attraction to Silvano is. My soul cannot illuminate anything, and I am unable to repress my desire to have him as my lover, Lucia said to herself, blushing as never before.

When the sermon was over and it was time to receive Holy Communion, the congregation formed a line to the altar. Then they knelt and, one by one, waited for their turn to receive the Sacrament.

"Don't ask me to go to the altar to get the host!" Angelina whispered to Lucia.

Farmer Peppe, Filippo, and the twins followed the line to Father Massimiliano, who held a host in his hand and put it on the tongue of the believers. Lucia was aware of committing a sin if she took Holy Communion, for she should have confessed her adultery to a priest in advance, but she was ashamed of telling Father Massimiliano that she had made love with Silvano.

After a moment of indecision, she joined the others lined up at the altar. If she had refused to receive the host, her husband would have definitely grown suspicious.

At first, Angelina remained stuck on the pew. She detested rituals. Furthermore, she had not confessed her sins to a priest. Finally, she looked inside herself and saw Jesus, who had already forgiven her sins as he had done with the adulteress mentioned in John's Gospel. So, Angelina felt clear of her sins and joined the others.

At last, Father Massimiliano concluded Mass by saying, *"Ite Missa est"* (in the rite of Mass preceding the Second Vatican Council, these Latin words meant that Mass was over). People left the church slowly and orderly. Father Massimiliano and the altar boy went to the sacristy to put their ceremonial robes away. At last, a friar closed the doors and the church fell into silence.

After Mass, the two families had dinner at Farmer Peppe's home. Angelina had cooked lasagna and roast chicken. A table had been set with wine and flowers in the courtyard. Angelina had a smile on her face the whole time. Farmer Peppe couldn't believe his eyes. He was the happiest man in the world.

My wife is not a bitch at all. No woman is a bitch by nature! I was the one who turned her into a wicked woman. I should not have married her! he thought.

The food was delicious. Angelina refilled the glasses of wine many times. Even the kids tasted some, watered down, of course. Between a glass of wine and other things, Father Massimiliano's sermon echoed in Angelina and Lucia's hearts: "If someone believes that a woman in love is like a bitch in heat, there is no reason why they should come to my church."

Am I a bitch in heat? No, I am not! I will find the strength inside me that I need to resist temptation. Then I'll be a real woman with a soul inside me, not a bitch in heat, Lucia thought.

I will not have prejudice against religions and priests anymore. I won't tar all priests and monks with the same brush. Deep down, Father Massimiliano is a sincere and honest man, Angelina thought to herself.

They enjoyed togetherness for about three hours. Filippo and Farmer Peppe agreed on the time they would meet the next day.

"I will pick you up at home at six thirty in the morning. Get ready with your children. It is dark at that time, but we can trust Caterina. She knows the way to Enna better than me," Farmer Peppe said to Filippo.

Suddenly, somebody rang the doorbell. It was Armando, a cousin of Farmer Peppe, with his wife, Cettina, and his daughter, Brigida.

Angelina beckoned them to come in and have a seat at the table.

Husband and wife were a typical Sicilian couple. They both were short with brown eyes and hair. Their daughter was a bit taller than her parents and wore a gray, close-fitting skirt and a purple blouse. As soon as Antonio saw her, his heart started. She was a few years older than he, long-limbed, with a coffee birthmark below her lower lip, and two blue eyes that looked like two pieces of the sky.

She took a seat next to him. Antonio noticed she already had a roundish bosom. He would have liked starting a conversation with her, but on seeing her, he blushed with emotion and had a lump in his throat. He was so enchanted by Brigida that he couldn't say anything!

"We are leaving for Belgium tomorrow. We can't find a job either in Calascibetta or in Enna. A friend of mine who lives in Belgium sent me a letter. He said that there is a position available for me in a coal mine near the town where he lives," said Armando.

"I heard that it is dangerous to work underground. Furthermore, you are going to inhale dust from the mine. It is harmful! It creates silicosis, a serious lung disease caused by breathing in dust containing silica. I advise you against going there to work in a coal mine. Keep in mind that the Sicilians who live there do all the jobs that the Belgians don't want to do," said Filippo.

"I have no choice but to emigrate. How can I live here without a job? Humans need to eat to survive. How can I buy food? I don't want to live like a beggar. Furthermore, I want to give a bright future to my daughter. I will earn money in Belgium, but I will not stay abroad for long. As soon as I find a job in Calascibetta or Enna, I will return to Sicily," replied Armando.

Antonio didn't miss a single word of their talk. He was still paralyzed by Brigida's charm. It was the first time he had felt attracted to a girl. *I will wait for Brigida! I feel that sooner or later she will return to Sicily and I will meet her again someday!* he thought.

Armando and his wife and daughter remained at the table in the courtyard for a few hours. It was a lovely afternoon. Although it was October, the weather was still fine. Everybody ate the apple pie Lucia had made and drank coffee, which Angelina served in small china cups. While Cettina, Angelina, and Lucia tided up the courtyard and washed the dishes, Armando, Farmer Peppe, and Filippo chatted with each other about this and that. Nunzio, who was less emotional and shy than his brother, took a seat next to Brigida and started chatting with her. She had fun and laughed loudly when she listened to the jokes he told her, while Antonio continued to keep silent. Who would conquer Brigida's heart someday? The taciturn Antonio or the humorous and talkative Nunzio?

Lucia Begins a New Life

It was six thirty in the morning when Farmer Peppe knocked on Filippo's front door. The children, though sleepy, put their satchels into the saddlebags and mounted Caterina. Filippo and Farmer Peppe followed them on foot.

Lucia went downstairs and opened her shop. She wore an invisible shield and armor to protect herself from temptation. *I am a human being, not a bitch in heat! If Silvano comes, he will find a block of ice instead of a woman,* she promised herself.

Despite Lucia's determination to hold out against Silvano, she was aware that the mere sight of him could easily overcome her resistance.

He will bewitch me with his cobra eyes. In that case, I can't help but follow him to the back of the store and have sex with him again. I must find a solution to overcome this tremendous issue. I have children and a husband that loves me. I must live up to their expectations! What to do? Yes, I have just found the solution to my problem. I will remove this goddamn curtain that separates the front of the store from the back. I will also lock the inner door that leads upstairs. From now on, I will walk the street to come and go from home to the store. I won't use the inner door anymore. This way, it will be impossible to have sex with Silvano again, thought Lucia, hopping like a little girl.

Lucia removed that filthy curtain from the ceiling and cut it into pieces, then she locked the inner door from the inside and went upstairs. Finally, she left the house through the main door and entered the shop from the street. She put the key for the inside door and the pieces of curtain into a garbage bag and went out to the farthest dustbin to throw everything away.

When Filippo asks me the reason why I made the changes in the shop, I will answer that I did so to give it a different look and separate the business from home, Lucia thought.

A few hours later, Fimminaru was standing in the corner of the street ready to step into Lucia's store again. Not to arouse suspicion, he had said to the other workers at the building site that he was going to buy a pack of nails and would come back soon. When the street was deserted and there were no customers in the store, he entered.

"Good morning, Lucia!" he said with a broad smile.

Seeing Silvano, Lucia strove to control her anxiety, but she felt that her cheeks were on fire. Her body trembled like a leaf in the wind, but she was still able to keep her self-control.

"Good morning, Silvano. As you can see, there is no curtain anymore. I tore it to shreds. Do you need anything in the store?"

"No, I don't. I have come here just for you, for I love you a lot. However, I can see a door on the left side of the store. Let's move behind the door. It will not take long for us to love each other there."

"Unfortunately for you, the door is locked. I have no key to open it, for I threw away the only key I had into the garbage bin."

"Let's go home through the street. Your husband and children are in Enna. We can spend a little time undisturbed. I love you!"

"I love you too, but to go home we have to pass through the public street. Somebody could see us walking together and entering my house."

"We don't need to walk together. You go home first, and then I'll come after a few minutes."

"Somebody could see you enter my home and report the fact to my husband. In that case, you could consider yourself a dead man. Filippo would definitely kill you. Do you want to endanger your life?"

Fimminaru turned pale. He knew what a bad-tempered man Filippo was. Why didn't he think about that before? Suddenly, he lost his boldness and started shivering.

"Give me a pack of nails, please. I will not come here anymore. I swear! If I need some tools, I'll send one of my hands here."

Lucia got the pack of nails and put it on the counter. Fimminaru handed her the money with a trembling hand and then ran away without waiting for the change.

After Fimminaru had gone, two men wearing black jackets and ties entered Lucia's store and put their briefcases on the counter. Seeing them, Lucia had the feeling of coming across two gravediggers dressed in black. They were hawk-nosed and wore black spectacles. They were the lawyer and engineer that were dealing with the lawsuit with her neighbors. Lucia knew them, but she had never talked with them. Filippo was the one who took care of the lawsuit.

They said that the lawsuit for the damage provoked by Filippo to his neighbors was going well, but they needed more money for their fee to cover the expenses for their traveling from Calascibetta to the court in Enna.

"Filippo is not here. Come back this evening and talk with him," Lucia said shortly.

"We know that Filippo is in Enna, but we also know that you are now the person in charge of the store. So, give us the money we need, or you may lose the case."

"How much money do you need?"

The lawyer and the engineer looked at each other and then nodded. Apparently, they had previously agreed on the sum.

"We have to go to the courthouse in Enna at least ten times. Furthermore, we have to stay there all day long. I have to study the case very carefully. On the other hand, the engineer has to make difficult calculations. We think one thousand lira should be enough for the moment. Five hundred lira each," said the lawyer.

"What?" cried out Lucia.

"Why are you so surprised? We ask you for money according to our professional rate."

"What kind of professional rate is that? Don't you know that I have to work hard for six months to earn one thousand lira? You two are bloodsuckers!"

"You're insulting us! We are two serious professionals!"

"I only now understand why my husband is always short of money. It is because of you two and this goddamn lawsuit. I'll solve the problem in my own way. Go away from my store and don't set foot in it anymore!" Lucia said angrily, pointing her finger at the exit.

After the two had gone, Lucia started thinking about how to make up with her neighbors. There was only one person capable of helping her.

I must go to Father Massimiliano right away. He is a good man. I am sure he will soften the heart of my neighbors, Lucia thought.

She closed the store—it was the time when customers seldom came—put on her shawl and went to the Franciscan monastery. She rang the doorbell and a novice soon came to the entrance.

"I am looking for Father Massimiliano. I am in a hurry to talk with him," Lucia said.

"Father Massimiliano is not here. He is at school," the novice replied.

"When can I see him?"

"Today is Monday. On Wednesday, his day off, he will stay at the monastery all day long."

"Okay, I'll come back on Wednesday. Please tell Father Massimiliano that I'll be here around ten in the morning."

"I will tell him."

On Wednesday at ten o'clock, Lucia went to the Franciscan monastery. Father Massimiliano came and opened the door. Seeing him, Lucia knelt on one knee and kissed his hand.

"I have a big problem, Father Massimiliano."

"I am here to help my neighbor. Let's go to the parlor."

They walked through the cloister and took a seat in the parlor. It was a wide room with a few green plants. The room smelled of peace and sacredness. Father Massimiliano looked into her eyes and smiled sweetly.

"What can I do for you, Lucia?"

"My children go to school in Enna. Every morning, my husband takes them there by walking through the valley."

"That is such a hard task! I can hardly believe that! How can Filippo manage his store?"

"I am now the manager in the store."

"That job doesn't fit a woman!"

"Why not?"

"Don't you know that there are some people without morals in Calascibetta? You are a very attractive woman. Somebody could convince you to follow him to the rear of the store and then take advantage of your weakness to make you commit adultery. It is a mortal sin! Is there still a curtain in the store?"

Lucia's legs quaked. It was clear that Father Massimiliano knew about her love affair with Silvano. *How did he find out about my adultery?*

The possibilities were only two. Either it was true what people said about Father Massimiliano's ability to read other people's minds, or Silvano had confessed his sin to him. The latter possibility was more plausible. Silvano had been badly upset since he heard that Filippo would have killed him if he had come to know he had had a love affair with his wife. Either way, Father Massimiliano was aware that Lucia was not as innocent as she seemed to be at first glance. He knew she was an adulteress! She should talk about this with Father Massimiliano. Otherwise, she would dig a chasm of incomprehension between her and him. He would mistake her reticence for mistrust.

Lucia remained silent for a few moments with her eyes on the ground. Then she gathered her courage and spoke.

"I want to confess a terrible sin I have committed."

"Wait here for a few minutes. I'll go get my stole."

Father Massimiliano came back with a violet stole around his neck.

"Tell me what sins you have committed."

"A terrible sin. The worst sin a married woman can commit. I am an adulteress. I made love with Fimminaru. Furthermore, he spread his seed inside me. I am likely to get pregnant."

"I know everything, Lucia. Pray to God that you are not expecting a baby from that stupid young man. Otherwise, the matter will be more complicated. You are a great woman. I know you cut the curtain in the store to pieces, and you even locked the inner door so as not to fall into temptation."

"How can you know that?"

"Somebody told me what happened, but I cannot tell you the name. It is a secret."

"I am so ashamed, Father Massimiliano! I, Lucia, the woman who wanted to become a Franciscan nun, am guilty of adultery! This is a paradox!"

"Don't blame yourself for what happened. Forget the past. Think of your husband and children. You are the chief support for your family. Under your management, the business will grow."

"I feel more relaxed after having confessed my sin! I have been very worried these days. I feel guilty and unworthy of being a Christian."

"I'll pray for you, Lucia. Everything will be alright. I absolve you of your sins. From now on, strive not to sin anymore! In the name of the Father, and of the Son, and of the Holy Spirit."

"I have come here not only to confess my sin, but also for another important reason. Only you can help me and my family in this matter."

"Tell me whatever you like. You know I will always try to help you."

"Thank you so much, Father Massimiliano! You are a holy man and my best friend. You have a great heart."

"Thank you, Lucia, but let's not stand on ceremony. What's the matter?"

"When Filippo was digging the ground to lay the foundations of our house, the wall of our neighbor's home remained unsupported for a few days. My husband was sure that the wall would be supported again after he laid the foundations of our house. Unfortunately, things turned out differently. One night, a storm broke, and the heavy rain caused our neighbor's wall to fall."

"Did Filippo start the digging in winter?"

"Not at all, Father Massimiliano! The storm came in high summer. Nobody could foresee such a thing happening."

"What happened later?"

"Filippo wanted to rebuild the fallen wall, but our neighbors said that it was not enough. They said that with the fall of the wall their house had also suffered serious damage, to such an extent that now it was not possible to live in it."

"Are they still living in their house, or did they move elsewhere?"

"Of course they live in their house. My neighbors are two vultures. They want to seize the opportunity to steal money from Filippo. They pretend their old crumbling house has been damaged. What they want is a new house on our money. This is absurd!"

"You could ask a lawyer for help."

"Oh, don't mention either lawyers or engineers. They are bloodsuckers. Two days ago, I kicked them out of my store. They asked me for the astronomical figure of one thousand lira in order to go on with their legal representation. I don't want to see them anymore!"

"You cannot win the case without a lawyer. You must realize this, Lucia."

"I want to settle the quarrel. You can help me, Father Massimiliano. I beseech you to talk with my neighbors. I want to pay for the actual damage. I want to rebuild their wall. Please, help me, my children, and my husband. You are a holy man. My neighbors will listen to you."

Father Massimiliano was reluctant to meddle in quarrels among believers, but he didn't feel like saying no to Lucia, for she was desperate. So, he made a deep sigh and, holding her hand, looked into her eyes.

"Okay, I will talk with your neighbors next week on my day off. I hope to convince them to make peace with Filippo. I'll do my best. Come here in fifteen days. I'll tell you how they want to manage the lawsuit. Meanwhile, I advise you not to burn the bridge with your lawyer."

Fifteen days went by. Lucia was now relaxed and peaceful. The previous night, she had had a heavy period. Fortunately, the danger of pregnancy was over.

She heaved a deep sigh of relief and went to the monastery overjoyed.

God has granted me my prayer. I am not pregnant! Today is a lucky day. Everything will be alright, she said to herself.

She entered the monastery skipping gaily like a little girl and headed for the parlor. Father Massimiliano was sitting in an armchair.

"Good morning, Father Massimiliano!" Lucia said, kneeling and kissing his hand.

"Good morning, Lucia. You look less worried than last time."

"I am happy, the happiest woman in the world! I'm not going to be pregnant."

"That is wonderful news!"

"Did you talk with my neighbors, Father Massimiliano?"

"Of course I did."

"What did they say? Tell me what you talked about. I want to know everything that passed between you and them."

"You look too anxious, Lucia. Keep in mind that anxiety is never helpful. I had a good talk with them. It seems that Filippo has been harsh with them, but they are disposed to talk with you."

"I have to go to their home alone?"

"No, we will go together. We will meet them next Wednesday at eleven o'clock. Come here at half past ten, and then we'll walk to their house."

"Thank you very much, Father Massimiliano. If they are disposed to meet us, it means that they are not bad people, I think."

"Keep in mind, Lucia, that nobody is bad, and nobody is good. If you open your heart to your neighbors, you can expect good things from them."

Now Lucia knew the power of a gift and the power of smiling. Both had worked well in convincing Angelina to come to Mass.

A kind smile and a gift given with all my heart can soften even the harshest being, Lucia thought.

The following Wednesday, she went to the monastery carrying a heavy bag.

"This is an apple pie for you, Father Massimiliano. I made it with my own hands," Lucia said while she took the pie out of her bag.

Father Massimiliano was surprised and happy. He liked pies so much.

"I'll share this gift with my brethren," he said.

"In that case, only a thin slice will remain for you."

"It doesn't matter. If I don't share what I have, I am not worthy to be a Franciscan friar."

Father Massimiliano and Lucia set out towards her neighbors' house. They crossed the main square and walked on narrow alleys. Then they stopped in front of an old house. Once there, Father Massimiliano rang the doorbell. Both husband and wife came and opened the door.

"Welcome, Father Massimiliano!" they said, looking askance at Lucia.

"Welcome to you, Luciano and Giulia!" replied Father Massimiliano.

Luciano was a policeman and wore a blue uniform with corporal's stripes. His eyes were blue and his hair white. He looked like a gentleman. His wife was bony, dressed in black, and goitrous. Behind them appeared their son, who looked like his father except for a nervous tic in his chin. Apparently, his tic made him feel uncomfortable. He tried to hold his chin still, but it quivered mercilessly.

"This is my son, Maurizio. Let's take a seat in the living room," Giulia said.

As soon as they sat down, Lucia took her gift for her neighbors out of her bag and put it on the small marble table.

"This is an apple pie for you, and this is a centerpiece I laced a few months ago. It seems to suit this marble table well," said Lucia, smiling from ear to ear.

Seeing Lucia's smile and looking at the gifts, Luciano, Giulia, and their son were dumbfounded. They expected the conversation to be about the lawsuit and the damages. Instead, Lucia's smile and her gifts, to them, seemed to be the dawn of a new relationship between the two families that so far had scowled at each other.

"I go get some plates. I want to taste the pie now," Giulia said.

Giulia cut the apple pie into pieces and gave the biggest helping to Father Massimiliano. She then made coffee and served it to everybody.

"Now, it's time to begin the discussion about the absurd lawsuit against each other," Father Massimiliano said.

"We didn't want to quarrel with your husband," Luciano said, turning to Lucia.

"Then what's the matter?" asked Father Massimiliano.

"Filippo refused to talk with us. He said that we had to discuss the matter with his lawyer and his engineer."

"And one day he even offended me by calling me handicapped!" said Maurizio, rising to his feet.

"Filippo is a good man. He just has a difficult character," said Father Massimiliano.

"We just want our supporting wall and henhouse that collapsed along with the wall to be rebuilt. We don't want money from Filippo. We want you to pay our trusted builder that will rebuild the wall and the henhouse," said Maurizio.

"Who is your trusted builder?"

"Fimminaru! In our opinion, he is the best builder in Calascibetta. Furthermore, he won't ask much for his work. Some time ago, he repaired the roof of our house perfectly for a small amount of money," said Luciano.

"Besides being a good-looking young man, he is also honest," added Giulia.

"May I go to the bathroom?" Lucia asked.

"Yes, of course. I'll walk you there," Giulia said.

In the bathroom, Lucia was about to pass out. She was upset and between two fires. If she said that Fimminaru was not the right mason to rebuild the wall and the henhouse, she would put the agreement with her neighbors at risk. Moreover, there was no valid reason why Silvano shouldn't do the job, for he was well known in Calascibetta as an excellent builder. On the other hand, Silvano working near her house would be a tremendous temptation for her. It was true that she had confessed her sin and proposed not to commit adultery anymore, but who knows what would happen if she was left alone with Silvano while her children and her husband were in Enna? It would be possible for her to fall back into evil ways. She was too shocked to get out of the bathroom.

Father Massimiliano knew why Lucia was lingering in the bathroom.

"Maybe Lucia doesn't feel well. I'll go see what is happening to her," he said.

He walked to the bathroom and knocked on the door. "Don't worry, Lucia. Let me deal with Fimminaru's work. I know what to do," Father Massimiliano whispered from behind the door.

"He will work too close to my home. I cannot resist temptation. I am sure about that," Lucia said in a tremulous voice.

"Don't worry about that! I will talk with Fimminaru. I know his character. He is a fearful guy. I'll tell him that I will excommunicate him if he dares to disturb you."

"I am coming out," said Lucia, feeling relieved.

Lucia washed her face, put herself together, and went back to the living room.

"I agree with you!" she said, turning to Maurizio. "Fimminaru will rebuild the fallen wall and the henhouse. I'll pay him for the materials and his work."

"Let's endorse our agreement!" said the son.

"We don't need to sign anything. I'll answer for the fulfillment of Lucia's obligation. Do you trust me?" said Father Massimiliano to the son.

"Yes, we trust you. Tomorrow, we will tell our lawyer to drop the case," Luciano and Giulia said with one voice.

Lucia was beaming with joy. "May I hug you?" she asked Giulia.

"Yes, of course! I am happy to have a neighbor like you. From now on, we'll be also good friends. I have always dreamed of having a sincere friend as my neighbor. Today, God granted my wish," said Giulia.

"My mission on earth is to bring love and peace to people. For that, I chose to be a Franciscan friar. Now it's the time I go back to the monastery. It's about dining time."

"Let's go together," Lucia said. "I'll walk you there."

While walking on the street, Lucia resumed her worries about the whole matter. "I don't know if I have enough money to make a single payment to Fimminaru."

"Don't worry about that. I'll give Fimminaru all the money he needs. Then you'll give me my money back when you can," answered Father Massimiliano.

"I am worried that when he works near my house, he will ask me to do a dirty thing. What I'll do in that case?"

"Fimminaru will not talk with you anymore. I assure you that he will be respectful to you. He has the terror of being killed by Filippo. Furthermore, I confirm that I'll tell him that he'll be excommunicated if he tries to seduce you."

"How can I repay you for your kindness?"

"Give thanks to God, not to me. I am just a means in God's hands. He makes miracles, not me. Be always happy!"

Fimminaru finished rebuilding the fallen wall and the henhouse within twenty days. It was done in a workmanlike manner. Father Massimiliano paid him. During his work, Fimminaru never dared to disturb or even glance at Lucia. The lawsuit was dropped and peace between the two families restored. Now, Lucia could go on with her life.

Lucia Wants to Move to Enna

In the store, things were going better and better day by day. Under Lucia's management, the sales of coffins quintupled. It was due to her character. Whenever somebody died, Lucia gave her condolences to the families, kept in contact with them during the mourning period, and helped them if they needed something. If poor people couldn't pay cash, she allowed them to pay in installments. Lucia's business was going so well that within three months she could return the money to Father Massimiliano that he had lent her for the reconstruction of the wall and the henhouse. She was even able to put some money aside.

It was wintertime, and her thoughts went to Filippo, Nunzio, and Antonio, who walked every day to Enna. It was a hard walk for both Filippo and the children. Suddenly, an idea flashed through her mind. *What about moving to Enna? We can create a business there! This evening, I'll ask Filippo to look for a business opportunity in that city.*

At dinnertime Filippo and the children returned home very tired and hungry. The more demanding task was that of the children. They had to do their homework. Middle school was quite selective. Their teachers would fail them if they didn't do well. The two hours lost to come and go to school were a heavy burden for them.

"We ought to move our business to Enna," Lucia said to her husband. "We cannot endure such a hard life for long, or we will all be exhausted. While the children are at school, you can survey the market to see if we can open a new store there. I heard that there is a big store located in the commercial area. The owner is quite old. Who knows, maybe he would be interested in a joint venture with us. You can talk to him about it tomorrow. With all the money I have earned, it should be not difficult to start a business in Enna."

"Tomorrow, while I'm waiting for the children to come out of school, I will walk the streets to get an idea about the market in Enna. Then I'll enter the shop you talked about and ask the owner if he is interested in a joint venture."

The following day, after he walked the children to school, Filippo took a walk in Enna's commercial area. There was no comparison between Enna's economy and that of Calascibetta. In Enna, the shops always had customers inside. He then went to the store Lucia had mentioned. At the entrance, two shop assistants stood behind the counter. They both wore gray jackets and black ties. It seemed like a funeral parlor, not a hardware store.

"May I talk with the owner?" he asked one of them.

"Our boss is engaged with a customer, but it will not take long."

"Okay, I'll wait here. Please inform me once he is available."

While waiting, Filippo had a look at the store. It was big, at least thirty times bigger than his small shop in Calascibetta. This store sold hardware, paint, furniture, timber, coffins, and so on.

Lucia's idea to enter into a partnership in this big store is absurd! I don't dare ask the owner to partner with us, he thought.

Filippo waited for an hour and a half. He couldn't stay longer because he had to go get the children from school. He was about to leave the store when he heard the assistant's voice.

"Mr. Gaetano Leone is waiting for you."

Filippo stepped back and headed for the owner's room.

"Please, come in!" said the owner of the store.

The room was large and bare. A white-haired man with a pointed beard sat behind a desk full of papers. In front of the desk were two old chairs. Other chairs were placed on the sides of the room.

These chairs must date back to the foundation of the store! Filippo thought.

The room looked grim. The paint on the walls was crumbling. There were many paintings hung on them, but they were covered with thick layers of dust. It was evident that nobody had cleaned the room for a long time.

"Please, sit down!" said the owner of the store.

He looked like a gentleman. He wore a black jacket and tie. Apparently, his work was a way to escape his inner void. He was at least seventy years old. Behind him, hung on the wall, was a portrait of a young woman.

That must be his wife when she was young, Filippo thought.

Filippo was tense and embarrassed and didn't even want to sit down. The store was too big for him. He was embarrassed to ask a wealthy man to enter into partnership with him. He was on the verge of shaking the owner's hand and getting out, but the old man calmed him down.

"Don't be tense! I don't eat men. Please, relax and sit down. We can discuss everything calmly."

Filippo sat on the dusty chair and introduced himself.

"My name is Filippo Reggiani. I live in Calascibetta. I am aware of the absurdity of what I am going to say. Surely, you will think I am mad, but my wife asked me to talk with you, and I don't want to disappoint her. She is running our store for the moment. It is quite unusual for a woman to run a business, but she is a good businesswoman, and above all, she is honest and loves me and our two sons. Since she took over the shop, our economic condition has improved, the store's revenue has quintupled. When I ran the business, we had a lot of debt; now we have none. We also have some savings. I owe much to my wife. She is an angel to me and my two children."

"Very well," said Gaetano, stroking his goatee.

"I am sure," Filippo went on, "that as soon as you listen to my words, you will burst out laughing and then kick me out of this room."

The old seller didn't lose his composure. He kept stroking his goatee and stared at Filippo in surprise with his black, piercing eyes. He was used to talking with his customers about business. Filippo's words were new to him. Then he calmly replied, "I am here to listen to you. Don't worry about anything. I want to help you. Whatever you will say, I will not kick you out. Give me your hand. Will you trust me?"

"I will," Filippo replied.

The old man spoke in a conversational tone. Filippo felt a bit relaxed. He thought that the best way to become friendly with him was to be true and talk with an open and humble heart.

"Mainly, I sell hardware in Calascibetta. As I told you before, my wife is in charge of the store. For the sake of my family, I walk every day from Calascibetta to Enna to take my children to school. It is a hardship for us. It takes one hour to get to the school and the same to go back home," said Filippo.

"Are you Lucia Bruno's husband?"

"How do you know my wife's name?"

"I also sell wholesale to retailers. Your wife ordered some wire netting and paint from my shop. The worker that delivered the goods told me that he was spellbound by your wife's smile and gracefulness."

"Yes, my wife is actually very kind, and she is also a very beautiful woman. Her smile is bewitching."

"The more you smile, the more you sell. That is a law of life. I made my business when I was in a happy mood. At the time, I was engaged to a blue-blooded girl, Countess Maria Antonietta di Belmonte. Do you see the portrait on the wall behind me?"

"Yes, it portrays a very beautiful woman with a sweet, warm smile."

"You are right, Filippo. Maria Antonietta was the most beautiful woman in Enna. I painted the portrait you see. I tried to make a faithful portrait of her. I painted her hair the same color as gold, her teeth as white as the fresh fallen snow, her eyes the color of toasted almonds, her skin the color of a rosebud, and finally I painted her sweet and dazzling smile."

"You did good work. The portrait is wonderful."

"Thank you, Filippo. I didn't want to make a poor impression on her family. I worked earnestly to make up for my non-noble origins with my wealth. I was cheerful and humorous; life smiled at me. Maria Antonietta and I had already planned our wedding, but a sudden incurable disease intervened. One year later, she died in my arms. Then, the smile disappeared from my store."

"I feel sorry for what happened to you."

"She died a long time ago. Time heals all sorrows."

"Your store is the biggest in Enna. If I had a store like yours, I'd be the happiest man in the world."

"Money cannot give you happiness. The rich never feel satisfied. The more money they have, the more money they want to have."

"If not money, what can make a man happy?"

"A smile!"

"Just a smile and nothing else? I don't understand."

"Can you tell me your name again?"

"Filippo."

"Listen to me, Filippo. If you lose your wife and your children, is your store still meaningful to you?"

"Of course not! My family is much more precious than my store or any material thing."

"The same went for me. I couldn't find a woman that could fill the void Maria Antonietta left in me. I continued to develop my business. Mine is the biggest store in Enna. It is true. But there is no smile in it. Here I talk only of business. I want to bring back to my store the smile that pervaded it fifty years ago."

"I see."

"If you take a quick look at this room, you'll find it gloomy. There is no good energy in my store. It lacks in smile! I want to talk with your wife. If she is as my worker has depicted her, you will enter into partnership with me."

"I feel honored by your proposal, but I want to be fair to you. My store is at least thirty times smaller than yours. It is located in the small town of Calascibetta, a town with a limited market. It is true that my wife has quintupled the revenue since she took over the store, but we are too weak to enter a partnership with a rich businessman like you."

"In the business field, human beings outweigh facilities. You can own a good and well-equipped store, but if you don't have good sellers you cannot beat the competition. I am seventy-three years old. I have no heirs. Before I leave my earthly life, I want this store to be managed by someone with a smile on their lips."

"Do you have a car?" Filippo asked Gaetano.

"Of course I have a car."

"Can you come to Calascibetta next week?"

"Yes, I'll come to your home next Thursday, in the afternoon."

"My wife and I will be waiting for you."

The New Joint Venture

The school year drew to a close. It had been a year of hardships for both Filippo and the children. Farmer Peppe had been their guardian angel all the way. He had taken the children back and forth from Calascibetta to Enna the entire year. Filippo wanted to give him some money for his service, but Farmer Peppe always refused. For him, friendship couldn't be paid with money. At last, Antonio and Nunzio passed the final examination with good marks.

"What present would you like to receive?" Lucia asked the children.

"I'd like a bicycle!" answered Nunzio.

"And you, Antonio? What do you want me to buy for you?"

"I want a globe."

"What?"

"I saw a fantastic globe displayed in a bookstore window in Enna. It is in relief and revolves on its axis. There is a bulb inside it that I can turn on and off. The globe is amazing when it is lit. I want to keep it on my desk."

"Okay, I'll present you with the globe you have seen at the shop. Whenever you look at it, don't dream too much. It is quite unlikely that you will leave Calascibetta. Your future is in Sicily, not in faraway lands."

One week later, the bicycle and the parcel with the globe inside arrived from Enna.

Antonio put the globe on his desk and turned it to see the continents, mountains, oceans, lakes, rivers, and countries he had learned about at school. He dreamed of traveling to some faraway land someday, but for the moment it was just a dream.

Nunzio had a different character than that of his brother. He was more extroverted than Antonio and had many friends. While Antonio loved to study catechism at the Franciscan monastery, Nunzio enjoyed riding his bicycle.

On Thursday, Gaetano parked his car in Piazza Umberto in Calascibetta. Then he walked to Filippo's house in Via San Michele.

Lucia and Filippo were at the window waiting for him. As soon as Filippo appeared in the distance, they went out into the street to welcome him.

"Good afternoon, Mr. Gaetano!" Lucia said, bowing slightly and with a smile so broad that it showed almost all her very white teeth.

"Good afternoon, Lucia and Filippo," replied Gaetano.

"It is an honor for us to welcome so powerful a man."

"My worker was right. I have never seen a woman with such a beaming smile. You are a lucky man, Filippo, to have Lucia as a wife."

"Let's go home, Mr. Gaetano. Surely you would enjoy a cup of good coffee," said Lucia.

"Yes, I like coffee."

While Gaetano was sipping his cup of coffee, Lucia went to the bedroom to get the gift she had prepared for him.

"This is a picture I painted when I went to the Franciscan convent to learn embroidery. In the convent, there was a nun who was very skilled in painting. She taught me how to use the palette and paintbrushes. This painting portrays a marine landscape. If you'd like, you can hang it on the wall in your office. It will give you a feeling of peace."

"Thank you for your gift. I will definitely hang it in my office. It will light up the room."

"I have another painting in my children's room. If you'd like, I can also give you that."

"No, please, Lucia. Leave it in the children's room. By the way, I heard from Filippo that every day your children walk from Calascibetta to Enna to go to school. That is absurd! They cannot endure such a hardship for very long."

"You are right, Gaetano. It is a really hard task for them and for my husband, but I didn't want to have my children separated. If I could, I would move to Enna right away, but that is nothing but a dream."

"If you keep dreaming, sooner or later your dreams will come true. Only dreamers can succeed in life. Pragmatists can also succeed, but they cannot reach the peak of success. I am here to ask you to enter into a partnership with me at fifty percent."

"How can I pay you to acquire such a big stake in your business?" she asked.

"You can pay me little by little. I am sure that with you the business will expand. In the span of a few years, you will pay your debt."

"I am just a housewife who tries to be a businesswoman for the sake of her children. I don't have special skills. I have not even studied economics. How can you trust me?"

"I got information from a friend of mine who lives in Enna but quite often goes to Calascibetta to visit his old mother. He told me that in the span of a few months the earnings of your shop quintupled. He said that you were able to put an end to the age-old lawsuit with your neighbors. Keep in mind that to succeed in business the heart is more important than learning."

"We have a house here. If we move to Enna, where are we going to stay?"

"I have an empty apartment. You can stay there as long as you like."

"Okay, I trust you. We'll move to Enna. I just ask you to allow Filippo to work with me in the store. I don't want to move to Enna if my husband won't work next to me."

"Okay, Filippo will work in the business as well. I promise."

New Life in Enna

The apartment was located in a building on Via Rocca, the area of Enna that looked onto Calascibetta and the vast valley beneath. It had four rooms besides the kitchen and the bathroom. Antonio and Nunzio settled in independent rooms with a bed, a closet, and a desk. When they lived in Calascibetta, they'd had to share the same room and study on the same desk.

Nunzio was thrilled with the new apartment, while Antonio would have preferred to remain in his old house in Calascibetta, for he loved the narrow alleys, Piazza Umberto, and the peace of his small hometown. In Calascibetta, the houses were detached and on a human scale, while in Enna some buildings looked like honeycombs. People went in and out of their apartments and greeted one another formally. Antonio seldom had the chance to meet those who lived in the other apartments. However, he had to stay with his family. He was too young to lead an independent life, but sooner or later he would be an adult, and then he would spread his wings to fly towards a better place to live. Enna was not his ideal city!

Since Lucia had set foot in the new store in Enna, the number of customers had increased significantly. Obviously, her smile had the power of drawing people into the store. According to the law of attraction, smiles attract good luck, while a sad face attracts only misfortune.

Lucia changed the look of the store. The windows were now clean, and the items well displayed. She took good care of making an inventory of the goods every month. The store was well-stocked. Customers came from nearby towns, even from Caltanissetta, because they were sure to find the items they wanted to buy.

Seven years after coming to Enna, Lucia was able not only to pay off her debt to Gaetano, but she also bought the other half of the store from him. Gaetano had become too old and had no family. He preferred to spend his last years on earth at a nursing home. He bequeathed part of his money to the nursing home and the other part to the Church of San Calogero.

Antonio and Nunzio had enrolled in the technical school, and this year they would have to take their final exams. Nunzio spent his free time outside his home, while Antonio preferred to read books and daydream about his future. From time to time he revolved the globe on his desk and imagined life in faraway lands. He quite often went to the library to read novels.

One day Antonio was reading a book in the library when, lifting up his eyes, he saw opposite him a girl whose features were more beautiful than any he had ever seen before. She was sitting at a table flipping through the pages of a magazine. She looked like Brigida, the girl he had met in Calascibetta in the courtyard of Farmer Peppe's house seven years before. She had now become an attractive and shapely woman. Even though she had changed a lot, there was no doubt that it was her. The coffee birthmark below her lower lip and her blue eyes that looked like two pieces of the sky were unmistakable. Apparently, she had returned from Belgium and now lived in Enna.

Brigida recognized Antonio at first sight and smiled at him. Seeing that she was smiling at him, Antonio blushed as never before. He didn't know how to interpret her smile. He wanted to stand up and walk to her table to greet her, but he was too shy. So, he remained at the table and kept reading his book.

The following day when he entered the reading room in the library, Brigida was already sitting at a table with her eyes in a book. Although Antonio's heart was thudding and his face was red like an ember, he strove to keep calm and took a seat next to Brigida.

"What are you reading?" he asked her.

Brigida didn't say a single word. She just showed the cover of the book. It was *Wuthering Heights* by Emily Bronte.

"What about you?" she asked.

"I'm reading *Jane Eyre* by Charlotte Bronte," Antonio replied.

"It's unusual that two sisters are both authors."

"As a matter of fact, there were three sisters—Emily, Charlotte, and Anne Bronte. They were all excellent writers," he said.

Antonio felt heartened because she continued to talk with him. If she had disliked him, she would have stood up and moved to another table.

"Do you remember me?" Antonio asked.

"Yes, we met in Calascibetta at my father's cousin's house about seven years ago," she replied.

"You have a good memory!"

"You have not changed much."

"Instead, you have changed for the better. I have never seen so beautiful a girl in my life."

"That's very kind of you, Antonio."

"You still remember my name!"

"What about you?"

"How can I forget? Brigida! Would you like talking about our books?"

"Yes, of course. We can share our views on authors and books while walking in the street. On Sundays, I usually go to Mass in the Church of Saint Marc. It begins at eleven o'clock in the morning. Would you like to join me?"

"Yes, I'll be there this Sunday, and then we can have a walk together."

"Okay, let's meet on Sunday. Now I have to go home," Brigida said, smiling at Antonio sweetly.

Antonio was over the moon with joy. He felt he had already conquered her heart. It seemed impossible to him, a shy introverted guy, that a girl could fall in love with him, but this time he sensed that his love for Brigida was returned.

The Church of Saint Marc was the chapel of the cloistered Carmelite nuns. Below the ceiling were windows and balconies screened with iron bars all around the perimeter of the church. Since the iron bars were very thick, it was possible to see from the inside but not from the outside. Obviously, the enclosed nuns had contact with the world through those concealed windows, for they could see people in the church without being seen by them. The altar of the church was gilded, while the floor was laid with majolica tiles.

Brigida sat on a pew near the altar. When Mass was over, Antonio waited for her at the exit of the church, and then they had a walk on Belvedere. Every Sunday, Antonio and Brigida met, but once in a while, Nunzio joined them and they walked together on Belvedere.

Antonio came to love Brigida more and more. He dreamed about his future life with her. They would have many children as beautiful as their mother. He even imagined the names they would give to their children, but his daydream shattered against harsh reality.

One Sunday, Brigida didn't come to the Church of Saint Marc. Antonio was worried. Maybe something bad had happened to her. But he had no reason to be worried, for Brigida was in the Church of Saint Joseph sitting next to his twin brother, Nunzio.

A few days later, Antonio saw his brother and Brigida walking together hand in hand on Belvedere. Antonio couldn't believe that his beloved brother, whom he had trusted so much and for whom he had walked from Calascibetta to Enna to go to school, would steal the girl he loved.

At home, he asked Nunzio why he had behaved so badly toward him. His answer chilled him.

"Brigida doesn't like you! You have no hope to conquer her heart. I like her and she likes me, so why should I not ask her to become my girlfriend?" Nunzio replied coldly.

Antonio looked at his brother with astonished eyes. At first glance, Nunzio's reasoning was flawless. If Brigida didn't like Antonio, there was no reason to stop Nunzio from loving her, but inside he began to harbor envy and even hate against his brother. He felt an unbearable urge to leave Enna and begin a new life in another country with different people and without brothers who betrayed their brothers. But it was just an illusion. The world is the same everywhere. No country is immune from treacherous beings.

In Enna, Antonio's only friend was Father Lucio, a handsome young priest who was tall, red-haired, and stout. He had shown his talent at the seminary. As soon as he was ordained a priest, he was given the care of the parish of San Calogero near the Castle of Lombardy. He was able to speak French and English fluently. Besides having deep knowledge of the Holy Scriptures, he knew Latin, Ancient Greek, philosophy, and even Hebrew. In a nutshell, he was an extraordinary man. Not only did he have a notable store of knowledge, but he also had a good heart—and above all, he was honest. He was not Sicilian. He was from Rome. He had entered the Seminary of Piazza Armerina, the diocese to which Enna belonged, because he loved Sicily and its culture and traditions.

Lucio and Antonio were almost the same age. They both loved good reading, philosophy, religion, and music. It was natural that they were attracted to each other. In the evening, they used to listen to music in Lucio's room. Sometimes they went to the cafeteria to drink coffee or beer. Some beautiful girls attended the parish, but Lucio ignored them. The most important thing for him was his mission as a shepherd of souls. Every time Antonio had an argument with his family, he ran to Lucio and asked him for advice about how to behave with them. He considered him his brother, not Nunzio.

Under Lucia's management, the family business developed considerably. Since the premises became inadequate to the size of the company, Lucia bought two new pavilions. She entrusted one pavilion to Antonio and the other to Nunzio, with the task of managing the trade in iron equipment for scaffolding, tubular scaffolding, and similar equipment.

While the business run by Nunzio thrived, Antonio generated only liabilities. He was not cut out for business, for he was too credulous and not talkative. He often sold on credit, but most of the credits went unpaid. Since his business was always in red, Lucia thought it best to tell Antonio that he should leave the family firm.

"You'd better take a rest. We don't need your help. Please stay away from the company for a few years, but don't feel disappointed! You are not cut out for business. In your hands, our firm would fall apart," said Lucia coldly.

"How can I live without working? Do you want me to look for a job elsewhere?"

"No. You don't need to work," she replied. "We will create a limited liability company formed by your father, myself, and Nunzio. The manager will be Nunzio, but you will have a small stake in the company. Therefore, every year you will receive a small amount of money. You can live well on such profits and even support a family if you get married someday."

Antonio's pride was wounded. He put his head down for an instant, then he looked up at his mother. She seemed to be a stranger. Business had hardened her heart.

"I don't want any stake! Yes, you are right. I am not cut out for business. I'll spend my time differently. I'll try to find a job that suits me."

"Why don't you become a priest?"

"That is none of your business!"

His mother was appalled by his answer. She couldn't imagine a more disrespectful answer. Obviously, the thin thread of filial love was already broken. So, she calmly replied, "Go take a walk on Belvedere and then come back home for dinner."

Antonio thought about becoming a priest, but he felt he was not cut out for an ecclesiastical life either. He couldn't endure celibacy. His sex drive was very high. If he met a woman he liked, he would try to conquer her heart. He was sure about that. How could he ever be a priest in such a condition? However, he decided to talk about this issue with Father Lucio.

He walked to the Church of San Calogero to meet him, but he was not in the sacristy, so Antonio passed through the narrow hallway that connected the church to the apartment of the parish priest. The door was wide open. There was a mess at the entrance. Father Lucio was packing without wearing a cassock.

"What happened to you, Lucio? Why don't you wear a cassock?"

"I resigned as a priest!"

"Why did you do so all of a sudden? Where are you going?"

"I'll return to Rome and try to find a job there."

"Are you still my friend, Lucio?"

"Yes, of course."

"I don't think so."

"Why?"

"If I had not come here today by chance, you would have left without even saying goodbye to me."

"No, Antonio. You are still my best friend. I kept your address and telephone number. I would have contacted you from Rome."

"If you don't mind, may I know why you quit your job as a priest?"

"The reason is very simple. I fell in love with Sofia. She is now my girlfriend. Sooner or later, when I am able to maintain her as my wife, I will marry her. Do you know Sofia?"

"Yes, I do. She also goes to the city library now and then."

"I heard that there are some priests that have relationships with women. They keep the relationships secret while still running the parish. I cannot do that. I am not a hypocrite. I am not one that doesn't practice what he preaches. Tomorrow I am leaving for Rome, while Sofia will remain in Enna for now. When I can afford to marry her, I'll do it. I'll find a job quite soon. I can speak English and French fluently. My mother in Rome informed me that next month there would be a competitive entrance examination for the Ministry of Foreign Affairs. I plan to take it."

"Do you have a good recommendation from a politician? It is impossible to pass a competitive examination without political support."

"I have no recommendation, but I trust in God."

"Are you still Catholic?"

"Of course, yes. I have just left the priesthood, not my faith. You don't need to be a priest to be a good Christian. When I was about to step down as a priest, I prayed to God. At that time, I felt that Jesus himself suggested I follow the voice of my heart. I did it, and then I proposed marriage to Sofia, who accepted."

"You are fortunate to leave this gloomy city. In Rome, you will breathe cleaner air."

"Why are you talking like that? You seem to be pessimistic."

"I haven't a brother anymore. He took the girl I loved from me. My mother expelled me from the business. I have no friends in Enna but you. I wish you a happy life in Rome. God will help me overcome this difficult time."

"I'll keep in touch, Antonio. If I find a good job for you in Rome, I'll let you know. Someday things will change, and the sun will shine again in your life. Be always happy and smile. Keep in mind that God helps cheerful people."

Antonio Emigrates

Six months later, Antonio received a parcel from Guatemala. The sender was Lucio. He had passed the examination to be a diplomat and had married Sofia. He now worked at the Italian Embassy in Guatemala City. In the parcel was an air ticket and all the material Antonio needed to get an extended-stay visa from the Guatemala Embassy in Rome.

Antonio exulted. Lucio had not forgotten him! Within a month, he got his visa. Now if he wanted, he could leave the country. His only concern was how his family would react. Would they oppose his moving to Guatemala? What to do in that case? The answer was quite clear. He would leave Enna whether his family liked it or not.

Things went smoother than he had predicted. His family members didn't even try to change his mind. A veil of incomprehension separated him from them. He had become a burden both for Nunzio and his parents.

"I'll drive you to the airport in Catania," said Nunzio.

"Take this money. I wish you all the best," said his mother while handing him a wallet full of banknotes.

"Take this small holy picture of Our Lady of Visitation. The Virgin Mary will protect you during your journey," said his father, an inveterate anticlerical that had turned into a fervent Catholic.

"Goodbye," said Antonio, waving at his parents from the car.

At Guatemala City Airport, Lucio welcomed Antonio and led him to Antigua, the old capital of Guatemala, by taxi. Lucio had secured a job for Antonio as a waiter. It was not a great job, but it was better than begging money from his brother and parents.

Antonio lodged with a family in a house with a panoramic view. His room had a separate entrance to allow him to come and go freely. Antigua stood near three volcanoes. Two of them were inactive; the other, called Fuego, was still active. The plumes of smoke from its peak were continuous and amazing.

Walking in Antigua, his attention was drawn to the many ruined churches. Although the places of worship had been built well and with good materials, they didn't withstand the earthquakes. In Guatemala, the ground shook quite often.

He went to Saint Francis Church every evening and meditated for a few minutes in front of the statue of San Benito of Palermo. The Franciscan saint was popular in South America. He was considered the protector of colored people. In fact, he was a refugee from Ethiopia who was later adopted by a Sicilian family. Standing in front of the statue of San Benito of Palermo, he felt at home. He had a fellow citizen who protected him in this faraway land! Even though he lived in another continent, Sicily was always in his heart.

The restaurant where he worked was located in the tourist area of Antigua. He had been hired because they needed someone able to speak foreign languages. It was the right job for him, for he was a humble person that enjoyed serving others.

When he was off duty, he went on excursions to the towns and villages nearby. He was fascinated by Guatemala's amazing history.

One day he went on a trip to Ciutad Vieja (Old City), the second capital of Guatemala. It lay at the foot of Volcan de Agua (Water Volcano). He walked up to the peak of the mountain. There was a small church inside the crater! It was said that Beatrix de la Cueva, governor of Guatemala, had twenty maids attending her. In 1541, she wanted to be proclaimed the queen of the local population. For her enthronement, she organized a sumptuous ceremony in the cathedral. When she was about to be anointed, a huge mass of water came down from Volcan de Agua, and Beatrix de la Cueva was submerged in the water, disappearing with all her followers as well as the city itself.

Overall, Antonio's life flowed smoothly. He had not made many friends, his salary was small, but he felt satisfied at being independent and far from Enna, which had become too gloomy for him. He even got accustomed to the earthquakes that once in a while rocked his bed at night as a childminder rocks a baby in her arms and softly sings a lullaby. The house where he lived was low with a wooden roof, so he had no reason to be afraid of earthquakes.

One night, something unexpected interrupted his quiet stay in Antigua. Life can change for the worse or the better according to the will of God! At three in the morning, while he was sleeping soundly, he thought he heard knocks at the door. He woke up with a start and ran to the door.

"Who is knocking?"

"It's me, Lucio. I have to tell you something important. Open the door, please!"

Lucio had brought his wife, Sofia, who had grown fatter and big-bellied since the last time he saw her in Enna. She was pregnant. Seeing them, he had the feeling that the sun entered his room and illuminated it. He hugged Lucio and shook hands with his wife.

"*Ummuliva ca Luciu viniva cca sulu di notti* (I didn't want Lucio to come here alone at night)," said Sofia, who always spoke with Antonio in the Sicilian dialect.

"What's up?" Antonio asked Lucio.

"Yesterday, I met a Mexican businessman. He said that in Mexico it is feared that the regime will topple soon. A few very rich businessmen have made a lot of money over the years in politics. If the regime is overthrown, they will have their assets confiscated by the government. To prevent such an eventuality, they need a figurehead—that is, a trusted person to whom they can fictitiously transfer the property of their assets.

"He asked me whether I knew someone to trust. I thought of you as the right person to be their figurehead. If you accept, you will move to Mexico. Tomorrow, at ten o'clock in the morning, an airliner will take off from Guatemala City Airport to Cancun in Mexico. You'll find a car with a driver at the exit of the airport in Cancun. The driver will take you to Merida, the capital of Yucatan. Then a lawyer will put the properties of these three businessmen, who are about to leave the country, into your name," Lucio replied.

"*Fussuvu u cchiu riccu du Messicu!* (You would be the richest man in Mexico!)," said Sofia, beaming with joy.

"Do you accept, Antonio?" asked Lucio.

"I don't understand what you have just said very well. It seems to me a somewhat complicated matter. Do you think the new revolutionary government is made of gullible men? Won't they find out about the scam? People are not stupid!" Antonio answered.

"In the field of law, things are not as simple as you imagine. Nobody is allowed to confiscate a person's assets without a process that proves the illegality of the property purchase. Supposing that the new revolutionary government sues you for illegitimate purchase of assets, you would have excellent lawyers to assist you. The lawsuit would take years. The businessmen are sure that the new revolutionary government will be toppled within two or three years. Furthermore, to pacify the country, the new rulers will grant amnesty for almost all common crimes. You have nothing to worry about."

"What will happen if the revolution is crushed or the revolutionary government is overthrown?"

"In that case, you will have to give back the assets to the businessmen, but what matters is the present. We can't predict the future. However, until the assets are in your name, you will get the fruits. It is a considerable amount of money! Don't you think so?"

"Lucio, you have to know that I am not cut out for business. My parents and my brother expelled me from their company because I was unfit to do business. How can I manage those properties, which may also include factories, I'd guess?"

"You have to take care of nothing, Antonio. A trusted administrator will manage the assets. He will deposit the profits into your bank account."

"Lucio, if you advise me to do this, it means that it is a good thing for me. I trust you, but I still have doubts. You once used to be a priest. You studied morals and religion in the seminary. Tell me one more thing. Isn't it a sin to scam?"

"No, it isn't. You commit a sin when you harm somebody. In this case, you are doing a good deed. You are helping three businessmen. Without you, their properties will be irremediably lost."

"I think the revolutionary government would act well if it seized the properties of the three businessmen and then shared them among the poor. If I prevented such a distribution of goods to the poor, my role as a figurehead would be immoral."

"In that case, it would be the first time for me to see a government distribute properties to the poor. However, if you don't want to accept..."

"*Ppi piaciri ascuta sa cchi ti dici Luciu. Iddu parla ppo to bbeni* (Please, listen to what Lucio says to you. He speaks for your own good)," said Sofia, shivering with excitement.

Antonio felt he could trust Lucio and Sofia. After all, they were the only friends he had, but there was something more that prevented him from accepting Lucio and Sofia's help.

"I'm a very humble person. I'm shy and a bit introverted. When my parents and my brother expelled me from the family company, I became demoralized and developed an inferiority complex. Can I ever act the role of a rich businessman? Of course not! It's like awarding the first prize in a horse race to a mule. Everybody would notice that the race has been fixed. I want to be honest. I am not the right person the businessmen are looking for. Do you agree with me, Lucio?"

Lucio always had the right answer to Antonio's questions. Even this time he replied to Antonio without hesitation.

"Do you think you are the only one in the world to suffer from emotional disorders? The rich are weak too. They may be depressed, anxious, or they may live an unhappy life like any person. They can also be humble and generous. Usually, the rich are neither miserly nor boastful. A rich person can even become a saint. One of them was the Blessed Pier Giorgio Frascati. He belonged to a rich family, but he used his riches to help the poor, so don't worry about your look as a rich man. Just continue to be yourself when you become rich. Don't get a swelled head from your new condition. Earthly riches may appear and disappear; they are impermanent. Be natural. Don't worry. Everything will be alright."

"Let me ask you one last question, Lucio. Last night, the earthquake in Antigua was a bit more violent than usual. I thought about death. Sooner or later, I will disappear from the surface of the earth. What's the use of wealth, honors, and power when one dies and then disappears into eternal nothingness?"

"We don't know what will happen after we die. However, if we humans have been born on this earth, there must be a reason. Although temporarily, we have been presented with the gift of life. Don't you think we should be thankful for the gift we have received, instead of giving it a kick and throwing it away? Life is now giving you another gift, that of becoming a rich man. Do you want to refuse it?" Lucio asked.

At that point, Antonio had no more valid arguments to contrast with Lucio's.

"Okay, you've convinced me. I'll come to the airport. Just give me a little time to pack and leave a note for the landlady. I'll ask her to inform my employer about my departure. I will also leave the room rent on the table for her."

"A cab is waiting for us. We'll go together to the airport, and then Sofia and I will go home in the same cab."

The road was empty at night, so they got to the airport quickly.

"*U Signuri ti bbinidica* (God bless you!)," said Sofia, hugging Antonio with tears in her eyes.

"Keep in touch, Antonio. If you have any problems or questions, don't hesitate to call me on my home telephone," said Lucio, who also hugged Antonio.

Antonio Gets Rich

The plane took off on time and landed at the airport in Cancun without delay. At the exit, a man with white gloves held a placard in his hands that read: "Antonio Reggiani." *He must be the driver that Lucio talked about.* Everything had been organized to perfection.

"Good morning, Mr. Reggiani. Welcome to Mexico. Please, follow me," said the man.

Antonio entered the car, and after about three hours, they arrived at a country house where the three businessmen were impatiently waiting for him. Two of them were of mixed race with olive complexions; the other was a white man. All of them had black eyes and hair. They looked humble and genteel. Apparently, Lucio was right. Not all the rich are boastful.

"My name is Miguel," said the white man.

"My name is Fernando," said another.

"My name is Adolfo," said the third man.

"My name is Antonio Reggiani," said Antonio.

The three men shook Antonio's hand warmly.

"Would you like to have a cup of coffee, Antonio?" asked the white man, who must have been the owner of the house.

"Yes, please. I couldn't sleep last night, so a cup of coffee will keep me awake."

"Maritza!" he called out.

A young colored maid with white gloves and a white lace apron on a black dress came in and waited for orders from her boss.

"Please, Maritza, bring some coffee for Mr. Antonio and us. Try and be quick, because we have to leave soon," ordered Miguel.

Coffee was served in no time. Miguel, Fernando, and Adolfo had to leave the country soon, for the revolutionary government was about to take over. There was no time to lose.

"Now we will go to the lawyer's office. He will transfer all our properties to you. I guess Lucio has already informed you about our predicament," said Miguel.

"Yes, I know everything. I'll do my best to help you," Antonio replied.

The same driver that had picked Antonio up from the airport now drove them to the lawyer, who had all the papers ready for the signatures. Miguel, Fernando, Adolfo, and Antonio signed the deed for transferring their properties into Antonio's name. Antonio also signed another deed. If Miguel, Fernando, and Adolfo returned to Mexico under a new government, Antonio would have to retransfer the properties to them.

Miguel introduced Antonio to another man. He was a half-breed and had a severe look.

"This is the administrator of the properties. He knows what to do. Ask him whatever you need," said Miguel.

The three businessmen said goodbye and rushed to the exit of the lawyer's office, while Antonio remained with the administrator, who had already gotten Antonio an extended-stay visa and a house in an area of Merida called Prato Northe. It was a nice house with a garden and a swimming pool. There was also a bookcase with many books in English. Having nothing to do, he spent part of the day reading them. He was particularly interested in the history of the Mayans.

In the evening, he went to downtown Merida. It was not difficult to get there, because all buses were bound for the center of the city. He liked Mexico. Every evening there was music and dancing in the main square. What impressed him was the harmonious sound of the trumpets.

Day after day, the administrator deposited earnings into Antonio's bank account. Antonio was becoming richer and richer. In Mexico, the new revolutionary government seemed to hold up well, and it even had the support of the general population. It would not have been easy to topple.

When Antonio got acquainted with the area, he visited the places around Merida, starting with the relics of the Mayan civilization. The pyramids where majestic. There was usually an altar on the top of a pyramid where the ancient Mayans offered sacrifices to their gods.

Sometimes he went for a swim in a *cenote*, a small underground lake. The Mayans also used to make sacrifices in them. The beaches near Merida were also nice. One of them, called Progreso, was a unique place to see the sun rising from the sea at dawn and disappearing into the sea again at sunset.

After a year of this peaceful life, his strong ego took the lead. He wanted to show his family in Enna and his fellow citizens in Calascibetta that he had become rich. He bought a luxurious limousine and embarked it on a ship bound for Italy.

When he arrived in Enna, his parents and brother where incredulous that he was the same Antonio that had left Enna two years before. When he left Enna, he was shy and depressed. Now he looked strong and self-confident. But money cannot change a person's mind and heart. He was still the same weak man that had emigrated two years earlier.

He bought the old house on Via San Michele in Calascibetta from his parents, remodeled it, and transformed the old store into a garage for his car.

After he spent one month in Sicily, he returned to Mexico. Nothing had happened during his absence. The revolutionary government was stronger and stronger, and day after day his bank account increased. Nobody checked on his assets. But life is not stable. Things can change unexpectedly, like waking up suddenly after a dream.

Two years later, on a sunny Sunday after Mass at the Cathedral of Merida was over, he took a walk in the nearby square. To his surprise, two tanks were standing there. There were also a few soldiers near the tanks. He approached one of them and came to know the reason why they were occupying the square. There had been a coup d'état. Things had changed radically. Now the revolutionary government was on the run. The three businessmen would return to Mexico to lay claim to their assets.

When Antonio called Lucio to inform him about the new political situation, he already knew what had happened in Mexico.

"Go to Calascibetta right away. Let me negotiate with the businessmen. I'll try to get as much as I can for you," said Lucio on the phone.

Antonio Returns to Calascibetta

Antonio returned to his house in Calascibetta in a hurry. What a difference between Merida and Calascibetta! In his small town in the center of Sicily, life flowed slowly. One day seemed to be never-ending. Lying in his bed, he saw the images of his life in Mexico before his eyes, like in a movie already shot. He missed everything in that faraway country, even the fragrance of bananas and the unique taste of vegetable juices. He missed the Mexican songs and dances in the main square of Merida, the cenotes, Progreso Beach, and above all the warm heart of the Mexicans.

He missed Rosa Maria, a woman with whom he used to go to Mass. She was not very beautiful but was friendly to him. She must have been a descendant of the Mayans, for she had almond black eyes and dark skin. She sang in the church choir with her melodious voice, while her nephews played the guitar. They were two fantastic guitarists. In Calascibetta, he had nothing to do but wait for news from Lucio. He was doomed to lose his properties. There was no doubt about that.

Ten days later, a big car passed by Piazza Umberto and went onto Via San Michele in Calascibetta in the middle of the night. The driver knew where to go, even though he was not from Calascibetta. The car pulled in front of Antonio's house. Then, four figures dressed in black, and one young man in white pants and a blue jacket, got out of the car and headed for Antonio's house. The young man knocked on Antonio's door.

"It's me, Lucio. Get dressed quickly. We have to go to Switzerland right now," said Lucio from behind the door.

He was with the businessmen and the lawyer that three years ago had dealt with transferring the assets to him. Now the lawyer would do the opposite. Antonio had to retransfer his properties to the businessmen. He had deluded himself into thinking he owned those assets in Mexico. Unfortunately, he was just a figurehead.

Antonio got into the car, and they arrived at the airport in Catania about an hour later. Everybody boarded a small plane that was ready to take off. After about two hours, the plane landed at Zurich's airport. Then, Antonio was led into an apartment on the twenty-seventh floor of a building in downtown Zurich. He had no choice but to sign the deed that the lawyer handed him. By signing it, he lost everything. The idea of not signing never flashed into his mind. He was honest by nature. He couldn't betray the trust that Lucio and the businessmen had put in him. However, Lucio had negotiated with the businessmen well. In exchange for retransferring the assets, he got good compensation for Antonio. The businessmen deposited a considerable amount of money in his bank account in Calascibetta. He had enough cash to live well for years to come. He didn't need to work anymore.

They parted at Zurich's airport. Lucio went back to Guatemala, the businessmen to Mexico, and Antonio to his hometown. Mysteriously, after Antonio returned to Calascibetta, he forgot Lucio. They didn't keep in contact. Lucio, the man who had helped him so much, his best friend, disappeared from Antonio's memory. How was that possible? It was a mystery. Surely, if he had kept contact with him, his life would have been different, but fate had already taken its inexorable course.

He was terribly bored in Calascibetta. He had no friends. His parents and his brother lived in Enna. He could have visited them, but a veil of mutual indifference had separated him from them for many years. He just didn't feel like it.

To escape from boredom, he started to frequent the cultural association in Calascibetta. Besides organizing trips to the theaters in Palermo and Catania, lectures, books presentations, and the like, the cultural association allowed members to play cards, and even to gamble in one of the rooms. He was so involved in gambling that, little by little, he became addicted to that awful vice.

From the Cultural Association he moved to the sports club in Enna to gamble. While at the cultural association, he used to lose a small amount of money; the losses were much bigger at the sports club. Every night he went there with a lot of money in his pocket, and when he returned to Calascibetta, his pockets were empty. He promised himself not to gamble anymore, but he didn't have enough strength to stay away from the green tables. Every night at the sports club he lost ten million lira. In two months, he lost six hundred million, a huge amount of money. However, even though he had lost a lot, he still had enough money left to live well until the end of his life.

He couldn't refrain from gambling. The charm of the vice prevailed over his determination not to gamble. He wanted to recover the money he had lost, but the more he tried, the more he lost.

He thought that Enna brought him bad luck, so he moved to Venice to play roulette at the casino. He remained in that city for a month. He used to stay in the hotel from morning to evening and then take a steamer to the casino. He played roulette and always lost. At the end of the month, he had no money left. Only his gold watch remained. He pledged it to the casino. Eventually, he lost that too. Finally, he left the casino and bought a train ticket for Calascibetta with the few lira he had left.

At home, he fell into depression and discouragement. He didn't even have enough money to buy food. He sold his car and got by for a few months. Winter was drawing near. Having nothing to eat, he would die from starvation. He also needed to buy some firewood to keep the house warm.

On a cold January night, the snow fell abundantly on Calascibetta. In Via San Michele, it had reached a height of twenty centimeters. Antonio stood motionless and looked out of the window at the snow that fell in large flakes. The town looked deserted. When he was a child, he liked the snow. Now, things were different. The snow was his enemy. He risked freezing to death.

He had become very thin. He had no food or firewood. He was sure he would die overnight. He lay in his bed and waited for death to come.

Suddenly, he heard a voice inside himself. "Come here, Antonio. I am waiting for you. Don't be afraid. I will remain with you now and in the years to come."

It was the voice of Father Massimiliano. People said he had supernatural powers. Maybe it was true. The voice that spoke inside Antonio was clear and unequivocal.

Antonio didn't have a watch anymore, but he realized that it must have been two or three in the morning. It was too late to disturb Father Massimiliano, who was likely sleeping, but the voice continued to talk inside him.

"The door of the monastery is open. Come soon before it is too late."

As if by instinct, Antonio put on an old greatcoat and left his home. He walked, sinking his feet into the snow, up to the end of Via Giudea. His face and hair were covered with snow. When he arrived at the monastery, the door was ajar. Father Massimiliano came out of the door, motioned for him to enter, and when he crossed the threshold, he hugged him affectionately.

"You were lucky to lose all your money. If you had worldly concerns, you could not walk the path that leads to God. What is more important for you? Money or God?" Father Massimiliano asked.

"God," Antonio replied, bowing his head.

"Have some food before going to your cell. You should be hungry, I guess."

Soup and some slices of bread warmed his cold body. He had escaped death for now.

"Now let's go to your cell. I have a surprise for you," said Father Massimiliano.

When they arrived at the cell, Father Massimiliano took a brown frock from the closet and a white girdle from the drawer.

"This frock belonged to a great friar that died before his time. This is yours now. The girdle has three knots to symbolize the main vows for a Franciscan friar: chastity, poverty, and obedience. You will live in this cell as long as you wish."

At the monastery, Antonio lived a life of prayer and read all the books Father Massimiliano passed to him. After five years in the monastery, his health worsened. The eczema that had been limited to his nose before now spread all over his body. Day after day, he became weaker and weaker. Doctors couldn't find the cause of his disease. He died with Father Massimiliano holding his hand. His brother, Nunzio, bought a tomb in Enna's cemetery for Antonio to be buried.

Thus ended Antonio Reggiani's life.

Chapter Eight

Walking in the Cemetery at Night

"Did you like the life story of Antonio Reggiani, Mario?"

"Yes, I found it captivating."

"Now let's go to the cemetery. I want to show you my tomb," said Luigi.

"Do you realize what time it is? It's a quarter to midnight. It is not the proper time to go to the cemetery."

"Why not? The cemetery is always the same. Do you think ghosts go out of their tombs at night and walk in the avenues of the cemetery? Of course not! The keeper once used to live there. His lodge was in the middle of the cemetery. I don't know whether he lived there with his family or not, and as far as I know, he didn't quit his job. Nothing ever happened to him. That is evidence enough that ghosts don't exist. They are in our minds, not in reality.

"Okay, I'll follow you. We can go."

It was midnight when we arrived at the hole in the cemetery fence near the graveyard of the poor. At that moment, four bluish lights hovered in the air over the graves. My hair stood on end. I was terrified. I thought I saw blue lights moving toward me, and then they went back to the starting point. They kept hovering over the graves for about two minutes until they vanished into thin air.

Luigi passed through the hole without caring about the lights, while I remained outside the cemetery. I felt petrified, as if those bluish lights had cast a spell on me. I couldn't move. My legs quaked as if there were an earthquake under my feet.

"What are you doing? Why are you standing outside like a statue? Come in. Don't be silly!" Luigi cried out to me.

"Didn't you see those lights over the graveyard?" I asked in a trembling voice.

"Yes, I did. They are nothing more than will-o'-the-wisps. Did you think they were souls of the dead wandering in the cemetery?" Luigi replied, shaking with laughter.

"What does it mean, will-o'-the-wisps?"

"It means small flames kindled by gas emanating from bodies in an advanced state of decay. You'll see this phenomenon only in the graveyard of the poor, because here the bodies are buried under the bare earth inside coffins that have not been sealed with zinc. So keep calm. Don't worry. You won't see blue lights beyond this area."

Luigi's words put my mind at ease. Gradually, I pulled myself together and then passed through the hole in the fence. I followed him as I used to do when we were children. He held a flashlight in his hand, which shed some light as we went on down the cemetery.

Absolute silence and peace reigned in the town of the dead. Only feeble lights came out from the candles in the tombs. We walked under a sky dotted with stars. The Milky Way was visible. My grandmother called the Milky Way Saint James's Stairway. According to her, the souls of the dead climbed up and down Saint James's Stairway when they came to our planet, and then they left Earth, bound to faraway planets and stars.

Walking in the cemetery, I didn't sense any ghostly presence beside me. Luigi was right. There were only bones and decaying corpses in the cemetery, nothing else.

Luigi's tomb was in the avenue of the rich and nobles. His father had built it from granite blocks. It was tall and quadrangular in shape. On the façade, the family name was carved in italic letters: *Chiaramonte*. The floor, the altar, and the eight niches inside the room were made of onyx. On the altar were just two framed photos, those of Luigi's parents.

"Before long, I'll occupy one of those empty niches. It will be paradoxical that a poor man will be buried in a tomb for the rich," Luigi said bitterly.

"I can't believe it. What happened to you? Why are you talking like that?"

"Antonio Reggiani's life is similar to mine. I was one of the richest men in Catania. Then I lost everything, just like him. I only own my old house in Enna. I'll live in Enna until I die. I'll spend my life praying and meditating."

"What about your agencies? I heard you were the best car dealer in Italy."

"Yes, I was very rich, but fine weather doesn't last long. Sooner or later, thunderclouds appear in the sky and obscure the sun. I owned ten car dealerships in Catania. Little by little, I was becoming old and couldn't take care of my businesses by myself. So, I appointed a trusted, renowned manager. It was my mistake. He sent the dealerships into bankruptcy in a short time. I lost everything. Evidently, I had put my trust in the wrong person!"

"Luigi, in some respects, Antonio Reggiani's life is similar to my life too."

"I didn't know you were a rich man, Mario."

"Even though I wasn't as rich as you, I had a lot of money at my disposal. I was a good lawyer, and my clients paid me well. Furthermore, I sold an apartment that my father had bequeathed to me. In a nutshell, I had one million euros in cash, which I deposited in the bank.

"You have to know that the biggest mistakes I made in my life happened whenever I followed others' opinions blindly. This was my Achilles heel! It also happened sometimes during my professional career as a lawyer.

"One day, an important manager of the bank where I had the money deposited called me at home. He asked me to come to the bank and have a talk with him; he had something important to tell me. I went to the bank and met him. He was sitting behind a desk with a laptop in front of him. He turned the laptop to me and showed me a graphic. The bank's shares were expected to increase in value in the coming years, according to the graphic. Therefore, he suggested I invest my money in shares of that bank. I followed his advice. At first, the shares increased in value, but two years later, a scandal involved the bank. Its president was arrested, and my shares lost their value. In a nutshell, I lost all my cash.

"Now I just live on my small pension, but I don't complain, for I am still in good health, which is much more valuable than money. Now, let's go to the upper avenue. I want to show you my tomb I finished building four years ago when I still had cash at my disposal."

While we were climbing the stairway to my tomb, an owl with a mouse in its claws fluttered its wings towards a cypress tree. Life was suddenly over for the little rodent. That is life! It is based upon violence. Without killing, carnivores cannot survive. The fish in the sea must eat the small ones so as not to depopulate the oceans. The eagles in the sky must bring some small animals to their nests, otherwise, their species becomes extinct. There is a fragile balance in nature. The life of one being passes through the death of another. Once, a Jehovah's Witness said to me that there will come a time on Earth when lions will live peacefully together with lambs; there will be no death, diseases, and violence. When will this time come? Surely not in a world like that in which we are living now. It would be another Earth.

What about human violence? There was a great philosopher named Georg Wilhelm Friedrich Hegel who considered war unavoidable. Was he right? I can just say that wars have never ceased since the beginning of the world. Man kills just like animals. There is not much difference between animals' violence and man's violence. Both of them kill not only to survive, but also to protect their territories, because of hate, jealousy, and even just for the sake of killing.

At the end of the stairway, we turned left and arrived at my tomb.

"I built it near my grandmother's tomb, the woman I loved most in my life. It's a common tomb, very simple with a room inside and no niches. I made a large red marble heart and put it above the altar. Too late, I realized that I had not only instincts but also a heart inside me. Better late than never! I engraved this poem on the marble heart:

> *I cannot force others to open their hearts.*
>
> *I can just open mine first.*
>
> *Then I will knock on another heart's door*
>
> *With the light of my love.*
>
> *Naturally, the door will open.*
>
> *If I can open one heart,*
>
> *that heart will be able to open another heart.*
>
> *More and more hearts will open*
>
> *as ripples spread out from where a stone has fallen.*
>
> *The landscape of life on Earth will change.*
>
> *No more violence, war, and hatred.*
>
> *Love will shine on our lives.*

"Your poem is very nice, Mario. You must be a good poet and a good writer, I guess."

"I'm neither. I just get inspiration once in a while. I don't know exactly where it comes from. I can only say that without inspiration I wouldn't be able to write anything."

"In my opinion, it comes from heaven. If a poet is not a mystic, he won't get inspiration from above. In Ancient Greece, the Muses, Zeus's daughters, were the source of inspiration for artists. They got ideas from the Muses and the desire to create poems, paintings, sculptures, music, and the like. These days, the names of the Muses, of Zeus, and of the Olympian gods have changed into only the name of God, but deep down, the same god was worshipped in ancient times, even though he was given different names."

"I agree with you, Luigi, but now we'd better leave the land of the dead and return to the world of the living. We've hung out in the cemetery too long this year. Don't you think so?"

"It's been well worthwhile staying in the cemetery at night," Luigi replied. "It has reminded us of our deaths. By being mindful of the impermanence and fragility of human life, we can live our daily lives differently. We can become a bit more spiritual, and who knows, we can have intuition about the meaning of life and the source of the universe and all things. We can go back home now. Before long, the rosy light of dawn will dispel the darkness of night. The cemetery will keep silent, while the city of the living will wake up and get ready for a busy day."

"I want you to be my guest at my home tomorrow, Luigi. I'll cook something delicious for you. We'll drink a glass of good wine and listen to beautiful music. Let's enjoy life as long as we are alive, and let's stay away from the cemetery for some time. We'll meet here again on November second next year. Meanwhile, someone will die, new tombs will be built to house new bodies, and new beings will be born to continue the endless flow of life on Earth."

We'd like to know if you enjoyed the book. Please consider leaving a review on the platform from which you purchased the book

CPSIA information can be obtained
at www.ICGtesting.com
Printed in the USA
LVHW041337310720
662069LV00001B/67